The Demon of Histlewick Downs

Books by Douglas J. Bornemann

The Demon of Histlewick Downs (Book 1 of the Dreamweaver Chronicles). This standalone novel explores historic events that set the stage for the rest of the Heiromancer Trilogy.

The Heiromancer Trilogy:
    Practical Phrendonics
    A House of Cards
    Hanged Man's Gambit

Shady Fortunes

Website: dougbornemann.com
Facebook: https://www.facebook.com/djbornemann/
X (Twitter) @DougBornemann

The Demon of Histlewick Downs

Book One of The Dreamweaver Chronicles

Douglas J. Bornemann

Published by Sorcelerity

Second Print Edition
ISBN 978-0-9906281-1-8
Copyright © Douglas J. Bornemann 2014

For Genelle...more than words.

Table of Contents

The Demon of Histlewick Downs

THE ROAD TO HISTLEWICK DOWNS

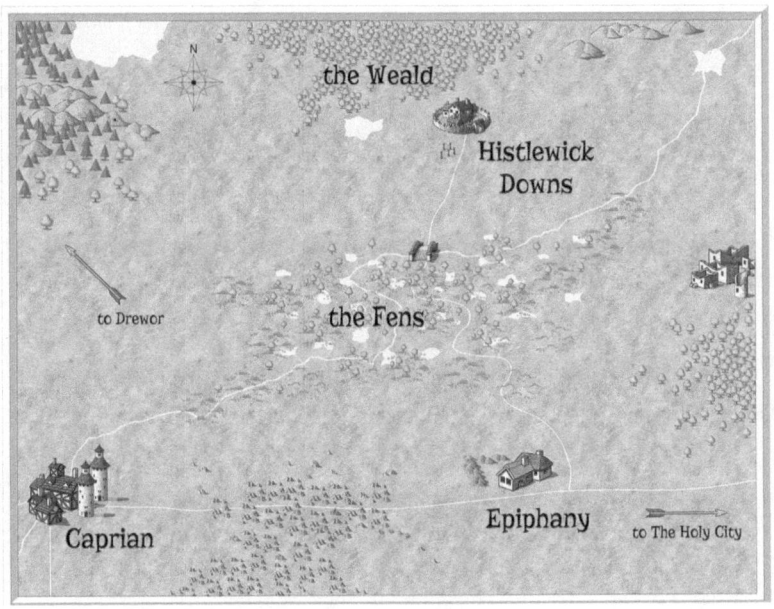

CHAPTER ONE

FAITH, HOPE, AND CHARITY

*C*ontrary to official reports, my father never was a heretic. There may have been a time early in his life when he aspired, but if that's true, it would have been more out of a sense of duty than any real interest. Rather, his was a passion for creating things with his hands—wondrous things of beauty and intricacy. He carved the mechanism for his first clock when he was seven and produced a working music box by eight, but despite his talent for crafting, his aptitude for the *craft* was nonexistent. It was a failing for which my grandfather never forgave him.

My father's vain attempts to please my grandfather paid off in a way neither of them anticipated, for although my father couldn't work a spell to save his soul, his grasp on the underlying theory was prodigious, and he gained a reputation among his father's peers as a discreet and reliable source of first-rate wands, rings, and other talismans suitable for enchantment. It didn't take much for a persuasive client to convince him that a lucrative future awaited him, if only he would relocate to Caprian.

The last great bastion of culture to the north, Caprian bordered vast forests peopled by barbaric Drewor tribes. To the southwest, one could find the bustling seaport of Azelon, and thereafter, the lands of Shunese heathens. To the east, the city-state of Trifienne held sway, known best for its patronage of the arts. Beyond Trifienne was the Holy City, domain of the Primal and seat of the Faith, whence came the Inquisition.

At the time, everyone believed Caprian to be the pinnacle of modern civilization, but those of us who lived through the Inquisition know the truth. Civilization is an illusion, a tenuous, intoxicating fog subject to the merest political ill wind. When the fog lifts, all too often it is precisely those who fancy themselves civilized who are slowest to wake to the danger. Like modern-day lotus eaters, they sit, vacuous and uncomprehending, blinking stupidly against the harsh glare of their new reality. So it was with Caprian.

Even as Inquisitors battered down his door, my father refused to accept that they could be doing so for any reason other than a simple misunderstanding. My mother knew better, but she couldn't bring herself to abandon him.

"Thoren, quickly," she said. "Climb out the upstairs window. Whatever happens, promise me you'll stay there until you're sure they're gone."

I scrambled out and flattened myself against the roof in a corner where the eaves of the original structure met the addition. It was a terrible place to hide. Since it was only partially concealed, I had to lie utterly motionless, only able to half-hear the horrors taking place below.

It was well past midnight before I worked up the nerve to climb down. The shop was a shambles. Display cases lay smashed and overturned, disgorged of anything of value to plundering Inquisitors. There was no sign of my parents. Sick with fear, I stumbled out the front door and headed to the neighbors for help.

The Hannikers had been the first to welcome my parents to the neighborhood, and they'd remained fast friends. Mr. Hanniker was a baker of some renown, and I still recall the delicious aromas emanating from the basket Mrs. Hanniker brought to welcome us. Their son Arin and I had made mischief together around town, and I took his loyalty for granted as I would a brother's. I knocked on the door, confident in the knowledge the Hannikers would rush to my aid.

After some time, a dim light appeared within the house, but the door did not open. As more time passed, I began to feel uncomfortably conspicuous, and rapped again. Bitter silence was my only reply. Presently, the faint light that had seeped through the shuttered windows winked out. With it went my innocence. As I began to fully appreciate my predicament, the image of myself as a street-person came to mind—the sort that even the gentlest of folk pass by as if they don't exist. They've done the math, you see. They know the magnanimity it takes to truly rescue such a wretch.

I sank to my knees in despair. Most are fortunate enough never to appreciate the intimate association between the will to live and the knowledge that someone exists to whom it matters. I no longer counted myself among them. Dawn would have found me wandering dazed and aimless, had not the impact of a pebble glancing off my skull brought me to my senses.

My head shot round in rage. Who had perpetrated this new indignity? Though only sixteen and small for my age, I vowed to go out fighting rather than meekly accept the taunts and jeers of miscreants prone to bullying vagrants. I didn't go far before I was pelted by another pebble, this time in the back. I whirled and caught a glimpse of the scoundrel disappearing down an alley. Obviously, I was being lured in. It was an old trick, but I was beyond caring. Let them ambush me. Maybe I could goad them into putting me out of my misery while they were at it.

With fists raised, I stalked into the alley only to discover that my bully consisted of a wide-eyed waif of a girl, no more than nine or ten. She stood at the far end and beckoned, clearly expecting me to follow.

"Who are you?" I called out. "What do you want?"

"Quiet, stupid. This way."

Not exactly cordial, but I got the impression her interest in me must somehow be connected with my predicament. Perhaps she'd seen something useful. Maybe she knew where they'd taken my parents. It was a faint hope, but the only hope I had, and I was determined to pursue it.

When I was younger, I prided myself on knowing more shortcuts and secret ways than anyone else in my neighborhood, but in a matter of minutes, this little girl put me to shame. She flitted ahead like a ghost, visible only long enough to keep me moving in the right direction. At the very moment I was convinced I'd lost her, there'd she be, beckoning impatiently, her big serious eyes skewering me with a look that implied my breathtaking ineptitude had to be deliberate.

It occurred to me that I had unwittingly placed myself in this strange girl's power. I wasn't entirely certain I'd be able to find my way back through the maze of culverts, back alleyways, and rent fences on my own. As dawn approached, I was stumbling from exhaustion. The only thing keeping me awake was the knot of hunger gnawing a hole in my belly.

I resolved to corner the girl at the first opportunity, but she proved too clever. Before I knew it, she'd jumped a fence, scurried across a trash-strewn yard, and was rapping with a stick at the back door of a boarded-up pub. Once I realized what she was up to, I kept well back, leery of who might lie in wait behind that door.

Presently a young man answered. Although he wasn't the slightest bit ostentatious, the quality of his clothing labeled him a man of means. He tousled the girl's blonde mop and dropped to one knee to hear her tale. After a few moments and with a quick wave of her hand in my direction, she darted past the man and into the pub. The man paused at the door, squinting pensively into the predawn glow. At last he stepped out into the yard, righted a toppled wooden bench, and took a seat.

"Lisbet tells me you've had a rough time of it," he said. "If there's something I can do to help, I'd be delighted if you'd let me."

I don't know what I'd been expecting, but it certainly wasn't this. Random acts of kindness? Oh please! More likely he was some sort of pimp or slaver. Still, considering my other options, I felt compelled to at least examine the offer.

"And what's in it for you?"

"Come sit," the man said, "and we'll discuss it."

"And give your friends in the pub the opportunity to surround me?"

"If that were truly my goal," he said, "you would already be my prisoner. Do you really imagine you're that well-hidden?"

He had a point. I was so tired I wasn't thinking straight. Chagrined, I stepped into the yard.

"Let me at least offer you a good meal and a clean bed."

"No way," I said. "I'm not setting foot in that place until I know who you are and what you want with me."

"That's fair. My name is Armand, and this building houses my charity. I do hope you'll excuse the mess—we only recently took possession. What I want is for you to have a place to sleep and food to eat until such time as you are able to fend for yourself."

Despite my skepticism, hunger and exhaustion weakened my resolve. It took all my willpower to deploy a final volley.

"What do you get out of it?"

Armand chuckled. "Although I do subscribe to the notion that virtue is its own reward, while you live under my roof, I would expect you to assist with the day-to-day operation of the charity according to the nature and measure of your abilities. Also, I would hope that once you are back on your feet, you would continue to give as you have received. I trust those terms are not unduly onerous?"

"They sound a little too good to be true."

Armand stood and beckoned me closer. "You have my word they are not. Come. Let's see to your bunk before you fall asleep where you stand."

There was still something about this situation that didn't add up, but I was too weary to put my finger on it. The last vestiges of my resolve finally gave way, and I found myself stepping forward to shake Armand's hand. All memory of the rest of that day is lost to me.

CHAPTER TWO

BRAND LOYALTY

I woke in darkness thinking I'd been dreaming. Reality reasserted itself in stages. The night sounds didn't seem right. The bed seemed somehow shorter and less comfortable than it should. While I searched my sleep-fogged brain for reasonable explanations, a snort erupted just above my head, a sound so strange and unexpected it caused me to fall out of bed and scrabble away in shock.

"Whoa! Easy there, mate."

The voice hovered above me, issuing from the same place as the snort. I finally began to breathe again, since I was now awake enough to realize where I was and that there must be a top bunk. I was suddenly grateful they'd put me on the bottom.

"Who are you?" I asked.

"I'm the guy who's going to be showing you the ropes."

"Do you have a name?"

The bunk creaked as he leapt down. He yawned and stretched. "You can call me Sly."

"Really? That's your name?"

"That's not the sort of question polite folks ask around here."

I blinked in confusion. His response left me with an over-whelming urge to backpedal, but I couldn't figure out what I was supposed to backpedal about. "I don't mean to imply there's anything wrong with it."

Sly tied back the scrap of blanket hanging over a tiny attic window. It was either very early in the morning or overcast, since there was still barely enough light to make out much more than his silhouette. He appeared to be around my age, or maybe a little older.

"Real names—we don't use 'em here," he said. "You don't ask, you don't tell, period. Got it?"

I nodded as though I did.

"Good." He rubbed his chin and looked me up and down. I was suddenly self-conscious, not just about the state of my clothes, but also that I was still lying sprawled across the floor.

"Flinch," he said at last. "That'll work." He held out his hand to help me up. "Welcome to Arm's Arms."

"Arm's Arms? Is what they call the pub, then?"

Sly chuckled. "Well, yes and no. It's what I've taken to calling this little troupe of misfits, wherever it happens to be. We move around enough that if we always adopted the name of the place where we're staying, I'd never be able to keep track of it."

His palm felt oddly rough as he pulled me to my feet. I stiffened at what that implied. He must have noticed, because he snatched his hand back.

"Yeah, I was branded," he said. "So were a lot of the people here. What of it?"

"I didn't say anything."

"No, but you thought it."

There was clearly no point in denying it. "So everyone here is a heretic?"

"Everyone here is a victim," Sly snarled, "and you'll do well to remember it. Or maybe you think Lisbet sneaks out during naptime to disseminate pernicious doctrine?"

"They branded Lisbet?" I asked, aghast.

Sly nodded grimly. "Guilt by association—it's the rage lately. She almost lost her hand from infection. Armand is hopeful she'll regain full function eventually, but he can't be certain. At least she was lucky enough to be right-handed."

When faced with a tale so horrific, the natural impulse is to respond with something sympathetic and profound. I'm ashamed to say that the best I was able to muster was a simple "I'm sorry." It was followed by an awkward silence.

"Well, no sense dwelling on the past," Sly said at last. "You must be starving. You slept the whole day yesterday. What say we find you something to eat?"

He smiled then, and the darkness passed.

"If you can find me a privy first," I said, "I'll be your friend for life."

He raised an eyebrow at that. "Careful what you wish for. Come on, there's one this way."

He led me down several flights of stairs, and after I made a quick detour out back, he took me to the pub's kitchen. Although the room was a shambles, the portly man stoking the oven was ecstatic.

"It works!" he cried. "An actual, honest-to-goodness wood stove, and it works!" He danced a little jig on the spot.

"That's great news, Chef." Sly said. "So when's breakfast?"

Chef stopped dancing long enough to favor Sly with a sidelong look. "Masterpieces don't just spring fully formed from the aether, you know."

"No offense," Sly said, "but we aren't looking for an experience, just a little something to take the edge off Flinch's hunger. He hasn't eaten in over a day."

"You poor thing," Chef said. "I'll boil some oats straight away. It's not what I would have chosen as my first 'Opus Gastronomique' on a brand new stove, but I suppose I can view it as a test." Then he looked at Sly and a slow grin dawned. "In the meantime, Sly, my friend, I'll need you to go out and gather eggs. I'll need at least thirty."

"Thirty?" Sly groaned, as he grudgingly accepted Chef's proffered basket.

"If that's more than you can manage, you can always ask Lisbet to help. She never has any trouble."

"I'll make a deal with you," Sly said. "First oats, *then* eggs. For that kind of scrambling, I'm going to need something to sustain me."

"Well, I suppose it is still early. I guess you could clean up around here while the water boils. I've already done the worst of it, but there's still quite a bit that needs doing. Why don't you start by taking that clutter in the corner out back?"

"I'll help," I said.

Chef put his hands on his hips. "You sure you're up to it?"

I was starting to feel a little dizzy, but wasn't about to let on. "I'm fine," I said. "Just hungry is all."

"All right then," Chef said. "If you two do a good enough job, maybe I'll recruit Lisbet to help with scrubbing the place down later."

We set about scrounging through the trash, which consisted mostly of bits of bar stools and tables, broken beyond repair. As we took the first load outside, I turned to Sly.

"Flinch?" I asked. "Really?"

Sly was unapologetic. "Got to call you something, mate. Lisbet didn't do it, and I saw you second, so I got dibs."

I shrugged and let it drop. I didn't expect to be around long enough for it to matter. Once my parents sorted things out with the Inquisition, I'd be returning to my former life at the shop.

Chef's boiled oats were shockingly good—in fact, they were far and away the best I'd ever eaten. He'd done something that made them smooth and nutty with a hint of maple and some other spices I'd never tasted before that gave them both warmth and a welcome bite. I wolfed them down in a few gulps and then suffered pangs once the bowl was empty, not of hunger, but of nostalgia—they were that good.

"Where did you learn to cook like that?" I asked.

Sly gave me a warning nudge and cleared his throat. "Did I mention Flinch just arrived yesterday?" he said.

"Is that so?" Chef asked, eyeing me up and down. "No wonder I haven't seen him around."

"What I meant to say," I stammered, "was that those were the best oats I've ever tasted."

Chef smiled indulgently. "If you think the oats were good, wait until you've tried my soufflé. Speaking of which, isn't it about time you boys got started gathering those eggs?"

Sly was sullen as we left with the basket, but I was now so eager to try the soufflé that egg-gathering seemed a small price to pay. Once we started though, I understood Sly's reticence. We didn't know the good nesting spots, and even when we found a nest, we weren't certain whether the chicken belonged to someone. Several times we found ample stashes, only to be chased off as thieves when the hen objected. We were exhausted by the time we filled our quota and started back to the pub.

During the egg hunt, I'd been able to pick out some of the taller city landmarks, and felt I had a good shot at finding my way home. If my calculations were correct, it wasn't far—it had just seemed like it in the dark because of Lisbet's circuitous choice of paths. When I looked down my clothes and noticed how filthy they were, I decided it was time to find out if my parents had come back yet.

"So, Sly," I asked. "What are you doing after breakfast?"

Sly snorted. "Cleaning up the kitchen, I imagine—at least if Chef gets his way."

"Do you think we'd have time for a little trip this afternoon?"

"Dunno," he said. "Whereabouts?"

"I was thinking maybe we could see if my parents are back yet."

Sly's jaw dropped in horror. He nearly dropped the eggs as well. "You still don't get it, do you?"

"Get what?" It seemed like every time I turned around I was saying something I shouldn't. It was starting to get old.

Sly sighed with exaggerated patience. "Look, if Lisbet brought you here, it means your parents aren't coming back."

"I don't believe that," I said. "Either way, I'm going to go check. Do you want to come with me or not?"

Sly's eyes widened in alarm. "You really don't want to do that."

Heat crept into my tone. "Oh? And why not?"

"Because once they realize you got away, they'll send someone to look for you. If they really want you, they'll put a bounty on your head." He held up his left hand to reveal the angry red "R" burnt into his palm. "Do you really want to end up like *this*?"

"They're my parents. I have to try. I'll be really careful, and if they aren't there, I'll come right back. I promise."

Sly shook his head sadly. "I'm afraid that won't do you much good, mate."

"Why not?"

"Because if you go, when you get back, we won't be here anymore."

CHAPTER THREE

SUMMONS AND COMPLAINTS

He was pulling my leg—he had to be. No one in his right mind would relocate an entire charity just because one of the needy went to check on his missing family. I laughed, admittedly a little nervously, to see whether he'd confess to the prank, but his brows only drew more tightly together.

"I know you don't want to hear this right now, but believe me, it's not going to get any easier. Your parents aren't coming back, and anyone else who might be waiting for you doesn't have your best interests in mind. I know you don't appreciate yet how lucky you were that Armand got to you first, but at least try to recognize that he's gone out on a major limb for you. If you're determined to muck it up, the least you can do is wait until he decides it's time to move again for some other reason."

"How long will that be?"

Sly shrugged. "Could be weeks. Could be months—it's hard to say."

"Months?"

"If you're lucky, they might even have stopped looking for you by then."

I dropped the subject. I had no idea whether Sly knew what he was talking about, but I had little doubt he believed what he said.

Breakfast at the pub was a bustling affair. Chef had scrounged up some of the old dishware and, while his first soufflés were baking, patiently instructed Sly and me on the proper etiquette of their deployment. The meticulously arranged place settings, situated as they were on mended bar tables, seemed oddly out of place to me, but Chef was insistent.

As the appointed time approached, ragtag groups of two and three drifted in, either from upstairs or outside. Now that I was sensitive to it, their branded palms stood out, either because they pointedly made no attempt to hide them, or more frequently, because they did.

Apparently Chef's emphasis on formality was common practice. As the would-be diners seated themselves, each unfolded a strip of worn bed sheet and placed it carefully in his or her lap. Some chatted amicably while they waited to be served. Others sat, staring vacantly into their plates.

Lisbet wandered in just as Chef appeared with a tray of steaming soufflés. Her face and clothes were smudged with dirt, her hair, wild. Chef took one look at her and shot a glance heavenward. Then he caught Sly's eye and nodded in her direction. Sly hopped up to catch hold of her arm and escort her out, presumably for a good scrubbing. They were delayed when a fat toad squirmed its way out of her pocket. Reveling in its newfound freedom, it undertook a whirlwind tour of half the bar before Lisbet finally managed to snatch it up again.

They'd been gone for only a minute when Armand made an entrance. He paused briefly at each table he passed to exchange a smile and a pleasantry. Then, spying Sly's vacant seat, he made his way over.

"May I?" he asked.

"By all means," I said. Judging by Lisbet's appearance, Sly would be gone awhile.

"I trust Sly is helping your transition go smoothly?"

"He's great," I said, "and Chef's skill with oats is amazing."

Armand shook out his napkin and let it settle into his lap. "Yes, we're quite fortunate to have them both."

Just then Chef appeared at our table carrying the steaming tray in one hand. He cuffed me gently across the back of the head with the other. "Manners, Flinch. Elbows off the table. Do you want Armand to think you were born in a barn?"

Blushing, I put my hands in my lap.

"Easy, there, Chef," Armand said. "The boy's had a rough few days."

Chef sniffed. "Shouldn't matter. If properly instilled, good manners are second-nature. I only point it out for his own good."

Armand chuckled. "I never doubted it. Now how about doing something for *my* own good? Dish me up some of that breakfast. It smells amazing."

Chef beamed with pride as he served up his creation. "That's nothing," he said. "Wait until you taste it! And yes, that is saffron you smell. Even though my supply is dwindling, the recipe sang out for it, and I was powerless to resist."

Armand patted his midsection. "I am sure we shall all greatly appreciate your lack of willpower, even as we regret the lack of our own. I see you're as resourceful as ever. The larder must be pretty bare so soon after a move."

Chef grinned. "Well I did have help from Sly and Flinch. I couldn't have done it all myself."

"I'm glad to hear it. We should talk this afternoon about how best to replenish it. Will you be around?"

"I'll be in the kitchen for the foreseeable future. There's still a great deal to be done before it's functional."

"I'll find you."

Chef nodded and moved on to serve the next table.

Armand then turned to me. "It seems you're adapting remarkably well.

"It was nothing. I just helped Sly gather some eggs."

"On the contrary. Look around you. If you and Sly hadn't helped, these people might not have eaten today. Many of those who come to us are too traumatized to make contributions like yours for quite some time. You should be proud."

"It was the least I could do. You offered me a bed and a roof when I needed it."

Armand nodded slowly. "I think you'll make a fine addition to our team. When you are feeling up to it, I'd like to talk to you about how we can make the best use of your talents."

"I'm happy to help out any way I can for as long as I'm here, but when my parents come back, they're going to need my help."

Armand's smile became suddenly strained. "Yes, well, we should probably discuss that too, I suppose."

My mouth went dry as Armand's reaction told me what I'd been refusing to admit to myself—that Sly had been telling the truth. Before I could press him further, however, Chef signaled everyone had been served. Armand rose to say a brief grace. If those whom the Church had branded had any objections, they did not voice them.

Looking back, I'm sure the soufflé was perfection on a plate, but I was too distraught to taste anything. Although Armand was heartily enjoying his, I ended up only picking at mine. I looked up to meet Armand's sympathetic gaze.

"They aren't coming back, are they?" I asked.

Armand sighed. "I know this is difficult, but you're going to need to keep your strength up."

"But it was all a mistake. They didn't do anything wrong."

Armand shook his head sadly. "We can only play the hands we're dealt. Sometimes all the good cards end up in your opponents' hands."

"This isn't some stupid game. These are my parents."

"What would you have me do?"

"Let me go check to see if they've come back."

Armand chose his words carefully. "I certainly understand your desire to go, but I must warn you that I think it would be dangerous, and ultimately fruitless."

"How do you know?"

At that moment the front door of the pub opened, and a collective intake of breath rippled among the diners. The vestments of the young man who stepped across the threshold bore the pattern of intricate embroidery that marked him a member of the Inquisition.

He scanned the tables until his eye finally lit on Armand. "Ah, there you are."

Armand was dumbstruck. "What are you doing here?"

"Looking for you." He assessed his surroundings as he approached. "What is this place, anyway?"

Out of the corner of my eye I saw several diners slip out the back. The others simply sat frozen in their chairs, eyes wide and jaws slack.

Armand rose to meet him. "I'm going to have to ask you to leave. You have no business here."

"*Au contraire*, dear brother," he said. "I have news for you."

"I'm not the least bit interested in your news. Please don't make me ask you again."

"No can do, Armand. Even though I wasn't thrilled about it, I promised I'd deliver the message, and I'm a man of my word."

"All right then," Armand said. "Deliver your message, and go."

"My pleasure," the Inquisitor said. "This shack has about as much charm as a funeral. What are you doing here anyway? Harboring heretics?"

"Not that it's any of your business," Armand said, "but they're not heretics. At worst, they're nouncers, who for the dreadful sin of knowing someone accused of heresy, have lost everything they own, have been ostracized by their families, and, if that weren't bad enough, have been branded on top of it."

Quick as a snake, the Inquisitor reached out and snatched up my wrist. "Oh yeah? Where's the brand on this one?

Armand hesitated only a moment. "He's my assistant."

The Inquisitor raised an eyebrow. "Your assistant?"

"You have a problem with that?"

The Inquisitor smiled and released my arm from his iron grip. "Not at all," he said. "Tell me, though. How exactly does the boy 'assist' you?"

"I don't see how that is any concern of yours."

"I'm merely asking so he'll know what to prepare for his trip," the Inquisitor said. "This is probably also none of my business, but would I be too terribly forward if I were to suggest he start with a bath."

Armand stepped closer, his eyes defiant. "He's not going anywhere. The boy stays with me."

The Inquisitor held up his hands and took a step back. "I wouldn't dream of having it any other way. That's why both of you will be going. You see, that's the message I'm here to deliver. It seems the Inquisitor General has gone and gotten himself burnt to a crisp by some self-Sacrificing heretic, and our father's been appointed to take his place. For reasons I can't fathom, he's decided that he could use your help. Did I mention his carriage is waiting outside?"

"I can't possibly leave right now," Armand said. "I have far too much going on here."

"I don't think he was offering you a choice. You have one hour to prepare." He looked around once more with obvious distaste. "I trust you'll forgive me if I wait outside."

Only when the door finally slammed behind the Inquisitor, did I realize I'd been holding my breath. To my surprise I noticed that Armand and I were the only people remaining in the bar. Plates of half-eaten soufflés littered empty tables.

"I'm truly sorry about that," Armand said.

"Does this mean this pub is going to be abandoned?"

"Yes, but only by the two of us. There's no way my father would have sent Darron here without swearing him to secrecy first. That's the only way any of this makes any sense. And that means the others should be safe here, at least for the time-being."

"So you're kicking me out?"

Armand shook his head. "Not exactly. In some ways that would be easier, but since Darron suspects you're a heretic, it's too risky. I miscalculated when I named you my assistant. Now, if you refuse to play the part, there's a chance he'll send someone to apprehend you. Unfortunately, necessary or not, my brother always prefers to bargain from a position of strength."

CHAPTER FOUR

EPIPHANY

I was in hot water, no doubt about it, and not just the bathwater Chef had kindly heated for me on his stove. As I scrubbed away at the grime left over from Lisbet's excursion, I wracked my brain to decide if I should go along with Armand's charade or just try to sneak away. It was pretty clear Darron suspected me of Phrendonic heresy, that is, of casting spells—the very thing my father had lacked the ability to do. Simply understanding the theory of how the spells worked (one of my father's specialties) wasn't technically supposed to be heretical as long as you didn't actually cast them, which explained why my father reacted the way he had when the Inquisitors arrived.

If Darron had his way, he'd probably bring me up on formal charges. If found guilty, I'd be given the opportunity to renounce the heresy, but then, like Sly, I'd be forever branded a nouncer. While nouncers are technically absolved, most people view them with suspicion and treat them with contempt. That's why the idea of facing the Inquisitor General with Darron breathing down my neck tied my gut in knots, but sneaking off wasn't a particularly attractive option either. Even if I managed to avoid capture by Armand's brother, my prospects for surviving alone on the streets were next to nil. At least with Armand, I'd have an ally. I'd been over that several times, and I kept coming back to it.

Armand had stood up to his brother when he'd grabbed my wrist, and I could think of no reason for him to do that unless his motives were genuine. In turn, that gave rise to the hope, however slight, that I might be able to get Armand to intercede with his father on my parents' behalf. Despite the danger, I couldn't let that opportunity slip by.

There was no time to wash my clothes, but there was no need. Sly pretty much insisted I take his spare set, and when I protested, he offered to take my dirty ones in trade. I was so grateful I could have hugged him. I threw on the clothes and headed out to the main bar to find Armand waiting. At his urging, I made a show of carrying his hastily packed bags out to the carriage, trying my best to ignore Armand's brother as he scrutinized me from atop his gray stallion.

Moments later, Armand and I were seated across from each other in the carriage, waiting for Darron's signal. At last, he gave the driver a nod. As the carriage lurched forward, I caught one last glimpse of Sly watching from an upstairs window. Lisbet was with him, and just before they disappeared from sight, she raised her hand in a tentative wave.

Armand steepled his fingers against his chin as he sized me up.

Unnerved by the attention, I asked something to break the silence. "Where are we going?"

"I'd be lying if I said it was someplace safe," he said. "Yet, it may prove less dangerous than other circumstances you could have found yourself in—assuming you can keep your wits about you. Do you suspect that might be a problem?"

"To be honest, sir, it might depend on the situation. Since I have no way of knowing what I've gotten myself into, I feel like I'm in over my head."

Armand chuckled at that. "Funny," he said. "I've got that same feeling, but for the opposite reason. Let me summarize what I know, and then you can ask me what you like."

I nodded.

"What I've told you is true—I do run a charity. However, the fact that it caters to victims of the Inquisition could cause us some difficulties. If that were generally known, certain elements of the Church, particularly the Primal, would find it troubling."

"The Primal? The leader of the whole Church?"

"I'm afraid so. Unfortunately, a recent attack by heretics in the heart of the Holy City has him convinced that Phrendonic heretics are conspiring against him. His paranoia was bad enough before, but the loss of the Inquisitor General will likely drive him beyond all reason."

"And your father has been appointed to replace the Inquisitor General?"

"So it seems. As a result, he'll be the Church official responsible for running every aspect of the Inquisition. I can only assume he accepted the position to prevent the situation from escalating to genocide. It's not a job I'd envy."

"And he knows about your charity work?"

Armand nodded. "He disapproved, but tolerated it. Unfortunately, I expect that to change."

Implications swirled in my mind, but despite the chaos, something finally registered. "Does that mean you sent Lisbet to find me?"

"I did," Armand said. "Or rather I sent her to search for survivors the Inquisitors may have overlooked. Lisbet's case drove home to me the importance of being proactive. I may not be able to do anything for the suspects themselves, but if I'm lucky I might be able to help their families, particularly if I can get to them before the Inquisitors do. All too often, once the Inquisition is through with them, it's too late."

"But that means you know my parents are innocent."

Armand regarded me with sympathy. "I'm afraid I don't, but even if that's true, it would be unlikely to help them. The Church has long viewed the Theratigan name with suspicion. You would do well to leave it behind and not look back."

"Could you do the same in my place?"

Armand raised an eyebrow. "As a matter of fact, if my father's new position goes awry, I might do just that. While there may be a certain bleak nobility to clinging to your heritage in the face of overwhelming odds, great deeds are rarely accomplished from beyond the grave."

I was stunned. "Could it really come to that?"

Armand nodded. "Opportunists are drawn to madness like vultures to a carcass."

"Is he really mad, then? The Primal, I mean."

Armand rubbed his chin thoughtfully. "Perhaps mad is not the right term. It might be more accurate to say that his fears eclipse his reason, and that makes him susceptible to those willing to exploit those fears to their own advantage."

I was appalled to imagine the Primal in such dire straits. "But can't they see what they're doing? Innocent people are being killed."

"Oh, they know. They no doubt congratulate themselves for it as evidence of their increasing influence. When grasping for power, the closer one comes, the more the heat of it warps the conscience. So there you have it. Now that you have a little better idea what you are up against, will you be able to play this charade, or do we need to devise a way to have you quietly disappear before anyone important gets around to noticing you?"

My pulse pounded in my ears at the thought of rubbing elbows with corrupt Inquisitors, but I couldn't give up a chance to plead my parents' case before the Inquisitor General. "I can do it," I said. "You went out on a limb for me, I'd be grateful for the opportunity to return the favor. How should I prepare?"

"First you'll need to memorize your duties. That will be harder than it sounds, since you will no doubt be called upon to perform them as though you've done them before. You'll need to know my needs and preferences, from how much sugar I take in my tea to which vestments are required for which occasions."

"Vestments?"

"I tend not to wear them at the charity, since the connection to the Church could make some of the residents uncomfortable, but since I am a priest, in other venues I prefer to dress accordingly."

I swallowed my surprise. "Should I be taking notes?"

Armand shook his head. "Your ability to write will be helpful, but notes of that sort in the wrong hands would be disastrous. We'll just have to trust your memory. We only have a day or so to prepare, so I suggest we begin immediately. I think we should start with your name. You can keep your first name, but we'll definitely need to change the last name to something else. Any ideas?"

"How about Flinch?" I asked. I'd already started getting used to it, and with everything else going on, I didn't fancy having to memorize another.

"'Flinch' it is."

The rest of the day was spent memorizing the minute details of Armand's habits. After the first hour, my mind was already reeling, and I doubted I'd ever be able to keep everything straight. Armand reassured me that my performance need not be flawless, just good enough to convince his brother that I had actually been in his service for at least a short while.

The lessons continued as the carriage left Caprian behind. We headed east along an ancient stretch of road known as the Pilgrim's Penance, through rolling fields greening with the first tender shoots of spring. After a time, the patchwork fields gave way to rugged grazing land peppered with roaming knots of goats and sheep, and thence to unclaimed wilderness. Here the rocky landscape was littered with low-lying grasses, struggling brush, and the occasional stunted tree. Once we caught a glimpse of a pack of wild donkeys picking their way among the rocks near the road. Shortly thereafter, Armand pointed out a cave that had sheltered a notorious band of highwaymen. Although the Caprian authorities had rooted them out long ago, older merchants still tended to hurry through the region with their eyes peeled and a weapon near at hand.

Just as dusk was falling, the carriage passed a sign dangling from a twisted branch. Painted across it in faded red letters was the single word "Epiphany."

"We're almost to the inn," Armand said. "You're still sure you want to go through with this?"

I forced myself to nod.

Armand slapped my shoulder encouragingly. "That's the spirit. You'll do just fine."

The carriage finally rolled to a stop outside a large inn surrounded by a barn and several outbuildings that together seemed to comprise the entire town. The buildings were sheltered along the north and west by a small ridge, barely taller than the inn itself. As we hopped out of the carriage and stretched, I ran frantically over everything I'd memorized, praying I wouldn't forget anything important.

Darron was waiting at the front door. Armand went to greet him, while I gathered up his luggage.

"Any trouble on the road?" Darron asked.

Armand eyed him in surprise. "Should I have expected some?"

Darron frowned. "These days, one never knows."

I lugged Armand's baggage up to his room, unpacked several articles he would need for bed, and started a fire in the fireplace. I then returned to the common room where I found him at a table chatting with his brother and several others sporting Inquisitorial embroidery. I stood quietly until Armand finally acknowledged me.

"Yes, Mr. Flinch?"

Darron's glittering eyes darted back and forth between us.

"Your room is prepared, sir," I said.

"Thank you, Mr. Flinch. I shan't be needing you anymore this evening. Get yourself a bite to eat and some rest. I'm told we depart at dawn."

"Very good, sir," I said, executing my best stiff nod. I turned and headed to the bar for an ale.

As I waited to be served, I saw Darron cock an eyebrow at Armand. "I suppose you expect me to believe that's the same filthy lad I saw at your pub this morning?"

Armand spared a glance in my direction. "Mr. Flinch, you mean? I presume he must be. I only have one assistant. If you doubt it, I could call him over to show you his wrist where you bruised it."

Darron eyed me dubiously. "That won't be necessary. Tell me, though. Does he begin every breakfast by rolling himself in dirt?"

Armand set down his drink and leaned forward. "Darron," he said, "what is this fixation you have with my assistant?"

Darron folded his arms in front of him. "These are danger-ous times," he said. "I like to be certain who I'm associating with, and frankly, I would never have pegged you as the type to take on a servant."

Armand sat back and took another drink. "Running a char-ity is a bigger undertaking than you might imagine. I'll be honest. I never saw myself as the type either, but there's noth-ing like necessity to adjust your preconceptions."

"How's he working out?" Darron asked. "He looks a little young to me."

"He is young," Armand said, "but I'm not looking for someone with silver hair and flawless etiquette. My needs are more diverse and practical than that. For example, this morning, when it was discovered the larder was empty, Mr. Flinch volunteered to help collect the eggs for our breakfast. Someone older, and with more experience as a manservant, might well have balked at such a task. And as a reward for his generosity, you nearly broke his arm."

Darron's compatriots, who had been watching the ex-change with mild amusement, now turned to him with raised eyebrows, as though they thought perhaps some explanation was in order. He ignored them.

"You almost make me want to take on an assistant myself," he said. "Does he have a brother?"

Armand grinned impishly. "If he did, do you think I'd tell you? If this works out as well as I think it will, I may just take on a second."

For the first time since Darron had appeared at the pub, my breathing returned to its normal rate. As their conversation moved on to other topics, I wandered off in search of food. I soon discovered that Armand had given me coin enough to eat for a week. A few minutes later I was sitting contentedly near the kitchen, slurping from a bowl of stew, gnawing on a loaf of bread, and washing it all down with my glass of ale. Every once in a while, I glanced toward the Inquisitors' table in case Armand happened to need something.

During one of these glances I caught sight of something that chilled my blood. Seated at one of the inn's corner tables was a tiny woman, older, smartly dressed, her snow-white hair swept up under an elaborate burgundy hat. It was cocked jauntily over one eye and adorned by a single peacock plume. A bold cameo, nestled in stiff lace at her neck, lent her an air of crisp authority. My frenzied chewing ground slowly to a halt as we locked eyes. I stared openly, and she did not look away. Even that wouldn't have disturbed me particularly, except for one thing. Although I couldn't place her for the life of me, I knew with dead certainty I had seen this woman somewhere before.

CHAPTER FIVE

RELATIVE DIFFERENCES

I wolfed down my meal. Although I hoped this lady was having as much trouble placing me, I couldn't rely on it—and with Darron present, all it would take would be a cheery greeting across the room to ruin me.

Gathering up my bowl and glass, I ducked into the kitchen in search of an exit. I was not disappointed. In response to the startled expressions of the staff, I hastily thanked them for their efforts, dropped off my dishes, and with formal little bow of farewell, disappeared out the back way. My plan was to wait until it was late enough for everyone to retire and then quietly make my way back inside. Since we were leaving at dawn, I hoped to be gone before the lady's presence could become an issue again.

Like most plans, this one was not without its flaws. A cool wind out of the north smelled of rain, and just above the ridge, pulses of light danced amidst angry clouds. Determined to avoid spending the next day in soggy clothes, I made for the barn. As I got closer, I caught sight of two Inquisitors posted outside and veered off, deciding instead that biding my time in Armand's carriage might be more to my liking. I found it situated among several others on a graveled patch of dirt, horseless and silent in the darkness. I fumbled with the latch and hopped inside just as the first gravid droplets of the storm fell. I was still congratulating myself on my timing when there was a sharp rap on the door.

Expecting the driver, I opened the door with an apology at the ready—only to be confronted by a peacock plume perched atop a burgundy hat.

"Good evening, young man," the lady said, "I wonder if we might have a private word?"

Perhaps Chef was right about manners being ingrained. Her formality threw me (not to mention the fact that she would shortly be standing in a downpour). Despite my conviction that fraternizing with this woman could prove disastrous, I nonetheless heard myself granting her request.

"Of course," I said, holding out my hand to assist her.

Once she was in the carriage, I slammed the door as quickly as I could manage without seeming rude. She took a seat and indicated that I should do the same.

"So," she said. "Young Theratigan, is it?"

"I'm sorry, but you must be mistaking me for someone else." I wracked my brain to recall where I'd seen her before. She must have been one of my father's clients, but a mental rundown of the client list didn't garner me any matches.

"And you must be mistaking me for someone who is easily fooled. Best get that out of your system right off."

"What do you want with me?" I snapped. Her tone had set me on edge, and my embarrassment from my failure to deceive her wasn't helping.

"That depends. Before I can decide, I need to know how a Theratigan comes to be traveling in the carriage of the Inquisitor General."

"You have me at a disadvantage," I said. "Before I could discuss such things, I'd need to know who you are and why you want to know."

My admission seemed to genuinely surprise her. "You really don't know, do you?"

I shrugged.

"Well, it has been some years since the wedding," she said. "I suppose it's possible..."

And then I had it. This lady wasn't a client, she was family. She'd been at my uncle's wedding, and the way she had tried to run things, it was a good bet she was my aunt's mother. That she still recognized me all these years later had to be more a matter of family resemblance than memory, but at least it explained why she seemed so interested in me.

"Oh, I think I remember you now," I said.

"Well, it's about time. Now let's get to the point, shall we? What are your ties to the Inquisitor General?"

"It's sort of complicated."

A brilliant flash punctuated my statement, followed by the low rumble of thunder. The rain became a deluge.

"It looks like we have time for explanations."

Since this lady was related, even if only by marriage, I wanted desperately to trust her. For all I knew, she might be the only family I had left. I decided to level with her.

"The Inquisition came for my parents."

She nodded. "I'm not surprised."

"I got away, and Armand took me in when I didn't have anywhere else to go. He runs a charity to help nouncers."

"You've already gotten ahead of yourself. Who is Armand?"

"He's the Inquisitor General's son."

"And you're telling me the Inquisitor General's son runs a charity for nouncers?"

"He believes the Primal is overreacting, so he tries to help those he can, but he has to keep it secret, even from his brother."

"His brother?"

"His brother Darron. You probably saw him in the inn. He was one of the Inquisitors."

"So the Inquisitor General has two sons?"

"That I know of," I said.

"I see. All this is very interesting, but it still doesn't explain why you are traveling in this carriage."

"Because I'm Armand's new assistant, and when his father sent for him, I naturally had to go along."

"So the two of you are planning to meet with the Inquisitor General?"

I nodded. "I'm hoping to convince Armand to intercede with his father on my parents' behalf."

"And what makes you think that once the Inquisitor General discovers you've escaped, you won't share your parents' fate? Naïveté is a luxury you can't afford. The Church Fathers are long past responding to bids for sympathy—power is the only thing that moves them now."

"What other choice do I have? My parents are gone, and their shop is destroyed. I have no money and no prospects. It may be a long-shot, but it's pretty much my only shot."

The lady patted my shoulder. "I know it seems like that now," she said, "but you're young, and for the moment, you're still free. If you're clever and hard-working, that's all you really need to build a life for yourself. This course you've chosen, though—it's fraught with more dangers than you know. He who seeks the rainbow in the sky is more apt to discover the chasm at his feet. Don't squander what little good fortune you've had. Leave this place and these plans of yours behind and start fresh in a new city with a new name."

"And how do you expect me to do that? Sell the shirt off my back?"

"I didn't say it would be easy. But even walking cross-country would be safer than the path you're on now. If it would help, I could spare enough money for you to book passage with someone, but if I do, you must promise me you'll abandon this foolhardy plan and have nothing more to do with the Church." She opened her handbag and began to search through it.

My future seemed bleaker by the moment. "But that would mean abandoning my parents."

"It would mean being adult enough to approach the problem realistically."

"But Armand has given me no reason to doubt him."

She stopped searching and looked up at me in disbelief. "Do you have even the slightest idea how many innocent people this Inquisitor General of yours has tortured and destroyed? Any idea at all?"

Taken aback, I looked away and shook my head.

"I thought not."

"If I could just talk to Armand about it first, I'd have a better idea of what my chances are. If it looks as grim as you say, maybe then I could leave."

"Well then," she said. "I can see that despite my best efforts, my advice is destined to fall on deaf ears. So be it, but when things go foully awry, don't say you weren't warned." She went back to searching through her handbag. At last she produced a small pouch and held it out to me.

"What's this?"

"A little something to help you keep an open mind. Take it. With any luck, sometime between now and dawn you'll come to your senses. If not, and you make the ill-fated decision to travel in this carriage once more…well, at least my conscience will be clear."

I couldn't help myself—I took the pouch. "I'll pay you back someday. I swear I will."

She stood then, her strained smile intimating she didn't think there would be much chance of that. "Best of luck to you, young man. You're going to need it."

She pushed open the carriage door and stepped out. Although the rain had lessened, it was still a steady downpour. I rubbed the fog from the window with my sleeve to catch intermittent storm-lit glimpses as she made her way back to the inn, a huge umbrella protecting her from the worst of the weather. That struck me as odd—I hadn't noticed an umbrella before.

Once she was gone, I poured the contents of the pouch into my hand. True to her word, she'd provided me sufficient funds to hire a coach, but that wasn't all. In addition to the coins, my palm also held a glittering pocket watch. I held the watch up to the window for a closer look, but the lightning revealed precious little detail. A quick search of the carriage produced a box of candles and a pack of lucifers, and soon I was attempting an inspection by candlelight.

Although the light was still not ideal, I could see the watch was ornate and likely contained a fair percentage of gold. A cabochon gemstone in the center of the front cover bore a striking resemblance to an eye. Floral scrollwork adorned the back. I pressed the post and the lid snapped open to reveal a white face with crisp italic numerals. I fussed for a bit with the latch on the back cover, and in a few moments I was examining the device's internal workings. Even by candlelight, I could tell the craftsmanship was remarkable—on a par with my father's best work. At first, the mechanism seemed unwieldy for a watch so well-designed, but upon closer inspection the opposite was true. The mechanism controlling the watch movements was actually quite compact. What made it seem unwieldy was the presence of a second independent mechanism. Intrigued, I attempted to trace by eye the intricacies of its springs and gears, but after several attempts, I still hadn't figured it out. Reluctantly I gave up, promising myself to try again in better light.

The patter of droplets on the carriage roof told me the rain had diminished to the point where I might be able to dash to the inn without drenching myself. I closed the watch and slipped it into my pocket, replaced the candles under the seat, and made a run for it. Fortunately, the common room was devoid of both old ladies and Inquisitors. I let myself into Armand's room and made my way by the glow of the fireplace embers to my assigned pallet.

Sleep did not come easily. Even when it did, it was troubled. Now that I had the means to leave, my mind was at war. Every rational argument I could muster told me I'd be a fool to stay, but my heart steadfastly refused to give ground, and with dawn fast-approaching, their conflict raged relentlessly across the battlefield of my unhappy dreams.

CHAPTER SIX

PRISONERS' DILEMMAS

Dawn was upon me, and still I wallowed in indecision. I resolved to ask Armand's opinion, praying he could help me find some way to avoid the Inquisition without abandoning my parents. When at last I heard him stir, I hopped up, lit a lantern, and rummaged through his luggage to lay out his vestments for the day—the sooner I saw to my duties, the more time I'd have to broach the subject. I still had no idea how to do that without seeming ungrateful.

"Good morning," Armand said.

"And to you, sir."

"I trust everything is all right?"

Paranoia gripped me—had he found out about my meeting with the lady? Was he testing me?

"Yes, of course," I said. "Why do you ask?"

Armand raised an eyebrow. "I was a little concerned when the storm hit and you weren't around. I trust you managed to stay dry?"

I nodded. "I was out for a walk, and I hopped into the carriage when the rain started. I was stuck there for a while, but at least I didn't get wet."

"Good thinking. Until we have time to find another set of clothes for you, you'll want to be careful with the ones you have. We're unlikely to find any where we're going."

"About that," I said. "Where *are* we going?"

Armand lathered up for a quick shave while I finished repacking his luggage. "Histlewick Downs," he said. "It's a bit north of here."

"Can I ask you a question?"

"Certainly," Armand replied. "What's on your mind?"

"I was just wondering whether…"

A staccato rapping at the door usurped Armand's attention. "Oh bother," he said, wiping the lather from his face. "Could you get that, please?"

Darron paced the hallway outside. His eyes narrowed when he saw me. "Where's Armand?"

"I'm right here," Armand said, throwing on vestments and coming to the door. "Are we late?"

"We've had a complication, and I want to know what you make of it."

"What sort of complication?"

"Come with me to the barn. You'll want to see for yourself."

Armand's forehead creased. "The barn? Is this about the prisoners?"

"That's what I'm trying to figure out."

On the way there, Darron explained that he'd gone down early to prepare his horse for the day's journey, only to find both Inquisitors asleep at their posts.

"And the prisoners?" Armand asked.

"That's the odd thing. They're still right where they're supposed to be."

"Doesn't that suggest someone's been working the men too hard?"

Darron snorted. "Had it just been one of them, maybe I'd buy that, but both?"

Several Inquisitors were now gathered around the barn door, including those who'd dined with Armand and Darron the night before.

Armand greeted them and let loose with a barrage of questions. At first I tried to keep up, but once I realized I had no idea where the questions were leading, my mind began to wander. My hand happened across the watch in my pocket. I pulled it out and popped it open, curious to know whether it was accurate. I was pleased to see that it registered six a.m. sharp, which I guessed was just about right, judging by the rosy glow in the eastern sky. When I looked up again, Armand and the others had disappeared into the barn. I scurried in after them.

What I saw staggered me. Four prisoners sat bound to chairs surrounding a supporting beam, their brass shackles attached to a ring set high enough to keep their hands suspended above their heads. The Inquisition was known for taking prisoners, but never in my wildest dreams would I have expected they'd be treated like this. Their faces were wholly concealed by leather masks with smooth surfaces broken only by small holes where their mouths should be. Their misery was palpable, but what was most disturbing was that one of them was a woman, and two of them were just children. My thoughts went immediately to my parents. Had they also been treated like this? I must have gasped, because suddenly all eyes were on me.

"What's he doing in here?" Darron asked.

Armand quickly interceded. "Mr. Flinch, if you would be so kind as to wait outside, we shall be done here presently."

Numb with horror, I backed away.

Once outside, I cast frantically about for some means to escape what I'd seen. Over by the patch of gravel, several wagons, carts, and carriages were being readied, but I ruled them out when I noticed the Inquisitor General's driver among them. Trying to book passage right under his nose struck me as a recipe for disaster. I considered checking the common room for another traveler, but I couldn't imagine how I'd be able to leave that way without the Inquisitors noticing, unless I tried to buy discretion as well—and with so many Inquisitors about, I doubted anyone would be fool enough to agree to that.

Then I spied the ridge behind the barn. With luck, I could hide out in the wilderness for a day or so, and then book passage. Unfortunately, all Darron would have to do to spoil that plan is leave one Inquisitor behind to watch for me. Faced with these alternatives, my only choice was to continue on as I had been, and hope Armand wasn't playing me false. I took a deep breath and waited.

For a minute or so, the discussion in the barn grew heated, but I couldn't make out the words. Then, abruptly, there was silence. Moments later Armand stepped outside.

"Mr. Flinch," he said. "Could I trouble you to collect my bags and load them on the carriage? We'll be leaving shortly."

"I'll see to it immediately, sir."

As I turned to comply, I caught sight of Darron eyeing me over Armand's shoulder. Though I didn't give him the satisfaction of looking back, I could feel the weight of that stare all the way back to the inn.

Packing up Armand's belongings took only a few minutes. I loaded the bags on the carriage and climbed aboard. The instant Armand joined me, the carriage surged forward. He sank down across from me, took a deep breath, and regarded me for a long while, his expression deadly serious.

"I'm going to ask you some questions," he said, "and I want you to consider your answers very carefully. As long as you are honest with me, I will still support you as best as I can. If you are not, I can make no such guarantees. Do I make myself clear?"

I nodded solemnly and, I hoped, calmly, but my palms were sweating. "I'm ready," I said.

"Now I'm aware your parents were accused of Phrendonic heresy," he said, "but despite the Inquisition's tendency to arrest entire families, I have been presuming the children to be innocent. Yet, I've been told of instances where children as young as twelve have convincingly incriminated themselves. I am therefore compelled to ask: are you a Phrendonic heretic?"

I didn't even have to think. "No sir, I am not," I said. "While I know a thing or two about the underlying theory of Phrendonic magic, I've never once tried to cast a spell."

Armand raised an eyebrow. "Although your definition is technically correct, at least as I read the canons, you do realize most Inquisitors would not recognize such a fine distinction?"

"Which is why I would never tell them that, but you asked me to be honest."

"So I did," Armand said. "Next question: did you have any involvement with the Inquisitors at the barn or their prisoners last night?"

I shook my head. "I headed initially for the barn, but when I saw the Inquisitors standing there, I changed my mind and waited out the rain in the carriage. As for the prisoners, I didn't even know they were there."

"So the Inquisitors were awake when you saw them?"

"Yes."

"And when was that?"

"It was right before the storm hit. It really wasn't that long after we arrived—an hour, maybe?"

"I don't suppose anyone saw you get into the carriage? Darron knows you still weren't back by the time I turned in. It will likely take more than just your word to convince him."

I couldn't bring myself to mention my meeting with the lady. If she'd actually done something to those Inquisitors, her status as family, distant though it was, would lead Darron's suspicions right back to me. If she hadn't, after what I'd seen in the barn, putting Inquisitors on her trail would be unconscionable. I had to think fast.

"I can do better than that," I said. "I can prove I was here in the carriage—I lit a candle."

"Did you, now?" Armand asked. "Let's have a look."

He reached down under the seat for the box containing the candles and with a smile, he retrieved the one that I'd used, now somewhat shorter than the rest.

"Oh, this is encouraging," he said. "It seems my faith in you was not misplaced. While in the carriage, did you happen to notice anything unusual or suspicious?"

"No sir. The windows were fogged and the candle made it even more difficult to see outside."

Armand nodded. "So the good news is that we can rule you out as a suspect. The bad news is now we don't have a suspect."

Actually, the good news was that Armand was persuaded by evidence. The Inquisition had a reputation for ignoring reason and relying on preconceptions and dogma, but if Armand's father was anything like him, my parents might actually stand a chance. Before I could plead my case, though, I'd need to gently press Armand for as much information about the workings of the Inquisition and the current situation as I could. I'd be a fool to go in blind.

"What was I suspected of?"

"Darron is of a mind that someone used Phrendonic heresy on the Inquisitors guarding the prisoners to put them to sleep."

"Someone was in league with the prisoners?"

"Possibly."

"If someone could do that, wouldn't he also free them?"

"Not necessarily," Armand said. "The guards didn't carry the keys to the shackles."

"So someone tried, but botched the rescue?"

"It could be something far more insidious. You saw the manner in which the prisoners were being held?"

I nodded, cringing a little at the recollection.

"I know what it must have looked like, but necessity, not cruelty, is the underlying motivation for their treatment. There's no safe way to confine a skilled Phrendonic, and it's impossible to judge a Phrendonic's skill by looking at him. Masking is far kinder than the alternatives. Unfortunately, they can still be incredibly dangerous, as the former Inquisitor General discovered."

"What happened to him?"

"He was killed by the leader of the Accipitrine Order, a group that still boasts quite a number of highly trained Phrendonic heretics. He pulled it off even though he was bound and masked."

I risked another subtle test. "I don't understand. If he was masked, he shouldn't have been able to vest a spell on anything other than himself."

"It seems you do have some grasp of the theory," Armand said. "In fact, we believe that's exactly what he did."

His continued acknowledgement of my facility with Phrendonic basics without balking was a huge relief. As he'd said, many Inquisitors would have concluded that understanding Phrendonic heresy was tantamount to practicing it—as bogus a proposition as assuming if you can appreciate music, you must therefore be a concert pianist. I decided to push him further. I needed to be absolutely certain where I stood.

"But then whatever the prisoner did would have affected him too."

Armand still didn't bat an eye. "It did. It's been dubbed the 'Infernal Sacrifice.' By centering the blast on himself, he managed to kill the Inquisitor General and several nearby aides, though of course, he did not survive it either. The Primal has since decreed that all suspects must be transported in the presence of family members. While that won't stop a determined Sacrificer, he believes the presence of spouses and children will act as a deterrent."

Armand's expression had soured during the explanation.

"I take it you don't approve," I said.

"I don't. Apart from the cowardice inherent in using children as shields, the whole endeavor is doomed to fail. History has shown time and again that application of enough force can change almost anything—except a mind."

My heart sank. Armand's views might actually be too moderate. There was no way his father could espouse the same views and hold the position he did. I clung to the hope that I could at least convince the Inquisitor General to adhere to the letter of the canons. First things first, though. If I was going to persuade him to hear my case, I still needed to know more about what was happening. I pressed on.

"So you think another heretic tried to keep the prisoners from revealing their secrets by Sacrificing himself in their midst, but ended up losing his nerve?"

"I don't think so," Armand said. "Such a heretic could simply have killed the prisoners without harming himself."

"What was his goal then?"

"Many Phrendonics are little more than dabblers. A Sacrifice might very well be beyond them. Darron is concerned a more-skilled heretic may have tried to equip the prisoners with the capability."

Once more I found myself recoiling. "Wouldn't it be kinder just to kill them?"

"And deny them a chance at martyrdom? The psychology of noble causes is strange and unpredictable. We dare not make the same mistake twice. That's why Darron is riding ahead with a warning."

"So Darron suspected I could do something like that to another person?"

"In times like these," Armand said, "we can't afford to take chances."

"I guess it's a good thing I'm afraid of the dark."

Armand's brow furrowed. "Don't assume the burnt candle will exonerate you. "Darron is not prone to let pesky details interfere with his pet theories. At best, the candle provides only meager evidence of your innocence, but perhaps with everything else going on, it will suffice to keep him at bay." He smiled sympathetically. "I have some idea how you feel. I've been dancing this dance with him for years."

I shuddered. Darron's meddling could still spoil my chances with the Inquisitor General. Obviously, my best shot at minimizing that risk would be to rely on Armand's advice, at least until I knew more.

"And what am I to do in the meantime?"

"Be efficient and invisible. For my part, I'll try to keep this little visit as short as possible. With any luck, we could find ourselves on our way back to the pub in a day or so." He patted me on the shoulder. "You'll feel better if you get some rest. Why don't you try to nap?"

He took out a small book then, and while he read, I leaned back in my seat and attempted to clear my mind by watching the rocky landscape fly by. By now, I was so tightly wound I felt I might never sleep again, and yet, the next thing I knew, the sun was high in the sky. Across from me Armand had nodded off as well, his book still resting open in his lap.

Outside, the rocks and twisted underbrush had given way to low-lying wetlands dominated variously by tall reeds and grasses surrounding small stagnant pools or by brooding stands of gnarled trees, moss-draped and ancient. The land steamed in the sunlight, and the air was dense and oppressive. The reluctant breeze hummed with an unnerving cacophony of trills, whistles, thrums, and shrieks from unseen sources that I tried to convince myself must be birds. The horses suffered from the heat, and they now drew the carriage at a slow walk instead of their customary trot. The road meandered on amidst the pools and hummocks. I drank it all in, amazed that a road could even exist in such a place.

Armand stirred and rubbed at the kinks in his neck. "I see we've made the fens. We should be reaching the edge of the downs in not too long."

The sun was suddenly shrouded as the road took us beneath the boughs of a particularly large and impenetrable grove. Sheets of hanging moss slithered eerily along the roof of the carriage, dislodging all manner of bizarre and skittering creatures, many of which I couldn't begin to identify.

"We should be coming to the bridge soon," Armand volunteered. "The trees get thickest near the river."

Despite my aversion to several bright green frogs now clinging by overgrown toes to the glass, I pressed my face to the window. I was anxious for any sign that we were making progress, and a bridge seemed like just the thing. Unfortunately, the gloom from the canopy conspired with marshy vapors to obscure vision at any distance. I was just about to give up in favor of another nap when out of the corner of my eye, I saw swift movement. It was followed by a thunderous snap and a startled exclamation from the driver. The carriage lurched forward and then hard to one side, nearly keeling over as it left the road. A moment later it came to a gentle and disturbingly squishy stop.

Armand threw open the door and leapt out of the carriage. It tilted precariously, its wheels on one side mired up to the axles. The spooked horses struggled in deep muck as the driver strove desperately to release them. Behind us, an enormous tree limb lay where it had fallen across our path.

As Armand rushed to assist with the horses, three figures stepped out onto the road. Two of them calmly drew bows and nocked arrows. The third, after a brief adjustment of her burgundy hat, folded her arms in front of her and smiled.

CHAPTER SEVEN

A DESTINATION OF NOTE

Armand was so intent on his task that the horses were free of the carriage before he knew we had company. He froze at the sight of the men and their bows, despite the fact that he was standing in mud up to his shins.

"Mr. Flinch," he said, without taking his eyes from the nocked weapons. "Get down!"

I dropped back into the carriage, and then peeked out again. Had the lady reconsidered? Had she decided to save me from my folly by force?

She laughed scathingly. "My, my, my. It seems the rumors are true—the good Father does have a soft spot for heretics. How delicious."

Had she just called me a heretic? Could this get any worse?

Armand slowly raised his hands. "I'm afraid you have me at a disadvantage, madam."

One of the bowmen snorted. "I'll say."

The lady silenced him with a glance.

Armand, nodded to indicate the weapons. "Whatever it is

you want from us, I'm sure we can work out something that doesn't require the use of those."

The lady signaled her companions to lower their weapons. "Perhaps you're right. Why don't you climb up here out of the muck, and we'll chat."

Armand was visibly relieved. "Thank you," he said. "You won't regret this." When he tried to move forward, however, his feet were stuck. The bog, it seemed, was reluctant to surrender its catch.

I ransacked the carriage for a rope or something for him to grab onto, but before I could find anything, the driver tossed Armand reins from the horses and then gently led the anxious team back up toward the road. I poked my head back out of the carriage just as Armand pulled free. The moment they reached stable ground, the lady gazed at him with an unnatural intensity of a sort I'd only seen on the faces of those who'd commissioned complicated devices in the shop—when they were contributing those little finishing touches my father was so regrettably incapable of doing himself.

"Look out!" I cried, but it was too late. The lady made a dismissive gesture, and Armand collapsed where he stood. The startled driver rushed to Armand's aid—only to topple over next to him.

I ducked back into the carriage in shock. At some level I knew flight was hopeless. Armand's experience with the bog told me there was little chance of escape that way. That left only the road.

"Mr. Theratigan," the lady called out, "I'd like a word with you."

It had all happened too fast. I was still struggling to figure out how I could possibly save Armand and still salvage a meeting with the Inquisitor General. Even if I succeeded, how could Armand possibly support me now? Once he found out who'd attacked him, he was sure to think I was complicit. My head reeling, I declined to answer. Maybe if I ignored her, she'd go away.

Then she upped the ante. "It's about your parents."

Even though I suspected a trick, I still had to bite my tongue...hard.

"Very well," she said at last. "It's your choice. If you would rather cower in your carriage than find out where they took your parents, who am I to argue?"

I heard activity outside, followed by the sound of the horses being led away. It suddenly dawned on me that being stuck in the middle of a desolate fen presented its own set of challenges.

I poked my head out once more. "All right, you win. Where are they?"

The lady was waiting by the edge of the road where Armand had fallen. Neither Armand nor the driver was anywhere in sight.

"I am not accustomed to shouting my conversations across a swamp," she said. "If you wish to know, you will need to address me properly, and that means from a conversational distance."

After taking off my shoes, I leapt out of the carriage. I was getting used to choosing between hopeless alternatives. All my plans lay in ruins, but at least this way I'd have a chance of finding out something important about my parents.

I had less trouble crossing the bog than Armand did. Either the trick was to keep moving, or perhaps I was lighter. Either way, I made it to where the lady stood without sinking deeper than my ankles.

"All right," I said. "Where are they?"

She held out her hand. "First things first. The watch, if you please."

At this point, I'd have given almost anything to hear what she had to say. I handed it over. "You want the money too?"

"Keep it," she said. "It might come in handy."

I took that as a promising sign. "Does that mean you're going to let me go?"

"We shall see. For now, we need to get off the road. Come." She led me past the tree whose broken limb now blocked the road and into a grove situated on a patch of high ground. In the midst of the trees was a clearing, its perimeter well-concealed by draperies of hanging moss. The horses were tethered to one side. Nearby, Armand and the driver were laid out on blankets. The lady's companions had disappeared. To my great relief, I could hear Armand's gentle snoring, barely audible over the sounds of the swamp.

"What are you going to do to them?"

"That depends on you," the lady replied. "Wait here. I'll just be a moment or two. In the meantime, you can check for yourself to see that your friends have not been harmed."

As she stalked off deeper into the grove, I shook Armand and the driver, but to no avail. As I'd suspected, theirs was no normal sleep.

All at once, I heard snippets of conversation among the nearby trees. After a quick glance to make sure no one was looking, I tiptoed through the marshy underbrush toward the sounds. Concealing myself behind a fungus-encrusted trunk, I peered through the moss. There, in a dappled patch of sunlight, the lady stood engaged in an animated discussion—seemingly with herself.

"So they suspected the boy?"

Although I heard no response, she nodded as though there'd been one.

"Well that complicates things, doesn't it? Nevertheless, there's no turning back now."

I'd been naïve. Whatever this lady was up to, it wasn't only about me. In fact, it probably wasn't about me at all. Then it finally sank in—she had been the prisoners' late-night visitor.

A piercing screech filtered down through the foliage. I would not have marked it as unusual given all the ambient animal sounds, but the lady took immediate notice. As she craned her neck toward its source, I caught the glint of sunlight off the pocket watch in her hand.

"They're coming," she said. "I have to go."

She snapped the watch closed and slipped it into her bag.

I barely made it back to Armand and the driver before she stepped into the clearing.

"We have visitors," she said. "Don't move until I return." Without another word, she disappeared down the trail toward the road.

Ignoring her order, I snuck after her. Once I found a concealed spot with a good view, I settled down to wait. Moments later, I heard hooves approaching.

An open cart pulled into view, driven by the two Inquisitors I'd seen at the barn. The prisoners huddled together in the bed of the cart. Their manacles rendered them powerless even to wave away the biting insects that swarmed them.

When they reached the fallen bough, one of the Inquisitors jumped out to inspect it. The other picked up a loaded crossbow. It did them no good. The Inquisitor on the cart went limp, followed by the one near the branch. An instant later, one of the bowmen leapt on the cart and gently removed the prisoners' masks. The other searched the Inquisitors.

The lady stepped out into the open. "We don't have all day," she said. "We need to get moving before anyone else happens by."

The bowman searching the Inquisitor looked up. "No key here."

"Check the other," the lady said. "If he doesn't have a key either, get them up to the grove. I have a workaround that will free them."

I was right. They were here to rescue the prisoners. But if that was their goal, why bother to stop Armand's carriage? My heart sank as I realized it was my fault. I should never have babbled all my plans. After what I'd told her, it made perfect sense. As long as she was here anyway, why not save the misguided boy from his own stupidity?

Within a few minutes, they'd loaded both the Inquisitors into the bed of the cart.

At that point I decided I'd best get back to the grove before I was missed. Fortunately, the lady stayed with the wagon, or I might not have made it in time.

Once in the grove, the two bowmen laid the Inquisitors out next to Armand and the driver. Meanwhile, the lady began picking through the charms on her bracelet.

"Ah, here it is!"

She fiddled with the chosen charm. After a moment it erupted in a hiss so startling I can only liken it to the magnum opus of a choir of angry cats. From the charm, a hacksaw materialized, which she caught in one hand.

I gaped in awe. She'd Evoked it from thin air. I'd just witnessed Phrendonic magic of the highest order. Usually such a deed requires extraordinary skills, multiple spells, and ample planning. That she'd been able to do it instantaneously suggested all the necessary spells were present on the bracelet—Patterned there earlier to be triggered at need. This lady wasn't fooling around. Precious few of my father's clients would have been capable of such a feat.

She handed the saw to one of the bowmen. "Here, try this."

As the man set to work on the manacles, the lady turned her attention back to me.

I couldn't hold my tongue. "What are you doing? When the Church finds out what's happened here, the Inquisition will go berserk. You're making it worse for everyone."

"Mr. Theratigan," she said. "Look upon the faces of those children in that cart and tell me the Church has not already gone berserk."

"They're alive," I pointed out. "And they're still whole. It could be much worse."

"Oh, it will be," she said. "Of that you may be certain. Only this time, instead of women, children and innocent bystanders, it will be worse for those who truly deserve it."

"What about all the prisoners they've already taken?" I asked. "Think about what this will mean for them."

"I have thought about it, Mr. Theratigan. In fact, that's where you come in."

"Me?" I asked, backing away in shock. "I want no part of what you're doing here."

"A pity, particularly given what your refusal will mean for your parents."

"What does this have to do with them?"

"Like my husband, your parents were taken to Histlewick Downs. As you so perceptively pointed out, after today, such prisoners are unlikely to see their circumstances improve."

"That would be true whether I help you or not."

"Not necessarily. If you were to help me, I would be inclined to add your parents' names to the ransom note. I think you'll agree there's a good chance the Inquisitor General will value the life of his son over the lives of three paltry heretics, particularly if, as you say, two of them aren't even guilty."

I recognized a corner when I was backed into one. "All right," I said. "What do you want me to do?"

"I would have thought that to be obvious," she said. "What good is a ransom note without someone to deliver it?"

CHAPTER EIGHT

TRICKS OF THE TRADE

The thought that I would be the one to inform the Inquisitor General of Armand's capture caused me to break out in a cold sweat. Even if these heretics actually succeeded with this ill-conceived hostage exchange, I couldn't foresee this ending well in the long run. And since Darron already viewed me with suspicion, he was sure to think I'd been in on it from the start. I didn't peg Darron as the sort to suffer betrayal lightly. Even if, by some strange quirk of fate, the Church were to find me blameless, Darron was unlikely to. I could think of only one thing that might help me, and that was to arrive in the company of someone whose loyalty was not in doubt. Only one person present fit the bill.

"Is the driver coming with me?" I asked. "Compared to Armand, he's a pretty poor hostage. Not only that, but I've never been to this place before. Someone's going to have to show me the way."

The lady considered for a moment before shaking her head. "We can't spare the horse."

"We could ride one horse together. I don't weigh much."

"Well…I suppose it would make for fewer hostages to manage. Very well, once everything is ready, I'll wake him."

Across the clearing the two adult prisoners climbed stiffly from the cart. The man lifted down his two boys, handing each in turn to his wife, who coddled and comforted them, all the while wiping away her own tears. Next he approached us and embraced the lady. He was dark-haired and lank, with a neatly trimmed beard that was only beginning to show signs of neglect.

"Joanna," he said. "How can I ever hope to repay you?"

"You've already been a great help," the lady said, "but I'd be lying if I said I didn't need more."

"Anything—anything at all," he replied. "All I ask is that we first find a way to get Ilse and the children to safety."

"Easier said than done," Joanna said. "I do have an idea that might work, but it is not without risk. If we were to disguise the cart and change out the horses, they should make it back to Epiphany without too much trouble. If we fill the cart with rushes, they would look like a poor family gathering reeds in the swamp. Chances are the Inquisition would consider them beneath their notice."

The man nodded. "I'll talk to her," he said. Then his eye strayed over to me. "Is this the Theratigan boy?"

The lady nodded.

He turned to me. "You have my deepest sympathies."

The lady faced me as well. "Ramos overheard the Inquisitors talking about your parents. That's how we know they were taken to Histlewick Downs."

"I recognized the name straight away," Ramos said. "I had a cousin who used to swear by your father's work. Went on and on about it. He'll be sorely missed."

"Not if I have anything to say about it," the lady said.

Ramos raised an eyebrow. "What do you mean?"

She nodded toward Armand, who still lay sleeping. "As you can see, yours was not the only vehicle to be stymied by a fallen limb today. Fortunately for us, the other happened to be carrying a very important person. As a result, we're in a position to make the Inquisitor General a little offer he can't refuse: his son in return for both my Marshall and the Theratigans."

"You've kidnapped the Inquisitor General's son?" Ramos asked, aghast. "Good Lord, woman, you'll bring the entire Church down on us."

"Let them come. For months now, I've stood idly by while Marshall offered the Church one concession after another in a vain attempt to keep the peace. You see how far appeasement has gotten him. It's high time they acquired an appreciation for the consequences of failed negotiations."

"And the Inquisitors who escorted us here?" Ramos asked. "What about them?"

"Throw them in the cart. If things go awry, they may prove useful."

"One more thing," Ramos said, "If I am to help you, Ilse must know nothing of it."

"Agreed. Let's get moving. Now that the pendulum is moving, every second counts."

With a bow, Ramos left to rejoin his family.

Next, the lady proffered me a sealed note. "Mr. Theratigan, your role in this is simple, but vital. You are to deliver this message directly into the hands of the Inquisitor General. If all goes well, I'll see you again at the point of exchange, together with your parents and my husband."

"And if it doesn't?"

"Then at least we tried," she said. "Or are you hinting that you'd prefer to back out?"

"I have a choice?"

"As I recall, I took some pains to provide you with a choice last night—a choice between your own safety and duty to your parents. Against my best advice, you chose duty. Are you telling me you're having second thoughts?"

"This isn't exactly the rescue I'd envisioned."

"I see. Well, I certainly didn't mean to interfere with your rescue plans. If you'd prefer, I can remove your parents' names from the ransom note. That way, you'd be able to pursue your plan in a manner more consistent with your original vision. Who knows? Maybe if you approach the Inquisitor General as a kidnapping victim, he will be even more sympathetic to your cause. If that's what you really want, say the word."

Something in the tone of her voice made my plan seem incredibly naïve. I also still hadn't come to grips with the mental image of Ramos and his family as prisoners in the barn. Together, these influences conspired, despite Armand's reasonable-sounding explanation, to convey the impression that sympathy wasn't the Inquisitor General's long suit. And although the idea of standing with these heretics against the Church terrified me, the thought of my parents bound, masked, and hopeless, terrified me even more. As much as I hated to admit it, her plan struck me as more likely to free my parents than mine did—but it would forever label me a heretic. My response was little more than an evasion.

"All I'm saying is that sometimes it's hard to tell whether I'm your prisoner or your ally."

She waved her hand at the spot where Armand, the driver, and the Inquisitors now lay. "Let me clarify. Prisoners, we sort into that pile there. Any more questions?"

I shook my head.

"Excellent. You should get going as soon as we are out of sight."

"What do you want me to do?"

"Go down to the road. We'll bring your driver friend and one of the horses. When he wakes up, urge him to take you directly to the Inquisitor General. The ransom note should do the rest. Oh, and maybe you should take this too, just in case." She pulled the watch from her bag.

"You're giving it back?"

"Consider it a loan. You may find it useful. Under no circumstances, however, are you ever to release the safety. Do you understand?"

"There's a safety?"

"Don't open the back, and you'll be fine. And one more thing... I want to say I'm sorry. If the world were a kinder place, we'd be running into each other at family picnics instead of doing this. You know, I don't even know your first name."

"It's Thoren."

"Joanna," she said. "Joanna Hockery."

For a moment, her stern exterior softened and her eyes misted up. "Well, Thoren, maybe one day we'll laugh about this over a good wine and a checkered tablecloth."

"I hope so."

She reached out and took my hands. "Good luck to you."

"You too."

With a nod of farewell she was off to make the final preparations, and I headed down to the road. While waiting there, I checked out the pocket watch. The time read precisely 3:34. I wondered if we could still make it to Histlewick Downs before sunset.

It wasn't long before the cart approached me, piled high with sleeping hostages. Ilse drove, a wide-eyed child huddled on either side. Ramos had claimed a horse and rode it bareback. Behind him, Mrs. Hockery sat astride her own horse, a spirited mare whose flowing mane sported burgundy ribbons that complemented her satin hat. The archers brought up the rear.

The archers dismounted long enough to lift the driver out of the cart and lay him alongside the road. One of them untied the reins of the horse trailing the cart and handed them to me.

The odd little caravan disappeared around a bend, and my stomach knotted with guilt that I hadn't been able to do more to rescue Armand. To make matters worse, that guilt made me feel I was being somehow disloyal to my parents. As I sank down next to the driver on the verge of tears, the driver stirred. Then he sat bolt upright.

"What happened?" he asked.

"They took Armand."

"Who did? The highwaymen?"

I nodded. "Are you able to ride? We have to tell the Inquisitor General right away."

"They left us a horse?"

I held the note aloft for his inspection. "They are trying to arrange a hostage exchange, and they want us to deliver the ransom note."

"I don't suppose they left us a saddle?"

"I'm afraid not."

"How are you at riding without one?"

"I've never tried it. Is it hard?"

The driver sighed. "In that case, we should see if we can salvage the carriage."

I glanced over at the carriage, now listing so badly, it was almost on its side.

"I don't think we have time for that," I said. "Mrs. Hockery doesn't strike me as the patient type."

The driver stared at me in disbelief. "Who did you just say?"

I shrugged. "Mrs. Hockery. You must have seen her. She was the woman with the archers and the dark red hat."

"You're saying she wants a hostage exchange? Did she say whom she wanted in return?"

"Yes, she did. She's pretty desperate to get her husband Marshall back. She must love him very much."

"Marshall?" he asked, grabbing me by the shoulders. "Marshall Hockery? Are you sure?"

I swallowed hard and nodded.

The driver shook his head. "Oh that's no good. That's no good at all."

"It can't be that bad," I said. "After all, no matter who this guy is or how bad he's been, I'm sure the Inquisitor General will be more than willing to give him up to save his own son."

"You don't understand," the driver said. "Marshall Hockery was the Grand Eagle of the Accipitrine Order. He not only killed the previous Inquisitor General, he killed himself, too. There's no way the new Inquisitor General could trade him— even if he wanted to."

CHAPTER NINE

SAFETY VIOLATIONS

By the time we had the carriage back on the road, the driver and I were both covered in noxious goo. Although the driver, whose name turned out to be Kendall, was not much of a conversationalist, he had a way with ropes and harnesses that was nothing short of genius.

Kendall jury-rigged a harness to allow the single horse to do the work of two. The going would be slow, but Kendall was adamant that we'd be better off that way than riding together bareback. By the time we were ready to move, night had descended, and so had clouds of vicious insects. I was eager to press forward, but Kendall convinced me that trying to navigate the swamp in the dark was asking for trouble. Given his skill with the horses, I was inclined to trust him. We huddled in the carriage, covering ourselves with blankets against a determined assault by the squadrons of keening blood-suckers that had somehow snuck inside. We slept little, and when we arose, our faces sported a host of nasty welts that both itched and burned. If the carriage hadn't been stocked with hardtack and jelly, we'd have been wholly miserable.

Although we were up with the sun, our progress was so slow we still hadn't made it to the river by noon. The horse was overburdened, and as brilliant as it was, Kendall's makeshift harness required frequent adjustments to prevent it from rubbing the horse raw. It didn't take long to discover he was passionate to the point of obsession about the horse's welfare. Frustrating though that was, the horse responded with an eagerness-to-please under circumstances that might have caused another to rebel.

At last, the river burst into view, its placid surface sparkling in the sunlight. A stone bridge stretched across it, jutting barely above water level. The land beyond sloped upward, eventually escaping the creeping undergrowth and stifling miasmas of the bog—a welcome sight indeed. We had planned to rest at the bridge, but the promise of dry land spurred us on. Although climbing the slope meant even slower-going, each and every step now felt like progress.

After a time the slope leveled and we found ourselves in the midst of a verdant expanse of rolling hills dotted with colorful patches of orchids, campions, and bluebells. We had finally reached the downs—the Inquisitor General couldn't be far now. Apparently my growing enthusiasm was not contagious, for Kendall looked troubled.

"What time do you have?"

I whipped out my watch. "Four-fifteen. Why?"

"At this rate," he said, "we'll never make the manor by nightfall."

"The road isn't so treacherous here. Can't we just press on after dark?"

Kendall shook his head. "Bessie's done in. We'd be heartless to keep pushing her after what she's already done for us. We should look for a spot to camp."

It was clear there was no point in arguing. When he suggested we stop at a small creek, I nodded, eager for the chance to wash the crusted mud from my clothes. They would never again be presentable, but with any luck they'd no longer smell. Kendall tethered Bessie to a shrub near the water's edge and brushed her down, while I cleaned up and set up camp. The sun was low in the sky by the time I'd gathered enough scrub for a small fire. After another lean meal of hardtack, Kendall rummaged through his trunk atop the carriage and returned to the fire with a bottle and a small stringed instrument.

"What's that?" I asked.

He took a long swig and handed me the bottle. "No campfire is complete without a mouthful of rakia and a gadulka," he said with a grin. Following his example, I took a swig, and almost spewed it into the fire, which, in retrospect, would not have been the safest thing I could have done. My mouth burned like I'd just swallowed hot coals.

"You like it?"

"It's not wine, is it?"

He slapped me on the back and laughed. "No, my friend. Wine, it is surely not. Have more."

He settled down near the fire and stroked the gadulka with a bow. The instrument responded with a low mournful melody, haunting and beautiful. He began haltingly at first, but his self-consciousness fell away as the rakia took hold, and soon he was singing along in full voice.

The music, the flickering fire, and liquor's warmth dulled my anxieties, and it before long, I nodded off.

Unwelcome images of shackled prisoners in expressionless masks crept into my semi-awareness, writhing in time to the gadulka's measured rhythm. At first they bore their suffering in silence, but as Kendall's baritone soared, in my mind, a prisoner raised his head and howled in despair. One by one the others responded in kind, until at last Kendall's voice was lost amidst a chorus of wails. I started at Kendall's nudge. To my dismay, although the music had ended, the howling continued. Kendall's expression was grave.

"Wolves," he said. "They usually steer clear of people, but they're spooking Bessie. I'm going to try to calm her down. There's a crossbow in the trunk on top of the carriage. Grab that out, just in case."

Still groggy, I clambered atop the carriage and pawed through the trunk. The howling seemed closer now, or maybe I was just more awake than I had been.

The crossbow wasn't hard to find, but it wasn't loaded. After a bit more searching, I finally located a bundle of bolts. I slipped one out, set it into the notch of the weapon, and tried to pull back the string, but it was strung too tightly to be loaded that way.

All at once the howling stopped. I turned to Kendall, wondering whether that might be a good sign. It was not.

Knife in hand, Kendall faced down a snarling wolf. The beast weighed easily as much as he did. Bessie snorted, straining against her tether. The whites of her eyes flashed in the darkness. Ghostly shapes leapt and danced in and out of the firelight.

"You said they avoided people," I cried.

"I was wrong! A little help here?"

There wasn't time to figure out the crossbow. Instead, I grabbed a bottle and threw it with all my might. It missed the wolf, but shattered in an explosion of shards and liquor beneath the beast's muzzle. The wolf yelped and leapt to one side. It dodged past Kendall to nip at Bessie's flank before fading into the darkness. That was the last straw for Bessie. She reared and squealed, snapping her tether. Before Kendall could react, the horse fled at full gallop, a growling throng of dark shapes snapping at her heels. Kendall ran after her, calling her name, until it finally sank in he had no hope of catching her. He returned to camp pale and shaken.

He picked up the neck of the broken bottle and shook his head.

"Next time you need a weapon, might I suggest the crossbow?"

"I didn't have time to load it."

He gathered up the gadulka and placed it back in the trunk. "We sleep in the carriage tonight. Tomorrow we proceed on foot."

I woke to gray skies and a stiff wind that held the promise of rain. Kendall had already been awake for some time and had prepared makeshift packs for us. The gadulka was strapped across of one of them, wrapped in some sort of tarp. I checked to make sure I still had the ransom note, and after a few conversationless bites of hardtack, we were on our way.

In addition to his pack, Kendall also carried the crossbow, now loaded. Despite the threat of wolves, I almost wished he hadn't brought it—every time I saw it I felt a twinge of shame. My pack was insanely heavy, but, eager to regain his good graces, I was determined not to complain. We trudged in silence. I wanted to say something, but I didn't know where to start and he didn't volunteer anything. Rain, when it came, only made matters worse.

Somewhere around midday a caravan of wagons passed us going north. We waved for them to stop but the Inquisitors didn't even slow down. Once we noticed that the wagons were filled with masked prisoners, I, for one, was glad they hadn't.

By two o'clock, I was ready to collapse. The pack dug into my shoulders, and the wet shirt underneath had rubbed my skin raw. My shoulders ached, my feet were blistered, and I was starting to get chills. Just when I thought I couldn't go any farther, we heard a carriage behind us. Once again we attempted to flag it down, but it passed us by—only to stop a little farther on. It was much like the one we'd abandoned, right down to the banner proclaiming its affiliation with the Church.

The driver hopped down and approached us with a look of incredulity.

"Kendall?" he asked. "Is that you?"

Kendall's eyes brightened in recognition. "Ricard, are we glad to see you!"

"What are you doing out here?"

"You aren't going to believe it," Kendall said. "But first, who's your client?"

"Father Graves—and his luggage. He must be important. I had to go all the way to the Holy City to fetch him. He's got more bags than a newlywed heiress."

"Think we could get a lift?"

"Both of you?"

Kendall shot me a sidelong look. "If it wouldn't be too much trouble."

"I'll see what I can do."

Before he made it back to his carriage, the door opened and a clean-shaven middle-aged man lifted his wire-rimmed spectacles and peered out.

"And who have we here?" he asked.

Ricard patted Kendall on the back. "Begging your pardon, Father," he said. "Kendall, here, is one of the Inquisitor General's drivers. He and his passenger have fallen on difficult circumstances and were hoping they could tag along with us."

Father Graves regarded Kendall critically for a moment and turned back to Ricard. "You know this man?"

"I do."

"You'll vouch for him?"

"I will."

Father Graves hopped out of the carriage and extended his hand. "Well then, welcome aboard. Things will be a little tight, but I'll be glad of the company. These long carriage rides are dreadfully dull."

He turned to me next. "And you are…?"

I shook his hand. "They call me Flinch, sir."

He smiled. "Flinch, eh? I sense a story in there somewhere. Once we are on the road, you can tell me all about it."

It took almost half an hour to rearrange the luggage to free up space, and even then a stack of small crates had to be wedged between Kendall and me. When we were once again underway, Kendall recounted Armand's kidnapping and the subsequent loss of Bessie.

The priest's expression grew heavy with concern. "May I see the ransom note?"

"It's sealed," I said, "and I was instructed to deliver it to the Inquisitor General directly."

"Sealed, you say? With wax?"

I nodded.

"Then under no circumstances are you to take it anywhere near the Inquisitor General. If, as it appears, these kidnappers are truly Phrendonic heretics, they may have placed a trap on the note to trigger when opened. In fact, I suggest the note be placed in a sturdy box to make certain there's no chance of it being damaged. I, for one, would not care to be the person to discover my hunch is correct. Shall I look for one?"

I nodded, a little embarrassed that Father Graves' reservations had not occurred to me earlier. I was certainly well-versed enough in the mechanics of such things to appreciate that his suspicions could very well be correct.

Father Graves pulled on a pair of thin white gloves and rummaged through some of the luggage pieces near him. "Any idea how far out we are from Histlewick Downs?" he asked.

"Ricard promised me we'd make it before nightfall, but between this delay and the weather, I'm not so sure."

Kendall took a long look out the window. "What time is it?" he asked.

I pulled out the pocket watch. "It's three-ten."

"It will be close," Kendall said.

"Here we go," Father Graves said. He produced a cigar box from one of his bags. As he handed it to me, he caught sight of the watch.

"What a beautiful timepiece. Mind if I have a look?"

Reluctantly, I held it out for his inspection.

He carefully took it for a closer look. "This must be worth a fortune. Where did you get it?"

"A relative left it to me. I really don't know that much about it."

"Does it chime?"

"It never has since I've had it."

"I can't imagine it wouldn't," he said. "Do you think it's broken?"

"Look," Kendall said, pointing out the window, "The standing stones. We're just shy of two hours out."

A series of five stone pillars dotted the landscape. Although generally similar, each sported unique features. They gave the impression of enormous chess pieces deployed across an unseen board. I was fascinated—I'd never seen anything like them.

"Aha!" Father Graves said. "Here's the problem!"

He'd opened the back of the watch to probe the insides with a stick pin. "There's a safety."

Before I could stop him, before I could even gasp, he'd released the catch.

CHAPTER TEN

A MIX OF MESSAGES

Father Graves snapped the watch closed and leaned forward to peer at my face. "Are you all right? You look a little pale."

"I'm just tired," I said. "I'm not used to that much walking."

"I suppose that's to be expected. Why don't you sit back and rest up a bit."

"Is the watch still working?"

Father Graves flicked open the case. "Still ticking," he said. "Here you go."

It was all I could do to keep myself from snatching it out of his hands. "Thanks," I said, slipping it safely back into my pocket. "A nap might be just the thing."

I closed my eyes, but sleep was the farthest thing from my mind. Joanna had been emphatic that the watch's safety was not to be released for any reason. Yet, releasing it seemed to have had no effect at all. If it didn't do anything, why had she been so specific? The watch still worked. If she'd feared a trap, no harm seemed to have come from it. I was at a loss, but I didn't have the luxury to think about it—my meeting with the Inquisitor General was only hours away. I tried going over what I would say and how I would behave. I didn't get very far. Too much depended on his responses. Perhaps Father Graves could help me.

I opened one eye to see him gazing out the window. "Do you know the Inquisitor General well?" I asked.

Father Graves nodded. "To the extent anyone can. Not only did we go to seminary together, I also introduced him to his wife. I even served as best man at his wedding. Even so, if you are asking if I know his mind, it would be an overstatement to say I do. As with many great men, his personality is one of complexity and contradiction."

"I don't suppose you have any idea how he's likely to react to Armand's kidnapping?"

"Ah, I see where this is going. If it makes you feel any better, Roman Goodkin isn't the type to shoot the messenger—at least not without good reason."

"And what would qualify as a good reason?"

"Hard to know in advance, but I expect if he did it, he'd have one."

"Thanks," I said. "I feel so much better now."

Father Graves chuckled. "I suppose that wasn't terribly comforting, but I don't want to mislead you. The Inquisitor General is already under enormous pressure. He's trying to satisfy the Primal's insatiable thirst for vengeance and to minimize collateral damage to innocents and the Church's reputation at the same time. Unfortunately, those goals are diametrically opposed. I'm not sure how he'll react to this additional stress."

"Do you have any advice?"

Father Graves stroked his chin for a moment. "If I were in

your position, I'd either want to appear inconsequential, or barring that, find a way to be indispensable."

I struggled to imagine a way to make myself indispensable to the Inquisitor General. When nothing sprang to mind, I tried to dream up a way for me to give him the news that his son has been kidnapped, and at the same time seem inconsequential. In the end, the only thing I decided was that Father Graves might not be the best source of advice for someone in my situation.

Taking advantage of the lull in the conversation, I leaned back, closed my eyes, and considered various ways of introducing myself to achieve minimum impact. The ransom note continued to be a major sticking point, and I eventually drifted off, having made no progress whatsoever.

The next thing I heard was Kendall's voice confirming Histlewick Downs had finally come into view. I had to move several boxes, but I eventually managed to see out of the window. Ahead of us, a castle-like structure of stark white stone dominated the landscape. Age and neglect had taken their toll. Perhaps in its prime, the shimmering walls would have been a proclamation of wealth and strength, but now the crumbling ruins muttered only half-remembered glories of a bygone age. The ruins presided over a village surrounded by a high wall built of the same white stone.

"Histlewick manor," Kendall announced.

"Is it still occupied?" I asked.

Kendall nodded. "Parts of it are, anyway. That's where we're headed."

"The Bey family has clung to that heap of rock for generations," Father Graves said. "If it weren't for Church support, I doubt they'd have been able to hold on at all."

"Why would the Church support a Lord?" I asked.

"As I recall, it was a reward for a particular service one

of the Beys did the Church long ago. It was supposed to be awarded in a lump sum, but at the time the Church was strapped for cash, and instead kept the principal in trust, doling out the income over time. While one might quibble about the appropriateness of the unilateral change in terms, the result is that we still have a Lord in Histlewick manor."

"What's that by the gate?" Kendall asked.

Father Graves craned his neck for a better look. "I'm not sure."

Just outside the village walls, a mound large enough to block our passage lay in the roadway. Ricard pulled the carriage to a stop a few feet in front of it.

Kendall moaned as he leapt from the carriage "Oh no. It's Bessie."

Sure enough, the makeshift harness still trailed behind Bessie's gnawed remains.

"What's she doing here?" I asked.

Father Graves bent down to inspect the scene more closely. "Looks like the carcass was dragged here. You can see the trail running off to the south. Was this your horse?"

Kendall nodded and looked away.

"Why would someone do this?" I asked.

"It's a warning," Kendall said. "The townsfolk are angry that the Church has commandeered the commons. They've been arguing that keeping their livestock outside the walls at night puts them at risk from wolves. It seems they have a point."

"What use is their commons to the Church?" I asked.

"They're keeping the prisoners there," Kendall replied. "It's walled, gated, and easily guarded."

"Well, if the townsfolk are indeed disgruntled," Father Graves said, "it might be better to get moving. I'd hate to incite them any further."

Father Graves climbed back into the carriage while Kendall, Ricard, and I dragged the carcass off the road. Moments later, we rode through the gate into the village of Histlewick Downs.

Narrow cobbled streets and rounded archways gave the little village a quaint and timeless air, but the faces that turned to watch as we made our way up to the manor were anything but welcoming. Even though a part of me now dreaded meeting the Inquisitor General, I was relieved to pass beneath the gated arch that announced our arrival at the manor.

The carriage pulled to a stop in a small courtyard formed on one side by the village wall and on the other by the manor. The shaded space was carefully tended, sporting hedges and a variety of exotic plants in containers and small beds. Well-dressed servants emerged to inquire of Ricard regarding the disposition of the luggage. They were followed almost immediately by Armand's brother Darron, still arrayed in his embroidered vestments.

Father Graves disembarked and turned back to face me. "Stay here for now. I'll go inform the Inquisitor General, and once we decide what to do about the ransom note, we'll send for you."

I nodded, grateful to be able to avoid Darron, even if for only a short time longer.

After several minutes, I pulled out the watch, curious to see what Father Graves had done to it. The time was 5:18, and the mechanism still seemed to be operating flawlessly. I had just flipped open the back when I first heard the voice.

If I were you, it said, *I'd tell them you'll open the note for them—even if they don't ask.*

I snapped the watch closed, pocketed it, and did a quick scan for the source. I hadn't been able to sense a direction—if anything, it had sounded like it was coming from all directions at once. Since it was obvious there was no one with me in the carriage, I even opened the door to peer outside, but no one seemed to be paying me any mind. I sat back, and pulled out the watch once more, presuming the sound must have come to me through some trick of the courtyard.

Because if you don't, they'll think you know more than you let on.

Again I put the watch away and looked outside, but all was the same as before. I suddenly recalled Joanna in the swamp chatting animatedly all by herself. It was then I first suspected the watch.

"Where are you?" I whispered, checking out the window to make certain no one was close enough to hear me.

Not far. Joanna asked me to look after you.

"Can anyone else hear you?"

Just you.

"You're the watch, aren't you?"

Yes.

"You must be Extending spells when the case is opened. Am I right?"

You know some theory, I see.

"Are you crazy? If the Inquisition finds out about this, they'll flay me alive."

Granted, there is some risk, but we were concerned that since Darron is already suspicious of you, they might decide to flay you anyway. At least this way, if you get in over your head, I might be able to help.

"I can't talk anymore. Darron's coming."

Indeed, Darron and Father Graves had reappeared and were heading my way. The look on Darron's face was not encouraging. When he got to the carriage, he reached in and grabbed me by the collar.

"All right, Mr. Flinch. What have you and your heretic friends done with my brother?"

Father Graves put his hand on Darron's shoulder. "I don't think your father wanted him harmed."

"My father doesn't know all the facts," Darron retorted. Still, he relaxed his grip enough for me to breathe.

"I had nothing to do with it," I said. "They just told me to bring the note."

A authoritative baritone voice rang out across the courtyard. "Put him down, Darron,"

Darron's mouth tightened, but he complied. "Father, what are you doing?" he asked. "Stay back and let us deal with this."

"Where is this note?"

"Last I saw it," Father Graves said, "the lad had placed it in that cigar box on the seat. He seemed unconcerned for his safety while doing so. If it's trapped, he either doesn't know, or he's a very skilled actor."

"All of you," the Inquisitor General commanded, "away from the carriage."

The drivers and the servants scrambled to obey. Darron practically lifted me out of the carriage by the collar.

Only Father Graves refused to move. "I'm not going to let you do this, Roman. We can't afford to lose another Inquisitor General, particularly not due to recklessness."

Roman Goodkin strode purposefully toward the carriage. "Albert, stand back. I need to see what's in that note, and I need to see it now."

"We should be able to devise a way to melt the seal from a safe distance." Father Graves said. "There's no reason for you to risk this."

"And how long would that take?"

"An hour at most, depending on how long it takes to assemble the equipment."

"We may not have that kind of time."

Father Graves reached into the carriage and retrieved the cigar box. "All right then, you stay back. I'll open the note."

"I can't ask you to do that. This isn't your battle."

"If you can't accept the risk of losing me, what makes you think I could accept the risk of losing you?"

Roman held out his hand. "The box, Albert."

I stood as tall as I could and cleared my throat. "If you need someone to open the note, I'll do it."

Roman gave me a long appraising look.

"Half an hour," Father Graves said. "That's all I need. In the meantime you can question the boy. You'll need to do that anyway."

"Very well. You have half an hour."

Father Graves clutched the cigar box close and scurried off. The Inquisitor General turned his attention back to me.

Darron tightened his grip, which he'd transferred from my collar to my arm. "You should keep your distance," he said to his father. "He's young, but that doesn't mean they haven't set him up for a Sacrifice."

"Unlikely," Roman replied. "I've been in range for some time now. If that were his goal, he'd have done it already. It's been more than a day since the abduction, so a set-up he's not party to is unlikely as well. Still, better safe than sorry. Chain him to one end of the table in the dining room. That should permit me to question him from a safe distance."

"One more thing," Darron said. "Armand picked this boy up as his manservant just before I arrived at that little charity of his to fetch him. It's possible there may be others there who were involved in this plot."

"Good thinking, son," Roman said. "Round them up and bring them."

I was horrified as I pictured Lisbet, Sly, and Chef, masked and shackled in the back of a cart, but now that I was a prisoner, there was nothing I could do.

CHAPTER ELEVEN

ḃONEST ꝳISTAKES

Razor-sharp fangs, inches from my face—I squeezed my eyes closed and tried to draw back, but Darron's bindings did not give. The best I could do was press the side of my face into the crushed velvet of the high-backed chair that held me captive. Dead and stuffed though it was, the reptilian beast's invasion of my space was still disturbing, which no doubt explained Darron's careful placement of the chair, at the foot of the table, but facing away—directly into the slit-pupil eyes of the beast.

The beast had ample company. The long dining-room table was the only thing that suggested the room served any purpose other than to proclaim the hunting prowess of the Lords of Histlewick Manor. Heads of once-proud stags, fearsome boars, and a menagerie of creatures less easily identified crowded the walls, their antlers, tusks, and teeth forever frozen in resplendent obeisance to the tactical superiority of family Bey.

The scrape of a wooden chair across the rough stone floor

told me I was no longer alone. The sound was followed by Roman Goodkin's commanding voice.

"Mr. Flinch, there seems to be some disagreement about your level of involvement in this kidnapping. Let's get to the bottom of it, shall we?"

I was momentarily mystified. Disagreement? Who was there to disagree? Had Kendall come to my defense? Father Graves, perhaps? There really weren't all that many options, but the thought that someone had actually dared to speak on my behalf buoyed my spirits. That Roman had been willing to listen was even more encouraging. I was now more determined than ever to win this man over and convince him to release my parents.

"What would you like to know?"

"Darron tells me you came to Armand's employ only a short time ago. I'd like to hear your version of the circumstances that led him to hire you."

Careful there, sport. Don't let him catch you in a lie. Best to just tell him you're not sure.

I ignored the voice in my head. If someone really had come to my defense, I wasn't about to betray his trust by telling lies at this point. Besides, if Armand were rescued, Roman would surely learn the truth then.

"Actually, it was Darron's doing."

"Go on."

"You know about Armand's charity, right?"

"I do."

Remember, the less said, the better.

"Well, I'd only been there a day or so when Darron showed up. He accused Armand of harboring heretics, but Armand denied it, saying they were at worst, nouncers. Darron grabbed my wrist and pointed out that I hadn't been branded. To defend me, Armand claimed he'd taken me on as his manservant. The whole thing sort of snowballed from there."

Whoa, whoa, whoa! You don't want to give him the impression you're in need of branding!

"Shut up!" I hissed.

"I beg your pardon?" Roman said. "I didn't catch that last bit."

"I screwed up," I said, more loudly, "but I only went along with it to minimize the chances Darron would get upset and start meddling with the charity. I was happy to accompany Armand when he asked, but it was never really about him needing a servant."

"If you weren't branded, then what were you doing at the charity in the first place?"

Oh, here it comes. Don't say I didn't warn you.

"Nouncers aren't the only ones unjustly brought to ruin by the Inquisition."

"Is that Armand's sentiment, or one based on your personal experience?"

"Both."

I heard the Inquisitor General's tired sigh all the way at the other end of the table. "All right, I'm listening," he said, "How did the Inquisition unjustly ruin your life?"

Listen to me! Whatever you do, don't mention your parents.

"They burst into my parents' shop, destroyed everything, and then hauled my parents away, even though they weren't heretics. That's why I was at the charity."

What are you doing? Are you out of your mind?

"And what makes you think they weren't heretics?"

"Because all his life my father was ridiculed for being unable to work magic. He was practically disowned for it, and then, after being punished all that time for being innocent, the

Inquisition showed up to punish him again for being guilty. But he wasn't guilty."

Ooh boy.

"And just who is your father?"

Don't tell him, you fool! He's named in the ransom note!

By this point, I was so ecstatic to actually be making my case before the Inquisitor General that I was only half listening to the annoying voice in my head.

"Carson Theratigan," I blurted, just as the warning sank in.

Father Graves' voice echoed in from the hallway. "The note's open. It wasn't trapped after all." He burst through the doorway, breathless and victorious.

"Let me see that," Roman said.

The voice in my head went strangely silent, and I wondered if the spells from the watch had run their course.

After a long pause, Roman spoke. "They want to make an exchange in the swamp."

"An exchange?" Father Graves asked. "For what?"

"It seems they want Marshall Hockery."

It took Father Graves a moment to respond. "But he's dead."

"I'd hazard a guess they are, as yet, unaware of that development."

Father Graves sounded puzzled. "I don't understand. How could they be well-informed enough to target Armand for kidnapping, but not know Marshall Hockery is dead? If they knew you'd become Inquisitor General, doesn't it follow they should also know Hockery died achieving that?"

My stomach did a somersault as I realized the whole mix-up was my doing. In my mind's eye, I saw Joanna in her burgundy hat sitting across from me in the carriage as I explained to her that I was working for the Inquisitor General's son. At the time I had no way of knowing we were thinking of two different people, but in hindsight it made perfect sense—after all, Armand had only learned of his father's promotion that morning.

"Do you suppose they targeted the carriage?" Father Graves asked. "Perhaps they were hoping it carried the Inquisitor General, but had to change plans when they found it was occupied instead by your son."

"I'd be inclined to believe that, except for one thing," Roman said.

"What's that?"

"The terms of the note. In addition to Hockery, they also demand we turn over a Mr. and Mrs. Carson Theratigan."

"And who are they?"

"They are, by his own admission, the parents of young Mr. Flinch, here," Roman said, "and since Mr. Flinch was actually in the carriage, I don't see how his co-conspirators could have thought they were waylaying either me or the previous Inquisitor General instead of Armand."

"You've got it all wrong," I cried. "The kidnappers only added that after they captured us. They were trying to use it as an inducement to gain my cooperation."

"Well, it seems to have worked," Roman observed.

"I meant, to deliver the ransom note, but I'd have done it anyway, if only for Armand's sake."

"I'm touched by your belated concern for my son's welfare," Roman said. "It will no doubt come in handy, since the note also specifically requires that you be present to mediate the exchange. Given that you seem to be so amenable to inducements, I shall add one of my own: any harm that befalls my son as a result of this outrageous scheme shall be visited upon you and your parents in equal measure. Do I make myself clear?"

Panic seized me as all my hopes evaporated. "But Hockery's dead. I don't have any control over how they'll react when they find that out."

"Perhaps next time you'll choose your co-conspirators with more care. Albert, have Darron see to it that Mr. Flinch is well-cared-for until we need him."

"In the commons with the others?"

"No. Have Darron check with Histlewick. See if he has somewhere we can hold him in the manor. I'd hate for anything to happen to him before we figure out whether we're going to need him."

"As you wish," Father Graves said.

Darron was none too gentle as he escorted me through the manor in shackles. At first I protested my innocence, but when it became clear that he wasn't going to respond, I fell silent. At last we came to a dank storeroom in the cellar of the sprawling structure. There we waited until an unkempt man appeared carrying a lantern and a ring of large keys. Dark circles underscored his eyes, which harbored a smoldering resentment very like that I'd seen among the villagers. I took him either for a gaoler, or a lesser servant of the sort generally reserved for particularly odious tasks.

I was shocked when Darron bowed. "There was no need for Your Lordship to attend to this matter personally," he said.

"If you don't mind," the man growled, "as long as I'm still Lord here, I'll be the judge of what needs my attention and what doesn't."

"Of course, Your Lordship. No offense intended."

Histlewick grunted and searched through the keys on the chain until he found one that suited him. He used it to open a verdigris-encrusted padlock on an iron-bound door. I winced as the hinges squealed in protest. Before us, the lantern illuminated a stairway choked with cobwebs, and beyond them, inky blackness. Histlewick went first, and I followed, clanking along in the dim light as best as I could. If I hadn't known they were going to need me for the prisoner exchange, they would have had to drag me beyond that point.

We were led down a maze of dank stairways, chambers, and narrow stone corridors that wound ever deeper into the bowels of the manor. Eventually Darron seemed to have second thoughts.

"Do you have nothing closer to the surface?"

Histlewick stopped so abruptly I nearly ran into him. He turned and looked Darron straight in the eye.

"You, sir, have some nerve. First, you commandeer my commons and convert it to a prison. Then, you invite yourselves into my house for a stay of unspecified duration. Then, as if that weren't enough, you allow the 'critically important' prisoner who for some reason couldn't be held in the commons with the others, to destroy my ballroom and kill one of my servants. And now, after requesting special accommodations for yet another prisoner, you object when those accommodations are not close enough to the rest of the manor to suit you."

Fire blazed in Darron's eyes, but he mastered it. "Forget I mentioned it."

After an uneasy pause, Histlewick resumed his forward march. At last we arrived at a door that required another of the keys. Contrary to the cell I'd been anticipating, the lantern revealed a beautifully appointed apartment, complete with bookshelves, furniture, and even a fireplace. Time and disuse had blanketed everything in dust and cobwebs, but it was clear that all it would take was a little elbow grease to restore the room's original splendor.

"What is this?" Darron asked. "I thought we were taking this prisoner to a cell?"

"Again with the complaints? You asked me to take you to the most secure place in the manor. Without question, this is it. If you prefer, however, I would be more than happy to find someplace less secure."

"There are no other exits?"

"None," Histlewick replied, "unless the lad wants to worm his way up the chimney."

Darron actually took a look to make sure the flue was too small for me before nodding in satisfaction. "It's a little more luxurious than I had expected, but it will do. What was its original purpose, anyway?"

Histlewick lit one of the room's many lanterns. "It's been this way for generations. How should I know?"

Darron eyed me a final time from the doorway. "All right, Mr. Flinch. Enjoy your stay."

He slammed the door behind him. As the key turned in the lock, I pulled out the watch. It was 8:37, but it wasn't the time I was interested in.

Well, that's a surprise.

"What is?"

You're still alive.

"I thought you were supposed to help me."

I can't help you if you won't listen.

"I'm listening now. What should I do next?"

Damn good question.

CHAPTER TWELVE

ÐABEAS CORPUS

*W*hat are you doing?

"I'm cleaning up. This place is filthy."

That's pointless. They're probably keeping you here in anticipation of attempting an exchange, and that's likely to happen sooner rather than later.

"Well, you haven't exactly been a wealth of other suggestions."

Don't blame me. You're the one who insisted on blabbering every last detail without regard for how it would play with your hosts.

I deliberately changed the subject. "This isn't doing me any good. I'm just smearing the dirt around."

If you insist on wasting your time, you might want to try using something other than your hands, particularly given they were not especially clean to begin with.

"Like what?"

You figure it out. I'm not your maid.

An armoire caught my eye. "Maybe there's something in here?" It was stocked primarily with moldering women's garments, which I considered tearing up for rags until I noticed a feather duster centered by itself on the top shelf.

I snatched it up triumphantly. "This should do the trick." Pushing a pair of candlesticks to one side, I tested the duster on the polished granite surface of a nearby end table.

What's wrong with the handle?

It was notched halfway along its length.

"Probably gnawed by mice," I said. "Maybe there are others." I ran my hand along the top shelf, but it was empty.

Gnawed in just one spot? That hardly seems likely.

I examined it more carefully. "Hmm, you're right. This looks like it was gouged out on purpose. I wonder why?"

You might try looking at it as something other than a feather duster.

And suddenly it clicked. "Oh, it's a promise stick."

That seems a fair possibility. At least it makes more sense to me than the mouse theory.

Finding a promise-stick was a real puzzle. They were tools Phrendonics sometimes used as the targets for certain spells. The notch allowed them to break the stick, and thus break the spell at a moment's notice, without the bother of actually having to cast another spell.

"So, based on the contents of the armoire, we can assume the previous occupant was both a woman and a Phrendonic heretic, right?"

Well, a Phrendonic, anyway. It only officially became heresy recently, and I doubt this room has been occupied for quite some time.

"Do you think Lord Histlewick is aware of all this?"

It seems likely, doesn't it? Why else choose this room, of all rooms, for confining a potential Phrendonic?

"Should I tell the Inquisitor General?"

Tell him what? That you found a feather duster with a notch in it? I hardly think that would help your cause.

"Well, I'd explain about how promise sticks are designed to break the spells on them when you break the stick."

And how does that help? If he knows already, you only seem more suspicious, and if he doesn't, why should he believe you?

"Maybe if we figured out what it's supposed to do first?"

Any spells on that stick likely dissipated aeons ago.

"Not if they were Patterned."

And what are the chances of that?

"Patterning is not as rare as you might think. My father worked with several colleagues who could do it."

Oh, it's rare—the few who could do it simply had reason to seek your father out.

"So, even if this is a promise stick, you're telling me it's useless. Not only should I not tell the Inquisitor General, but it's pointless to investigate it any further, since the chances that it's still enchanted are next to nil."

I wouldn't say it's completely useless. After all, you can still dust with it.

The smug tone of the comment pushed me over the edge. "Yeah, well for some reason I'm just not in the mood anymore." I broke the feather duster over my knee.

I froze as I heard something clatter behind me.

You just couldn't take my word for it, could you?

Turning to face the end table, I saw the candlesticks scattered across the floor. The end table itself was nowhere to be seen, and in its place lay the prone form of a man. The gentle rise and fall of his chest told me that, whoever he was, he still lived.

"Your word, it would seem, is less infallible than you make it out to be."

Really? So once again you think you're better off for having ignored me? Well, I'll be tickled to hear just how you're going to explain this new development to the Inquisitor General.

"Maybe I won't have to," I said. "Maybe this guy can just explain it himself."

As a rule, one who explains himself generally does so to his own best advantage. You may find it preferable to present your own version first.

"I suppose that would depend on who he is and how he got here, wouldn't it?" I reached down and give the man a shake.

Careful there, sport—you don't know if he's dangerous.

"He's either unconscious or faking it. I wonder if he's been magically Slept, like Armand was in the swamp?"

Any sign of who he might be?

"Let's have a look." I squatted to flip him over. When I did, I suddenly found myself staring into the unseeing eyes of Lord Histlewick. I ran my hand over his face to close them.

Well, well, well. We do have quite the knack for finding trouble, don't we?

"How can this be? Histlewick was just here. Is this his twin?"

Either that, or maybe Histlewick isn't Histlewick after all.

"You mean you think this could be the real Histlewick, and the one outside has taken his place?"

I don't think we have enough facts to know. Either way, the whole thing stinks, and you've just stuck your foot right in the middle of it.

"We have to warn the Inquisitor General."

I don't see why. It's not like he's overly concerned about your welfare.

"I don't think you understand. He's my only hope. If we rescue Armand, there's at least a chance he'll vouch for me, but if they replace the Inquisitor General again, Armand's word won't carry any weight."

You have a point. The way I see it though, the problem is not so much how to warn the Inquisitor General as how not to tip off Histlewick. If he insists on turning the lock personally like he did last time, both he and whomever the Inquisitor General sends will find out about this together—and if it turns out Histlewick is an imposter...

"He'll stop at nothing to keep the Inquisitor General from finding out."

Exactly.

"Then we just have to make sure the other Histlewick doesn't find out about this one."

In case you haven't noticed, you're in the fancy equivalent of a cell, and there's a body sprawled on the floor.

"You, my friend, need to start thinking inside the box."

The armoire?

"The armoire," I said. I grabbed the unconscious Lord beneath his arms and dragged him over to the armoire. After several minutes of pushing, shoving and rearranging, I finally finished tucking him inside and closed the doors.

"There," I said. "Problem solved."

What about the table?

I paused a moment to scan the room. The current arrangement of furniture did seem to emphasize the gap left by the missing table.

"Maybe it's time this room had a really thorough cleaning."

I hardly think dust-free gleaming surfaces are going to be distracting enough to take Histlewick's attention away from a missing piece of furniture.

"Oh, I have no intention of finishing. I just need to get a really good start."

I pushed all the furniture over toward the armoire, including the bookcases when I could move them. Those I couldn't move, I emptied of all books, which I stacked in piles near the furniture. I even tipped chairs over on tabletops in an effort to create as much visual chaos as possible. Once everything was on one side of the room, I picked up an old broom I'd found behind a bookcase and began sweeping the open space. I had to do it in short bursts to avoid choking from the dust, but in not too long, I had an open patch of reasonably clean floor. Next I set about dusting the empty bookcases.

When I noticed that the voice in my head had gone uncharacteristically silent, I checked the time. It was well after midnight.

You know, I think that could actually work...

"I'm glad you approve."

...but what if it doesn't?

It's late, I'm tired. We'll just have to cross that bridge when we come to it."

I really must caution you not to underestimate your enemy here. You saw what he did with Histlewick and that table. If he could do that, imagine what else he's capable of.

I have the vague impression that the voice in my head nattered on for quite some time, but I didn't take much notice, curled up as I was on a cracked leather sofa. Although the stuffing had gone flat, it was still the most comfortable place I'd been in a very long time.

CHAPTER THIRTEEN

TO TELL THE TRUTH

In the heavy silence of the catacombs, the key turning in the lock echoed like a thunderclap. I'd left Histlewick's lamp burning, fearful I wouldn't be able to relight it in the darkness. By its flicker I checked the watch. It was 4:00 a.m. The door swung open to reveal Lord Histlewick. I hastily rubbed the sleep from my eyes. To my surprise, Darron was not with him. While that would normally have been cause for celebration, given my latest suspicions about Histlewick, this odd development only raised my hackles.

I bowed as Darron had the previous evening. "Lord Histlewick."

He nodded reflexively, but his attention was on the room. He held up his lantern to survey the rearranged furniture. He did not look pleased.

"I've been doing a little cleaning," I said.

Histlewick eyed me warily. "So I see."

"Can I be of some assistance?"

"Possibly. Have a seat."

Curiosity warred with anxiety as I sank slowly onto the sofa. Histlewick drew up a chair and straddled it.

"You've met Joanna Hockery." I couldn't tell if it was a statement or an accusation.

"Only briefly, My Lord."

Careful now. Remember we aren't sure who we're dealing with.

Histlewick's world-weary eyes glinted with sudden hunger. "But you'll be seeing her again as part of the hostage exchange?"

"I really can't say, My Lord. The Inquisitor General has not seen fit to share his plans."

"They say you were witness to her heresies."

"I saw her cast spells to incapacitate Armand and Kendall."

"Did you see anything else of that nature?" Histlewick asked. "Anything at all?"

"Well, at one point she made a hacksaw appear out of thin air."

"You're not talking sleight of hand, I take it?"

"No, I mean one minute it wasn't there, and the next it was. She must have Evoked it. It hissed when it appeared."

For a moment he seemed taken aback, but then he leaned forward and eyed me with even greater intensity.

"You're absolutely certain?"

"The noise was pretty distinctive."

Histlewick stood. "You've been most helpful. If you should somehow survive this business with the Goodkins, seek me out. Perhaps I can return the favor."

I stood and bowed once more. "Will they be attempting the hostage exchange then?"

Histlewick snorted. "The Inquisitor General rarely seeks my counsel, and is even less inclined to offer up his own, except insofar as it requires my cooperation. Since you are here, one can infer he is still entertaining the idea. Were I you, I would be prepared for travel on short notice."

"Thank you, My Lord." I bowed as he let himself out.

Well, at least he didn't notice the table was missing.

"Or didn't point it out, anyway. What do you suppose he came here for?"

He seemed to be interested only in confirming Joanna's abilities. By the way, you might want to be more careful about revealing those, particularly given your relationship to her.

"I'm in no position to get caught lying."

You can tell the truth without pointing out every little detail.

"This is not a battle I'm likely to win on a technicality. From their perspective, a deliberate omission is every bit as serious as an outright lie. The last thing I want is to give them reason to believe I'm holding something back."

You have a point there.

"I would also prefer to be awake when they come for me."

You mean "if" they come for you. There's no guarantee they'll decide to include you in the exchange.

"I was being subtle. What I really meant was, good night."

That put an end to the discussion.

At almost ten o'clock the next morning, the door opened again. This time, Darron accompanied Histlewick. He tossed the shackles at me as he entered. There's something degrading about being expected to fasten your own shackles, but I was grateful to have been free of them for the night.

Neither Darron nor Histlewick seemed particularly inclined toward conversation, so we made our way back to the court-yard in silence. There, Kendall and Ricard stood by their carriages in neatly pressed uniforms, ready for travel. Several other carriages waited as well, draped with banners bearing the intertwined snakes that declared their affiliation with the Church. A small knot of men surrounded the Inquisitor General, including Father Graves and an older gentleman arrayed in the starched, brightly colored vestments that marked him as an Ordinal—a position surpassed in authority only by the Primal himself.

"Roman, I know it pains you," the Ordinal said, "but Barclay has the right of this. Since these heretics have targeted you and your family, it makes no sense for you to put yourself directly in their sights. We can ill afford to lose another Inquisitor General. In fact, since they may also be on the lookout for Darron, I think he should remain behind as well."

"With all due respect, Your Ordinence," Roman said, "if we can't afford to lose an Inquisitor General, we surely can't afford to lose an Ordinal."

"Nonsense. The Primal has a vast supply of sycophants who would be more than happy to step into my shoes on a moment's notice. Due to recent events, however, your shoes are not nearly so receptive."

"But he's my son."

"All the more reason you should remain behind. When a son is threatened, paternal instinct can supplant clarity of thought. My decision stands. Young Barclay will lead, and Albert and I will assist. You and Darron are to remain behind to see to the operation of this facility."

Roman did not immediately respond. When the silence became uncomfortable, Father Graves placed his hand on Roman's shoulder.

"We'll bring him back to you," he said. "I promise."

Roman looked Albert in the eye then looked away. At last he nodded. "You'd best get started."

All at once the courtyard was a flurry of activity. Servants loaded up carriages as armed, grim-faced Inquisitors climbed aboard. Darron escorted me to Ricard's carriage and practically threw me inside. Barclay hopped atop Kendall's carriage, and the Ordinal climbed into the one at the back of the line. A few moments later Father Graves joined me.

"Hello, Mr. Flinch," he said. "I'm sorry this has turned into such a big to-do."

"Father, before we leave, I have something to tell you," I said. "I think it might be important."

"What is it?"

"Last night, while I was locked in a special room down in the catacombs, I found someone else was already there, unconscious."

"Did you tell Darron?"

"I couldn't, or at least I didn't think I ought to—the unconscious man looked identical to Lord Histlewick—he could have been Histlewick's twin. Does he have a twin?"

"I have no idea. Where is he now?

"I stuffed him in the armoire. If Histlewick's some sort of imposter, I didn't want him to know I was on to him."

"That's quick thinking, lad. I'd best let Roman know before we leave. Whoever he is, we can't have him dying down there while we're gone. Thank you for telling me."

"I hope I did the right thing."

Father Graves hopped out of the carriage. "You did fine. I'll be right back."

You just can't stop yourself from getting in deeper, can you?

"If that man had died after I put him in the armoire, I'd have been in deeper still, wouldn't I? Did you ever stop to think Histlewick may have intended for it to look as though I'd killed him?"

If he'd wanted to do that, he'd have just disappeared after meeting with you alone last night.

"Not necessarily. It might have been too soon—after all, as far as we know, the Histlewick in the armoire is still alive. With any luck, Father Graves will make sure he stays that way, and I'll have improved my chances with the Inquisitor General for having been honest."

Speaking of Father Graves...

"Yes?"

If I were you, I wouldn't let him handle the watch anymore.

"Why not? He's handled it before."

Yes, well, fortunately for you, he happened to be wearing gloves.

It was ten minutes before Father Graves reappeared. The caravan started forward the instant he took his seat. "He's going to have Darron look into it," he said.

As the small caravan snaked through the village toward the gate, I peered out through the window to see if I could catch a glimpse of my parents.

"They're in the second to last carriage."

"My parents are?"

Father Graves nodded. "At least so I am told. We're hoping Mrs. Hockery will adjust her terms and release Armand in return for just them, since we obviously can't produce her husband."

"I don't think she'll agree to that. She only added my parents to the ransom note as an afterthought to encourage me to deliver it."

"Really? Barclay seemed convinced there was a family connection somewhere."

"If there is, it's very remote. If you really want her to co-operate, I think you're going to have to find something she wants almost as much her husband."

"I don't see where we'll have time for that between here and the swamp."

Despite my misgivings, I dropped the subject. I couldn't afford to annoy Father Graves. Instead I broached a topic of obvious interest to him—his luggage. Although some of the crates had been removed from the carriage, enough of them remained that adding more people would have been uncomfortable.

According to Father Graves, one of the first things Roman had done after being appointed Inquisitor General was to ask him to collect up all the Inquisition's confiscated Profanities—items "profaned" by heretical spells made permanent. Apparently Roman was hoping to use some for defense. Such a suggestion would normally have been met with moral outrage, but the previous Inquisitor General's dramatic death at the hands of a bound and masked prisoner had, temporarily at least, muted the opposition. Father Graves even removed several items from their packages to show me, but he stopped short of telling me what he thought they might be useful for. I neglected to mention that several of them had originated in my father's shop.

After an hour or so of this, we heard the drivers calling to each other for a halt. Father Graves seemed as puzzled as I, until he glanced out the window. Another carriage was rapidly gaining. Unlike our snake banners, however, the banners of this carriage were emblazoned with the symbol of the red wolf.

Father Graves lifted his spectacles for a better look. "It looks as though Lord Histlewick will be joining us."

"Which one? The real one, or the imposter?"

Father Graves sighed and shook his head. "I have no idea."

CHAPTER FOURTEEN

PASSING IN THE NIGHT

The caravan pulled to a stop as Histlewick's carriage drew near. Father Graves hopped out to apprise Barclay of the possibility of Histlewick's duplicity. A few minutes later he climbed back into the carriage.

"What did he say?" I asked.

"He thanked me for bringing the matter to his attention. However, the fact that the information was supplied by a young prisoner seemed to raise concerns about its legitimacy. I doubt telling him is going to make a difference, but I tried."

We were underway again in no time, with Histlewick's distinctive carriage bringing up the rear. As the procession plodded forward, I found myself trying to catch glimpses of the windows in the third carriage from the end, to no avail. I then tried to envision my parents as last I'd seen them, knowing deep down that few who survived the Inquisition emerged unscathed. It didn't help that Father Graves' expression was somber as he watched me. If even Father Graves couldn't find words of encouragement, there were probably none to be had.

The vibrant spring colors of the passing downs darkened my mood still further. I felt as if they were mocking me.

I soon realized unless I wanted to burst into tears in front of the good Father, I needed to distract myself. For inspiration, I resorted once again to Father Graves' collection. His eyes glittered as he selected various objects to present for my inspection, speculating with animated fascination on each as to its design and potential function. He apparently had precious few opportunities to discuss his obsession with anyone else who showed any interest. While unwilling to reveal that some of the objects bore my father's mark, I was happy to ask questions that directed his speculation in the right general direction. He seemed so astonished by my insights I even smiled once or twice. I didn't have the heart to tell him that most of his gadgets were probably little more than elaborate light sources.

One unusual item did catch my eye, however. It was a lens circled by a wire to which was attached a long loop of very fine chain. It sparkled in Father Graves' gloved hand as he turned it to and fro for my inspection. Although there were no visible seams in the glass, the lens was clearly divided into seven different wedges, each tinted a different color of the spectrum.

"Sometimes the colors fade out," Father Graves said, "and sometimes only a few are present. I suspect it might be a child's toy—a sort of primitive kaleidoscope, if you will."

I probably blinked a few times in shock before I recovered enough to nod in agreement. It was perfectly clear to me this object was no kaleidoscope. While I certainly had no desire to mislead the good Father, such an object in the hands of the Inquisition terrified me. If Father Graves were to recognize its true purpose, it would be a disaster for the heretics. A spell detector in Church hands? Sniffing out heresy would become trivial. With unassailable proof that a spell was present, the Inquisition would win a conviction every time. Unfortunately, the device didn't provide a means to identify the caster. Anyone in range would be a suspect, allowing the Inquisitors to pin the crime on whomever was most convenient. The legitimate uses were bad enough, but the potential for abuse was staggering. Worse yet, the monocle bore my father's mark. If that got out, he'd be infamous. I only started breathing again when Father Graves set the monocle aside in favor of the next item, a perpetually warm teacup.

"The manifold innocuous uses for this heresy never cease to amaze me," he said.

Once again I merely nodded. It would probably have been impolitic to point out that the same series of spells cast on a person instead of a teacup would cause a dangerous increase in body temperature. Favored historically as means of assassination, this combination of spells would ultimately kill, with symptoms difficult to distinguish from those of a good old-fashioned fever. Innocuous? The particular use, maybe, but the particular spells, surely not. To my relief, the next exhibit was another of the elaborate light sources that had become so fashionable of late, and I was able to identify a hidden triggering mechanism without the slightest twinge of guilt. Father Graves duly noted the discovery in his journal, and then went on to the next item.

He lifted a small rosewood box from its carton.

"We acquired this one only recently," he said. "I presume it was once filled with cigars. There may even be some left, but I haven't solved the trick of the latch. Any ideas?"

With borrowed gloves, I held the box up to the window. It only took me a moment to realize I'd seen something like it before.

"Here's the problem. The latch is a fake. If you hold the box up to the light you can see the glint of the hinges in the crack beneath the lid. If the latch were real, the hinges should be on the opposite side."

Father Graves took the box and squinted at it through his spectacles. "That's quite an eye you've got there. I might have fussed with that for hours and never figured it out. So there must be some sort of catch on this side."

"Sometimes they'll make it so the front panel slides."

He fiddled with the box a moment more. "Sure enough," he said.

The lid sprang open, accompanied by a terrific hiss. Startled, Father Graves cried out and lost his grip. The box dropped. As it fell, it sprouted a glittering column of glass and metal. Sinuous tubes shot out from it in all directions. I had to dodge to avoid being hit.

The carriage pulled to an abrupt stop.

Father Graves mopped his brow as he stared at contraption rising out of the box in his lap. He had to look up to see the top of it.

"Are you all right?" I asked.

He gulped and nodded. "A little embarrassed by my carelessness, but otherwise, I'm fine."

"Well, the box clearly Evokes something, but I don't think it's a cigar."

Father Graves squinted in consternation at the device. "True, but same idea, though. It's a hookah. Any clue how I get rid of it? I'd just as soon not allow this little incident to distract from the mission."

Barclay's voice filtered into the carriage. "What's going on back there?"

"I heard something." Ricard called back. "Checking on

them now." The carriage rocked as he hopped down from his seat.

Father Graves turned to me then, his eyes wide. "If you've got any ideas, now would be a good time."

I put my feet on the seat next to Father Graves, doubled up the chain connecting my shackles, and swung with all my might. The links connected with the glass chamber in the hookah's center, smashing it into a spray of smoking shards. Broken in half by the blow, the entire device erupted in a tempest of roiling vapors that obscured Father Grave's stunned expression for only a moment before vanishing completely.

Father Graves snapped the box closed, and I dropped my feet back to the floor as the door flew open. Ricard poked his head in.

"What are you two doing in here?"

"So sorry for the commotion," Father Graves said. "Mr. Flinch was merely shifting positions. I understand shackles can become quite uncomfortable after you wear them awhile."

"What about that hissing noise?"

"Hissing noise?" Father Graves asked.

Ricard's brow creased. "Are you two all right?"

We're both fine, but it was kind of you to check."

"All right," Ricard said. "We'll be underway again in just a few minutes." He let the door fall closed.

Father Graves sighed and sank back into his seat. After a moment he broke into a soft chuckle. "Thank you, Mr. Flinch. I wasn't even remotely prepared for that tiny little box to contain something quite so large. So that's what an Evocation looks like?"

"We were lucky. It could have been far larger than that. Evocation spells suck in air and assemble it according to a pre-determined pattern. You don't see them often because they're so difficult. Fortunately for us, if you break the spell, the object reverts back to air."

"Using the chain was quick thinking."

"Not really. When you're wearing shackles, they're never far from your thoughts. Did you want to take a break?"

"Not on your life. Who knows how long it will be before I get another opportunity like this? I'll just take a few notes on that box, and then we can check out the next item on the list."

His supply of confiscated artifacts seemed unending, and the process was repeated many times. Although I offered what insights I could, many of the objects, including a wide array of jewelry and wands, gave little indication as to function. In the absence of prior knowledge of the items, appropriate spells for testing them, or the gumption to try them outright, most of my comments were idle speculation. Of course, that didn't stop Father Graves from studiously jotting down every word. The sun was low in the sky by the time we arrived at the bridge that marked the edge of the swamp. By then we were both exhausted.

"What happens now?" I asked.

"I expect we'll head for the exchange location," Father Graves said. "Presumably we'll camp there until we are contacted."

"We aren't planning to stay here overnight, are we?" The welts I'd acquired during my last overnight stay still itched. I wasn't eager to add to them.

"Barclay will decide that, but I don't see much in the way of alternatives."

"How far to the exchange point?"

"According to the note, we'll know it when we see it."

The caravan pressed on despite lengthening shadows. Apparently Barclay didn't buy Kendall's cautionary tales concerning the treachery of swamp travel at night. Eventually, the moist scrape of moss across the carriage warned us we'd arrived. I was thankful that, unlike the drivers, I was riding inside.

We paused briefly to light the carriage beacons. In their flickering brilliance I could make out the silhouettes of the drivers. Their arms twitched as they tried to ward off a trailing convocation of pests. Although the beacons allowed continued travel, our pace necessarily slowed to a crawl. Father Graves dropped off into an uneasy slumber, and I used the opportunity to sneak a peek at the pocket watch.

It won't be much longer now.

"What are we looking for, anyway?" I whispered.

When you see it, you'll know.

I should have known better than to ask. Ignoring the watch, I settled in for a little nap of my own. If the rendezvous location was going to be so obvious, the drivers would see it long before I got a glimpse anyway. I'd no more than closed my eyes when the carriage ground to a halt.

Father Graves started. "Why are we stopping?"

I shrugged.

He opened the door and stepped out. "I'll be right back."

I poked my head out for a quick look. Some distance ahead in the road, an eerie green light hung in the air. Although it swayed gently, the light itself was remarkably steady. There was no trace of the flicker that unmistakably marked a flame.

Barclay and the carriage drivers converged on Father Graves, eager to hear his professional opinion on this new development.

"Gentlemen," he said. "I think we have our sign."

"Best not to let haste get the better of us," Kendall said. "Like as not, that's a corpse candle, come to lure us to our graves. These fens have a foul reputation for that sort of thing."

"Seems a tad on the stable side for a wisp, if you ask me,"

Barclay said, "but even if it is the sign we're looking for, it doesn't mean we should proceed carelessly. Father Graves and I will check it out, but not alone." He turned to one of the Inquisitors. "You there. Bring one of the prisoners. The rest of you, keep us covered."

At this point Father Graves noticed our carriage door was still ajar and pushed it closed. As a result, I caught only a brief glimpse as they escorted the prisoner past my window, masked and shackled. The prisoner's movements were ungainly and sluggish, more than even shackles and a mask could account for. I found myself denying it could be one of my parents.

You know, instead of just sitting there slack-jawed and useless, you might consider using this opportunity to accomplish something.

"Such as?"

Well, you might consider disposing of that monocle. You may never get a better chance.

"And if I'm caught? It's not like he doesn't keep close track of his inventory."

True, but what are the chances he'll discover it's missing before the hostage exchange takes place?

"And what are the chances I'll escape the gallows if he does? Other than Armand, he's the closest thing I have to an ally. I won't jeopardize that. If it's all the same to you, I'll just let him go on believing it's a kaleidoscope."

He only believes that because he hasn't had time to think it through.

"I don't care. I'm not doing it."

You do recall what happened the last time you ignored my advice, right?

"I told you, it's not worth the risk."

The carriage door opened suddenly. Father Graves' face was wrinkled with concern. "Who are you talking to?"

And now, of course, it's too late.

"No one," I said. "I talk to myself when I'm nervous. Was Kendall's green wisp the sign we were looking for?"

Father Graves nodded. "It certainly looks like Phrendonic heresy to me. They've left a trail for us to follow. Once we got close to the first light, we could see a second off in the distance. The only problem is that the trail leaves the road. We'll have to get where we're going on foot. "

"Does that mean waiting until morning?"

Father Graves shook his head. "Barclay is determined to forge ahead. The ground in that direction is firm, and there are sufficient lanterns among the carriages to light our way."

"Crossbows will be useless in the dark."

"Barclay is confident we have nothing to fear, and given his track record dealing with Phrendonic heretics, I'm inclined to give him the benefit of the doubt."

At Barclay's behest, the travelers abandoned the safety of the carriages to gather in the road. The shackles on my legs were exchanged for a set on my wrists. The same was true for the other prisoners. Their masks became a point of contention when Father Graves pointed out that the prisoners couldn't negotiate the swamp unless they could see where they were going. One of the Inquisitors suggested they be carried. Barclay decided that would take too long and ordered the masks removed.

My stomach knotted as Barclay's assistant Prentiss stripped off the heavy leather coverings. Relief flooded through me as I recognized my parents' faces in the glare of the beacons. I'd worried Barclay might try to foist off imposters on Joanna, but now it was clear that wasn't the plan after all. My joy at seeing them was short-lived, for if they recognized me, they showed no sign of it. Their eyes were hollow, and they stared vacantly into the distance, placidly moving when prodded, but showing few other signs of consciousness.

"What's wrong with them?" I whispered.

"They've been drugged," Father Graves said. "I know it looks dreadful, but it's a kindness. They will have little memory of this trip."

"So they'll be all right?"

"If the dosing is done properly, there should be no permanent damage. I've been assured that Prentiss is expert at such things."

Prentiss smiled and inclined his head. "I do my best, Father," he said. "The subjects should remain compliant for several hours."

"Then we'd best get moving," Barclay said. "There's no telling how far they're going to make us walk."

Histlewick and the Ordinal were the last to arrive. Barclay politely suggested they might wish to stay behind for safety reasons, but both declined. Barclay was less than pleased at the prospect of the two of them tagging along, but he didn't argue. Once the Inquisitors readied their packs, the caravan set off.

The ground near the first of the wisps was spongy, but solid enough to support a variety of reasonably tall trees. The green light emanated from a cork tied to a low-hanging branch. Father Graves, wearing one of his little white gloves, reached for it, but Barclay stayed his hand.

"We may need them to find our way back."

"Oh, excellent point."

"If you're really concerned about getting back," I said. "You might want to make some sort of trail of your own. Phrendonic lights can fade after as little as an hour."

There was a small conference at that, and Barclay finally assigned one of the Inquisitors to affix pieces of parchment to the trees along the way, marking them with an arrow to indicate the way back toward the carriages. By now, everyone was eager to press forward. The hum from the circling cloud of bloodsuckers was deafening, and the greater their numbers, the bolder they became.

I went first since I had a face the enemy would recognize. I set off at a measured pace toward the next wisp, aware of the difficulties encountered by those attempting to shepherd my parents, but also because I was worried my shackles would make it difficult to catch myself were I to trip. Fortunately we had enough lanterns that I could see most dangers before I stepped in them. The looming trees cast twisted shadows that prodded the imagination in strange directions. As I plodded along, I wondered whether the swamp was home to poisonous snakes, and if it was, whether they were nocturnal.

Three bobbing wisps later, we were still plunging ever deeper into the shifting, uncharted bog. As the land became soggier, the mists became denser. Once, as we waited for my parents to be guided over a fallen tree, I peered into a dark still pool. For a moment could have sworn I saw our lamps reflected in two glowing orbs that broke the surface almost a foot apart. When I blinked, all that remained was two expanding ripples.

At last we came to a dead end—the last green cork in the sequence. We stood at the end of a small peninsula, our way blocked by a sluggish river. The smell of decay was suffocating, and our steps squished, producing faint phosphorescent footprints. To go forward, we would have to swim a hundred feet across the rush-choked river, but there was no indication we were meant to go that way. I looked to Barclay for guidance.

He strode to the very tip of the peninsula and cupped his hands around his mouth.

"Joanna Hockery, we're here to deal. Are you out there?"

Nearby, another green light winked into being. This one illuminated a small canoe resting among the reeds.

Joanna's voice echoed through the mists. "Place your prisoners in the canoe where I can see them."

"We have to talk," Barclay said.

"There's nothing to discuss," she called back. "Produce the prisoners, or the deal is off."

"We'd like nothing better. Unfortunately, during questioning your husband invoked the Infernal Sacrifice. We were powerless to stop it. He took the Inquisitor General with him. Your hostage, I'm afraid, is the son of his successor. We are prepared, in accordance with the terms of your note, to give you all three Theratigans in return for Armand's safety."

My breath caught as I waited to hear the words that would determine my family's fate. For a long while, the only thing to break the silence was the croaking of frogs. Then a new voice spoke—this one belonging to Joanna's friend Ramos.

"We are prepared to exchange the Theratigans for two Inquisitors," he said.

"And what of Armand?" Barclay called back.

"We will discuss that once the exchange has been made."

"No deal." Barclay cried. "That's a gift, not an exchange. Why not trade all three of your hostages for all three of ours?"

"Really?" Joanna cried. "After what you did to my husband, you have the nerve to come here and expect an equal trade? Well, sir, if it's parity you want, parity you shall have."

Almost simultaneously Ramos' voice rang out. "Joanna, no!"

The Ordinal stepped forward. "They seem distracted," he said. "Can we get to them before they recover?"

"Not short of diving in or taking the canoe," Barclay said. "Lit up like that, the passengers would be sitting ducks. Either way they'll likely recover before we can get there."

"Remember," I said, "they have two archers who might not be distracted."

"All right then," the Ordinal said. "Keep them engaged. I'll send out Inquisitors to see if they can find other ways across. I don't intend to miss another opportunity."

"Lord Histlewick's from around here," Barclay said. "Maybe he has some insights? Where is Histlewick, anyway?"

Almost as one, the entire caravan looked around and shrugged. Histlewick was no longer with us.

"Damn it!" Barclay said. "The fool's going to get himself killed."

Once again Ramos' voice rang out through the mists. "We'll send you an Inquisitor for the boy. If that goes well, then we can chat about the rest."

"How do we know you'll keep your end of the bargain?" Barclay asked.

In answer, another canoe lit up across the water. One of Joanna's captive Inquisitors stepped into it, his hands held high in the air.

Barclay gestured in my direction. "Remove his shackles," he said. An Inquisitor stepped forward with the key, and my shackles fell away.

"All right," Barclay said. "Get in the boat."

My heart pounding, I clambered inside, grabbed a paddle, and had a seat. After a moment, Barclay nodded, and Father Graves gave me a shove off.

"Good luck, my boy."

Across the river, I saw the twin to my own boat slip into the water. I marveled for a moment at the simplicity of Joanna's process for making the exchanges. I dared to hope the rest of the exchanges would be equally smooth-sailing. And why not? After all, I'd certainly lived a charmed life until now.

CHAPTER FIFTEEN

ONE BEASTLY EVENING

I was relieved to hear my canoe slither across the reeds on the far side of the river. They'd probably used canoes to keep us vulnerable to spells or arrows in the event of a breach of promise. If Joanna was planning a double-cross, at least I'd been lucky that Barclay hadn't discovered it yet.

I wasted no time in disembarking—the longer I stayed in the canoe, the longer I remained a target. I splashed my way up to where Joanna waited on the shore, still sporting the burgundy hat.

She beckoned to me imperiously. "Quickly—the watch, if you please."

I reached into my pocket and produced the timepiece with a flourish. "Here you go," I said, opening it for her inspection. "Good as new."

She snatched it from my hands, fixing me with an annoyed look that said she knew full well why I'd opened it. She immediately snapped it closed and reopened it, her expression a curious blend of hunger and dread.

"I must know," she cried. "Are they playing me false? Is my Marshall truly gone?"

Her words echoed strangely in my mind, much the same as the voice from the watch. Indeed, I also heard the response. *From everything I could gather, they speak the truth. I am sorry.*

Even in the ghostly light from the canoe I saw her pale. Trembling, she bowed her head and closed her eyes, clenching the watch to her breast. Tears sparkled along her cheeks. She shuddered, allowing a single agonized sob.

Barclay's voice echoed across the river. "Let's end this, shall we? We'll send over the Theratigans in return for your remaining hostages. Then we can all be on our way. Are we agreed?"

Ramos touched Joanna's arm. "I need to tell them something."

With great effort, Joanna straightened and took a deep breath. "You can tell them to…" Her sudden smile chilled my blood. "On second thought, tell them they have a deal."

Ramos looked puzzled. "Are you sure?"

"It's over," she said. "Just do it." Without waiting for his reply, she strode away, deeper into the fen.

"As you wish," Ramos said. He stepped a bit closer to the river and called, "We are agreed."

My parents were in no condition to paddle a canoe. I turned, curious whom they would designate to do it for them. At that moment, I again heard Joanna's voice, although this time, it was only in my head. To anyone else, it would have seemed like gibberish, but having worked in my father's shop, I'd encountered spoken mnemonics before. Given that I had yet to see Armand, I took it as a bad sign.

On the opposite bank, Inquisitors herded my parents into their canoe. Prentiss pressed a paddle into my father's hands.

He dropped it several times before his drug-fogged brain registered that he was supposed to hold onto it. I was aghast. Could they really be planning to cast them adrift by themselves?

Behind me, Joanna appeared, pushing Armand and the other hostage ahead of her. Both men stumbled in their shackles as Joanna herded them toward the glowing boat. They were shaken, but otherwise unharmed.

Armand's eyes widened as he saw me. "I presume Mr. Flinch will be accompanying us."

Joanna shoved him with enough force that he stumbled once more. "If I were you, I'd spend less time presuming, and more time watching where I was putting my feet."

"Ready when you are," Barclay cried.

Moments later, Armand and the Inquisitor arrived at the boat.

"Get in," Joanna rasped.

Ramos eyed Joanna questioningly. "What about their shackles?"

"They should count their blessings they aren't masked as well. We wouldn't have been accorded the same courtesy."

"But if the boat should tip—"

"They'll just have to be careful. Shove them off."

As Ramos pushed them away from shore, Joanna pulled out the watch once more. Her voice still echoed strangely in my head. "Is there anything else I should know before we leave?"

Not that I can think of. I trust that means I've fulfilled my end of the bargain.

"You've been most helpful," Joanna said.

When can I expect you to fulfill yours?

"Unfortunately, despite your help, this mission has been a total failure. Therefore, it doesn't count. Until we find something that does, I'm afraid it's back to the chest for you."

I was afraid you'd say that. You realize you're leaving me no choice.

"Save it. I don't have time for your sniveling right now."

Remember, you brought this on yourself.

For a brief instant, a detailed image flashed across my consciousness. It disappeared so quickly I was able to retain only a vague impression of a bell ringing in a high tower. Simultaneously, the pocket watch chimed. Joanna went momentarily cross-eyed. Before Ramos or I could react, she collapsed. The watch fell and splatted against the spongy ground near the water's edge.

Ramos cried out and rushed to Joanna. While he was preoccupied, I snatched up the watch and shoved it into my pocket.

After a brief examination, Ramos rounded on me. "What did you do to her?"

"It wasn't me, I swear!"

He cast about wildly for signs of intruders. "We've been double-crossed," he cried. "Kill the hostages."

The archers stepped forward, approaching the bank with arrows nocked. Meanwhile, Ramos focused on Joanna and began muttering.

"Wait!" I cried. "It's not their fault!"

I dove at the nearest archer, trying to knock the bow from his hands. The other archer was too far away for me to reach. His bow sang. The arrow whizzed past me. Armand's agonized cry told me it had found its mark.

As the archer reached for another arrow, a crossbow bolt erupted from his throat. He fell clutching at the wound, dying before he drew a single breath. The archer I'd interrupted took one look at his fallen comrade and fled. Six steps and another bolt took him in the back.

Downstream, I saw a flash of movement. A shady figure

ducked behind a tree. I scrambled out of sight behind a decaying stump.

Ramos helped Joanna to her feet. It looked like they were going to make it to the protection of a nearby tree, but then another Inquisitor emerged from upstream. There was no way the tree could protect Joanna and Ramos from both crossbows at once. The upstream Inquisitor took careful aim, confident he'd not been seen.

"Look out!" I cried.

The Inquisitor tensed as he squeezed the trigger. At that moment a great snarling wolf lunged out of the darkness. The beast's jaws snapped, ripping away the man's jugular. Then, as quickly as it came, the beast melted back into the shadows.

Once again, I heard Joanna chant. Fearing the worst, I circled the stump to get out of sight. As she completed the spell, a veil of impenetrable blackness descended. While it wasn't the firestorm I'd dreaded, her Darkness spell still made my situation more difficult.

In my head, I heard Joanna speak one final time. *"Leave it. We don't know how many more there are. Mount up and ride. I'll be right behind you."*

Blinded by the spell, I felt my way out into the river. Unless I could make it back to the caravan, I'd probably never escape the swamp.

In up to my ankles, I already regretted the decision. The water was so cold I feared my chattering teeth would break. I steeled myself and inched forward through the darkness, knowing once I acclimated, I'd feel the cold less. My vision returned by the time the water was up to my knees. Darkness still hovered behind me, a great dome of inky blackness. Ahead lay the eerie green reflection of an empty canoe drawn up on the far shore.

You're not planning to swim this, are you?

I stopped short. The watch. I'd completely forgotten about it.

"I'm not sure I have a choice."

How are you planning to protect the watch mechanism?

"I think I'll have to play that by ear."

I can't say I like the sound of that.

"Sorry you feel that way."

You saw what I did to Joanna, right?

"I don't see how that really helps you under these circumstances."

Hmm. You have a point. Perhaps I should try a different approach. Are you going back to the caravan?

"The thought had crossed my mind."

Will Armand be there?

"Assuming he survived."

If he's there, you'd be better off staying on this side of the river.

"I don't see why."

Then maybe you aren't thinking it through.

I held the watch suspended just above the water. "All right, out with it. Unless you'd prefer a nice refreshing little dunk this instant."

Let's not be hasty. I'm not telling you anything you don't already know.

"Perhaps you can't tell," I said, "but this water's really, really cold. The longer I stand here, the more feeling I lose in my fingers, and the harder it is to hold onto things."

All right, all right. Given what Joanna's done to Armand, the caravan might not be such a safe place for a while, that's all I'm saying.

"What did she do?"

Didn't you hear her casting the spells?

"What spells?"

Oh, you know, Incinerate, Passive charges, things like that. Together I imagine you'd call it an Infernal Sacrifice.

"What? How long ago?"

If I had to guess, I'd say your boss and his closest friends have, at most, half an hour left to live.

CHAPTER SIXTEEN

Calculated Risks

I pushed farther out into the river. The current was not brisk and by the time I was halfway across, the water was only up to my waist. But the river continued to deepen, and although the bottom muck was not thick enough to slow my progress, the water had a stagnant reek that made my eyes burn as it crept closer to my face.

If this gets any deeper, we're going to have a problem.

I ignored the voice and focused on reaching the far bank. I finally detected an uphill trend in the slope of the river bottom, and moments later stepped out from among the reeds—into an area bristling with crossbows. All of them were trained on me.

"Where's Armand?" I demanded. "I need to see him right away."

The Inquisitors stepped aside to reveal the Ordinal. "To finish him off, you mean?"

"To save his life."

"It would seem your heretic friends have other ideas."

"That was a misunderstanding. Please, there isn't much time. It's important that I see him right now."

"I'm afraid, young heretic, that the only thing you'll be seeing is the inside of a mask." He motioned to one of the Inquisitors. "Shackle him."

Father Graves stooped to retrieve my recently cast-off shackles. "I'll see to it, Your Ordinence. Armand is ready for you now."

The Ordinal waited until Father Graves had snapped the shackles on my wrists before he finally stalked off. Father Graves then waved off the Inquisitors as well. "I'll deal with the boy," he said. "You make certain the perimeter is secure."

The moment they were out of earshot, he turned on me. "What, in the name of all that is holy, are you doing back here?"

"I'm trying to save Armand. They've set him up for a Sacrifice."

"Dear Lord! We must warn the others. They're all gathered round him."

"But if you warn them, they may not let me try to save him."

"What can we do? We aren't heretics—we don't traffic in spells. If the Sacrifice is already in place, Armand's fate is sealed. The others, however, we can save."

"You have a whole carriage of spells."

"Most of which we don't understand."

"There must be something in there we can use. At least let me go look."

"For what?"

"For something that could dispel the Incinerate, and barring that, anything that could interrupt the energy transfer. If I understand correctly, a basic Sacrifice probably entails some sort of Charge spell to supply the energy, and another spell to convert that energy into heat. Even something that could Extend a simple Light spell might steal the Charge away from the spell that generates the heat. Surely there must be at least one thing in the carriage that can do that."

Father Graves shook his head. "Even if there were, the carriage is halfway across the swamp. You'd never get there, find something, and then make it back here in time."

My mind raced as I tried to find a flaw in the Father's logic.

Father Graves did not wait for me to reply. "I've got to get the others away from Armand. Don't move until I get back."

Perhaps I can be of assistance.

The voice brought me up short. Given the role it had played in all that had just transpired, the timepiece's intentions were now suspect, but I was out of ideas.

"What did you have in mind?"

I was merely going to suggest the direct approach.

"And that is?"

Given what you have to work with, circumventing the Incinerate would be a very tricky proposition. Why not just have me diffract for Summoning? As long as I stay within thirty feet, your friend should be safe. You'd only have to manage it for fifteen minutes or so. How hard could that be?

"You can do that?"

I'm a multi-purpose personal assistant for the discriminating heretic. Protecting against unwelcome incineration is all in a day's work.

"Sounds perfect. Let's do it."

There is, of course, one tiny little condition.

"Figures. What is it?"

You'll first need to snap off the little safety latch inside the back of the watch.

Warning bells went off on my head. "Why would I need to do that?"

Do you really have time for me to explain?

As much as I hated to admit it, I didn't. After a quick glance over to where Father Graves was arguing with the Ordinal and Inquisitors gathered around Armand, I flipped open the back of the watch and looked for the latch. It was too dark to see anything. I edged closer to one of the glowing corks until I could make out the mechanism. It took a bit of bending back and forth with my thumbnail, but eventually I snapped off the tiny golden latch.

"I hope you know what you're doing," I said. "Can we get in range now?"

Once the chimes are finished.

"Chimes? I don't think that's a good…"

The image of a bell tower wreathed in flames flashed through my mind. As I shook my head to clear it, three melodic chimes rang out.

The nearby argument came to a halt, and all eyes turned my way. The Ordinal was the first to break the silence. "What was that?"

"It sounded like it came from the corpse candle," Barclay said.

"It sounded more like the chime of a pocket watch," Father Graves said. "Perhaps the boy's timepiece isn't broken after all."

"What timepiece?" the Ordinal asked.

"Quite a fine one," Father Graves said. "He showed it to me shortly after we picked him up along the road."

"You permitted a suspected heretic to keep a potential Profanity?"

Father Graves shrugged. "At the time, the boy was not considered a suspect. After that, with everything else going on, it slipped my mind."

"Will you please take care of it? I have an injured patient to attend to."

"Your Ordinence," Father Graves replied, "we must get

clear of Armand. If he has indeed been Sacrificed, there's no time to lose."

"Oh, very well," the Ordinal said. "Five minutes either way shouldn't matter. Everyone away."

As the men withdrew, Armand became visible. He was lying on a blanket they'd spread on the ground. A wicked-looking shaft protruded from his knee. I'd barely caught a glimpse before Father Graves blocked my view, his gloved hand held out expectantly.

"I'm sorry I have to do this," he said, "but the Ordinal does have a point—for all we know, that watch could be a danger."

"I'm sorry too, Father," I said, holding out the watch. As he reached for it, I dodged under his arm and sprinted to where Armand lay.

"Stop him," Barclay cried. "He's going to Sacrifice!"

His words had the opposite effect of what he'd intended. Instead of pursuing me, the Inquisitors backed farther away, but the Ordinal had the presence of mind to grab a crossbow.

I landed hard on the blanket next to Armand. The impact seemed to bring him around. He looked at me and smiled groggily as I flattened myself to the ground behind him to avoid the Ordinal's aim.

"So you escaped them after all," Armand said. "I was dreading to think what they might do to you."

"All right, Theratigan," the Ordinal called out. "You've had your fun. Put your hands in the air and step away from my patient, or I'll make a Sacrifice seem merciful by comparison."

"How much time yet?" I asked.

I'm not sure. Maybe one minute, maybe five.

"What's this all about?" Armand asked. He grimaced as he shifted for a better look at me. His face was deathly pale.

"Joanna's set you up for a Sacrifice," I said. "I think I've found a way to prevent it, but His Ordinence doesn't trust me."

The Ordinal took several wary steps closer, trying to get a bead on me, but just as he had me, Armand sat up.

"Please, Your Ordinence," he said. "There's no need for the weapon. Mr. Flinch assures me he's here to help me, and I believe him."

"Based on what?" the Ordinal sneered. "Forgive me, Armand, but despite all your efforts to keep them secret, I'm well aware of your heretic sympathies. Look how well they've served you."

Crouching behind Armand, I could hear the Ordinal approaching. He was less than fifteen feet away and closing when the night was suddenly swallowed by blinding light. Screams erupted from behind the Ordinal. As my vision returned, I peered over Armand's shoulder to see that the Inquisitor who'd come in the boat with Armand was now engulfed in flames. The Ordinal watched in shock as the terrified man ran blindly through the smoldering swamp, waving his flaming arms about him.

"Drop to the ground and roll!" the Ordinal cried. "Try to suffocate it!"

It was no use. The Inquisitor continued to flail, fanning the flames.

At last the Ordinal tossed the crossbow aside and ran toward the flaming man. He took only three steps before Father Graves tackled him.

"You fool!" the Ordinal cried. "What are you doing?"

He'd no sooner said it than a second flash engulfed the Inquisitor. He finally stopped flailing and collapsed, though he still writhed and wailed. A few moments later there was a third flash, and the Inquisitor finally lay still.

An eerie silence fell over the swamp.

At last Father Graves spoke. "Sacrifices are rarely encountered in multiples of one."

CHAPTER SEVENTEEN

IN DEFENSE OF OTHERS

Once Father Graves broke the stunned silence, the Inquisitors sprang into action. I thought I might be overlooked in the chaos, but then Barclay was on me, yanking my head back and holding a blade to my throat. The Ordinal pulled himself to his feet, brushed himself off, and helped up Father Graves.

"Albert," he said, "I believe you just saved my life."

Father Graves shook his head. "You're thanking the wrong person."

The Ordinal nodded toward the smoldering remains of the Inquisitor. "Nonsense. If you hadn't stopped me, I'd have shared his fate."

"I beg to differ," Albert said. "Notice how the vegetation is charred roughly in a circle around the poor fellow."

"It's actually more like a crescent than a circle."

"Exactly. And we are soundly within that crescent. If something hadn't prevented the effect of the Sacrifice where we're standing, neither of us would have survived."

"So you used one of your Profanities?"

"No, it wasn't my doing. To find the source, make a circle from the inner edge of the crescent and find the center."

The Ordinal scowled. "You mean…Armand?"

"I think that rather unlikely under the circumstances, don't you?"

"You can't mean the boy?"

"Well, if it wasn't me, and it wasn't Armand, he's the only other option."

"So he used heresy to fight heresy?"

"So it would seem. If he hadn't, we would not be having this discussion."

"What's your point, Albert? Surely you're not arguing for leniency on the basis of how the heresy is used. The Primal would never permit it."

"No? And just what do you suppose Roman is planning to do with the Profanities in my carriage?"

"That's different."

Albert's tone turned subtly sarcastic. "I think I see your point. Whereas Roman plans to use heresy to defend himself, the boy, at great personal risk, used it instead to defend the very people who abducted his parents and slapped him in chains. I guess if you look at it that way, the boy's actions were really much more noble."

"That's not what I meant."

"Regardless, the point is that if you're indebted to anyone, it's Mr. Flinch."

"Under no circumstances will I be beholden to a heretic. The Primal would have my head."

"When all is said and done, is it really the Primal to whom we must account?"

Barclay chose that moment to interrupt. "With all due respect, Your Ordinence, we really should get moving. There's no telling when the heretics will show up next. In the mean-time, what do you want me to do with this one?"

"Roman is going to want to have a nice long chat with him. Until then, we can't take any chances. Keep two crossbows on him. When we get back to the carriages, mask him. Oh, and will someone please take away that Profanity?"

Father Graves let out a long sigh. "If that's truly your decision, Ordinence, I'll deal with the trinket."

Tell them if they take the watch, they'll no longer be protected.

"Hold on," I said. "If you take the watch, it won't protect us anymore—it only works for me."

Father Graves paused and looked back to the Ordinal for guidance.

"Is that even possible?" the Ordinal asked.

Father Graves shrugged. "Heretics have proven themselves to be endlessly inventive. Who can say?"

The Ordinal considered. "We may not need any more protection, anyway. The heretics have fled and an hour has elapsed since any of us have had contact with them."

Barclay's assistant Prentiss stepped forward. "Not necessarily. We are a fair distance from the carriages, and transporting our patient through this wilderness will be slow going. It's entirely possible that by the time we get there, the heretics will be waiting for us."

"We just routed them," the Ordinal said. "Do you really think they'll have any stomach for more of the same?"

"You surprised them," Prentiss said. "They are unlikely to let that happen again. Not only that, but we've left behind a bait they just might find irresistible."

Father Graves jaw dropped. "Oh my Lord!" he cried, "the Profanities!"

The Ordinal raised his eyebrow at Prentiss. "You aren't suggesting we allow the heretic to keep that pocket watch, are you?"

Prentiss bowed his head. "I suggest nothing, Your Ordinance. I merely direct your attention to some details that may have eluded your esteemed consideration."

"We must get Armand back to the carriages," Father Graves said. "We've already wasted too much time on this."

Unless I did something soon, things were not going to end well for me. I assumed the most confident tone I could muster given the knife pressing against my throat. "Your Ordinence, I just risked everything to save you. Please don't let it be in vain."

The Ordinal's eyes narrowed. "I take it you're suggesting we may not be through dealing with your heretic friends after all." He signaled to Barclay to let me speak.

"I don't claim to know their minds," I said, "but I do know that it would be naïve to presume you are out of danger. You're assuming they cast the Sacrifices directly on their hostages, and the spells have therefore expired. Father Graves can correct me if I'm wrong, but wouldn't it make more sense for them to have cast the spells on something the hostages carried with them?"

"The lad has a point," Father Graves said. "It would be a shame for us to have survived the first Sacrifice only to fall prey to the next one."

"*Next one?*" The Ordinal cried. "How many are we talking about?"

"Without a soul to resist them, the spells could last much longer," Father Graves said. "On an object they could go on all night and well into the day tomorrow. To be safe, we should completely strip both hostages of all their belongings and sink them to the bottom of the river."

"I have a better idea," the Ordinal said, motioning to several nearby Inquisitors. "Strip Armand and place his belongings in a heap on the shore. You can go ahead and sink the other man's possessions, or what remains of them. When you're finished, I'll see if I can get Armand's wound patched up enough to transport him. Albert, you keep a close eye on our young heretic. Barclay, please see that we are prepared to move out the instant Armand is ready."

"What about the carriages?" Father Graves asked.

"I can only handle so many things at once. We'll just have to hope they're not a target."

Father Graves and I stood off to one side while Barclay barked orders to the rest of the troupe. When I was certain everyone else was too busy to be listening, I tugged at Father Graves' sleeve. "Where have they put my parents? I don't see them anywhere. Are they hiding them from me?"

Father Graves looked puzzled. "I thought you knew. We sent them across the river in one of the glowing boats as part of the hostage deal."

"You mean you didn't recapture them?"

"We were too busy dealing with Armand," he said. "Why would you think we recaptured them?"

"Because they never made it to the other side. Please, you have to send someone to find them."

"I can suggest it, but before I do, you might want to consider whether they would be better off if I didn't."

"But they could drown."

"But there's always the chance they won't. Even if they do, you should be aware that there are worse fates than drowning."

"I see your point. Forget I said anything."

"As you wish."

In short order, Armand was stripped down and wrapped in blankets while the Ordinal attended to his wound. I tried my best to watch the process, but when he went to remove the shaft, I had to look away. To my amazement, Armand didn't even cry out. Most likely either he'd lost consciousness or the Ordinal had done something to dull his pain. In several more minutes, they transferred him to a makeshift stretcher.

No one was more surprised than I when Armand's belongings erupted in a series of brilliant flashes that lit the night and charred the surrounding vegetation.

Father Graves favored the Ordinal with a sidelong look. "It seems, Your Ordinence, that the lad has come through for us again."

"Or he's setting us up. Keep a close watch on him."

Though his tone was gruff, I noticed he was no longer insisting they take the pocket watch. He also seemed unwilling to look me in the eye, which I took as an additional sign of progress. I decided to press my advantage.

"Ordinence, I request permission to travel next to Armand. As the Inquisitor General's son, he may still be a target. While I couldn't hold off a determined assault, I might be able to provide crucial extra minutes in case we are ambushed."

The Ordinal avoided addressing me directly. "Albert, I'm placing the lad in your custody. See to it he doesn't cause us any difficulties."

Father Graves nodded. "Of course, Ordinence."

Since Father Graves made no objection, I remained at Armand's side during the long walk back. The corks still lit our path, though with Armand and the charred corpse of the fallen Inquisitor both on makeshift stretchers, progress was painstakingly slow. Armand slept fitfully. Though his eyes would occasionally flicker open when he was jostled or bounced, he seemed to be generally unaware of his surroundings. I tried to wave the flies and gnats away from him as best I could with shackled hands, but they were relentless.

As we finally drew close to the road, Barclay sent ahead scouts to report on the status of the carriages. To everyone's relief, they were just as we'd left them. Although that still didn't rule out an ambush, it made it considerably less likely that Father Graves' Profanities had been the objective. There was some consternation at Lord Histlewick's continued absence, but the need to get Armand back to the Manor was paramount. Histlewick's own men would remain behind to institute a search.

The stretchers were placed on the road while the carriages were prepared to receive them. The fallen Inquisitor was assigned to the carriage my parents had traveled in, and Armand was to ride with the Ordinal. A sudden movement as they loaded him into the carriage jarred Armand back to his senses.

I smiled my best reassuring smile and squeezed his hand. "You're going to be all right," I said.

He snatched his hand away. "Mr. Flinch, I trusted you, and you lied to me." Before I could protest, indeed before what he'd said even registered, he was already in the carriage.

As the carriage doors fell closed, for the first time since I'd encountered Armand in that cluttered little back yard behind the pub, I truly felt all was lost.

CHAPTER EIGHTEEN

ÐISPENSATION

Once again, I found myself alone with Father Graves in his carriage. At first Barclay tried to have an Inquisitor ride along with us, but it was obvious that there wouldn't be room without a serious reorganization of the Profanities, and Father Graves finally waved the man off, insisting he couldn't justify the delay given Armand's injury.

The trip back to Histlewick Manor began in awkward silence. I was out of my mind with worry for my parents, and still reeling from Armand's rebuff. With my heresy now a foregone conclusion, Armand's high regard had been the only thing standing between me and the full force of his father's wrath. For some time, Father Graves didn't take his eyes off me, his expression a curious blend of incredulity and pity. It did not improve my disposition.

At long last, he spoke. "Why?"

"I don't know what you mean."

"Why did you come back?"

"That's complicated, but it had mostly to do with thinking that Armand didn't deserve to die, and maybe there was something I could do to stop it."

"Surely you must have known the risk you were taking."

"He was kind to me when no one else was."

Father Graves nodded slowly. "He's a great man like his father, but in different ways. I suspect in time, the Church will have cause to be grateful for your selflessness this day."

"You'll forgive me for not weeping with joy."

"Ah yes, your use of heresy. I'd be lying if I said that didn't complicate matters. Technically, using it to save lives should weigh in your favor, but under this Primal, embracing that stance openly is asking for trouble. Worse still, Roman is unlikely to take his son's injury in stride. When it comes to defending his own, he's nothing short of fierce. If he should view you as responsible, it may be difficult to get him to appreciate the bigger picture."

"It wasn't even my doing. When I said I never learned how to work spells, I was telling the truth—it was the watch."

"You do realize that using a Profanity is also considered heresy."

I looked at all the crates and boxes piled high around me. "What about all these Profanities? I thought you said the Inquisitor General was going to use them to defend himself. How is that different from what I did?"

"In rare situations, dispensation can be granted."

"And who has the authority to grant these dispensations. The Primal?"

"Yes, assuming he were so inclined. And of course, as Inquisitor General, Roman can too."

"So he's giving himself dispensation?"

Father Graves shrugged. "Given what happened to his predecessor, I doubt anyone is going to question it."

"Not even the Primal?"

Father Graves shifted uncomfortably. "Technically, Roman's authority to grant dispensations does not require the Primal's express consent."

"So you're doing all this behind the Primal's back?"

Father Graves' mouth tightened. "I hardly think that's a productive line of inquiry for someone in your situation."

"I meant no offense. Really, I'm just wondering whether these dispensations must always be prospective. I don't suppose they can be granted retrospectively as well?"

He relaxed a little. "I'm not sure that question has ever been addressed. I would have to research it to give you a definitive answer."

"It's not that important. Have you determined whether any of these Profanities will suit your purposes?"

"Unfortunately, no. It's one thing to confiscate a Profanity. It's another thing entirely to determine what it does. Frankly, I'm not certain whether most of these things even are Profanities. Absent some obvious manifestation, it's often next to impossible to figure out what they do short of triggering them, and that's assuming you can figure out the trigger. Even for Heretics with appropriate investigative spells, I'm told it's a tricky business. Your best bet is to hope you can find a record detailing the item's creation. The problem with that is, such records are often little more than coded schematics, using symbols understood only by the craftsmen who scribed them."

"The craftsmen won't reveal the code, even under interrogation?"

Father Graves shook his head. "Up until now, it hasn't really been a topic of great interest to Inquisitors. So far the most promising item we've come across is that watch of yours, and even that is of limited utility if, as you say, it only works for you. Are you sure about that, by the way?"

I held out the watch. "That's my understanding, but if you'd like to try it for yourself, I have no objections."

He drew back slightly, stared at it, and swallowed hard. "That's all right," he said. "I'll take your word for it."

I tucked it back into my pocket. "Perhaps we can use the rest of the trip to examine more of the items in your collection. Maybe we'll get lucky and find something useful."

He donned his little white gloves in anticipation. "I'd like that."

Traveling across the downs by lantern light, we discovered several more inscrutable items bearing my father's mark. Where I could, I pointed out likely mechanisms for activating those items, but of course, since Father Graves was not inclined to test them on the spot, we had no way of knowing whether they would satisfy his requirements.

Two of the items I'd actually done some of the work for. One was a ring that produced a pair of pince-nez eye glasses for a particularly absent-minded client, and the other was a jeweled pendant given as a gift by a client to his depressive wife—useful because so long as she wore it, the pendant could be activated to improve her mood. The first was useless because Father Graves already had his own glasses. The second would only function in conjunction with the client's trigger ring, and of that, there was no sign. When we finally gave up and drifted off to sleep, the birds were heralding the dawn.

It was late morning when we arrived back at Histlewick Manor. Both Roman and Darron were waiting as we pulled up. They wasted no time hustling Armand's stretcher into the Manor. Father Graves rushed off after them, leaving me in the custody of Barclay's assistant, Prentiss.

We didn't get off to a great start—his first act as my gaoler was to force a mask over my head. Then he marched me off someplace cold and clammy. Once there, he gave me a push from behind, and I fell face-first into a pile of musty straw. Unlike my previous gaolers, he remained nearby, forbidding me to remove the mask even to sleep. I drifted off to watery dreams peopled by drowned corpses with bulging, unseeing eyes.

It was Darron who finally came for me. He was less than gentle in yanking off the mask, but I was so glad for it to be gone, I didn't care.

"How's Armand?"

"Feverish," he said. "The Ordinal is hopeful he can keep the infection in check. Otherwise, he may have to amputate."

"Can I see him?"

"I don't expect he's likely to be on today's itinerary. Come with me."

"Where are we going?"

"Where do you think?"

"To the commons with the other heretics?"

"Possibly, but that won't be our first stop."

"I don't know then."

"You'll see."

He led me through a maze of tunnels and corridors until we arrived at the dining room. Darron pointed to the chair at the foot of table, and I sat. At least this time, the chair faced the table instead of the stuffed face of the beast.

It was not a short wait. I took to counting the number of times the cuckoo popped its head out of the clock, and made it to four before I finally heard footsteps in the hallway at the other end of the room.

I stood at the Inquisitor General's arrival.

"How's Armand doing?"

"Sit down."

I sat.

"Mr. Theratigan," he said, "you'll recall that the last time you sat in that chair I made you a promise. I made it clear that any harm that befell my son as a result of his abduction would be visited on you and your parents as well. Do you remember that?"

"I do." I took some solace in the fact I was able to say it without my voice cracking.

"Today my son returned to me wracked with fever and in mortal danger of losing his leg."

"I'm very sorry for that, sir. I did everything in my power to protect your son, but in the end, it was not enough. No one regrets that more than I do."

"Because of the penalty for failure?"

"No. Because when had I lost everything and had nowhere else to turn, Armand held out his hand to me. He was my friend."

The Inquisitor General regarded me skeptically. "It might interest you to know that Father Graves is of a mind that your efforts saved not just Armand's life, but also his own, the Ordinal's, and perhaps the lives of many more."

"If our roles had been reversed, Armand would have done the same for me. Father Graves too, for that matter."

The Inquisitor General raised an eyebrow. "You really think so? Even if it involved the use of heresy?"

"I'm sure I don't know your son as well as you do, but I know him well enough to know if there were any way he could save someone from a Sacrifice, he would do so, regardless of the repercussions."

"So you acknowledge that the use of heresy, even for the laudable purpose of saving lives, should still have repercussions?"

"That's not for me to say. What I can say is that if I had it to do over again, even knowing there would be repercussions, I would do exactly the same thing."

"Before you commit to that position, perhaps it would interest you to know exactly what those repercussions might be. You see, in recognition of your service, Father Graves has requested leniency on your behalf. I am inclined to grant it, provided you renounce any and all heresies from this day forward for any reason whatsoever. If you agree, your hand will be branded, and you will be free to go."

"Are you saying that I'd have to swear to stand idly by and watch my friends be Sacrificed even if I had the means to prevent it?"

"If the means involved heresy, that's exactly what I'm saying."

I shuddered as in my mind's eye I once again saw again the flailing form of the Sacrificed Inquisitor and heard his dying screams. I tried to imagine how I could ever face Armand again after having made such a bargain. When I considered what I knew about Roman Goodkin and his intentions for the Profanities collection, something about his offer didn't ring true. Was he testing me?

"I can't do it," I said. A cold wave of nausea washed over me as I heard myself say the words.

"So you're rejecting my offer?"

The words seemed to just tumble out. "I can't lie to you. You didn't see how he suffered. I'd leave here with all the best intentions, but if it ever came right down to it, I know I'd do whatever I could to stop a Sacrifice, even if I had to use heresy to do it."

The Inquisitor General sighed and sat back in his chair. "Then I have no choice but to impose the harshest penalty I have at my disposal. You're certain you don't want to change your mind?"

"I'm sorry."

"Very well then. Effective immediately, I am removing you from Armand's employ. From now on, Mr. Theratigan, you work for me."

CHAPTER NINETEEN

quid pro quo

In short order, I found myself in the kitchen standing before the Inquisitor General's manservant. Mr. Hollings cast a daunting shadow. His slicked-back hair and formal jacket conspired with an unapologetically dubious expression to make me feel instantly unworthy. I squirmed as his critical eye probed every aspect of my being, altogether certain that no matter what I did, I was about to be found wanting.

"Once again, the Master delights in challenging me," he said. "As if trying to make this ruin into some semblance of a home weren't challenge enough."

Nearby a buxom, middle-aged woman snorted. Her sandy hair was bound up in a bun, and her smock was stained with greasy handprints. She cranked a fireplace spit upon which roasted an entire boar.

"At least you aren't expected to produce something edible from a kitchen so antiquated our grandparents wouldn't have recognized it. Not only that, but unlike you, I'm expected to share."

"Well, after all, Saville, we are guests here," Hollings reminded her. "What did you expect would happen when you refused to cook for the natives?"

"Bah." Saville dismissed Hollings with a wave of her hand and focused on basting the boar.

Hollings turned back to me. "Now, Mr. Theratigan, whatever am I going to do with you?"

I opened my mouth, but Hollings cut me off. "The question was rhetorical."

"Sorry, sir."

"First, we'll need to find you something civilized to wear. I'll have a word with Jaccard. In the meantime, perhaps you could clean yourself up a bit. Although this wilderness environment may not afford us all the amenities we would wish for, when it comes to staff fashion, I draw the line at lice."

"Yes, sir."

He pressed a piece of paper into my palm. "Take this and go, but be back no later than three. Dinner is at five, and there is much to be done before you will be remotely presentable."

I wound my way through the warren of hallways that made up Histlewick Manor. Even with Hollings' directions, it was no simple task. I backtracked several times before I finally arrived at the baths.

A relic from the manor's heyday, the baths occupied an imposing space with soaring ceilings and louvered skylights. A colorful colonnade topped by rounded arches encircled two mosaic-lined pools—one for cold water, the other warm. They apparently stoked the furnace only during the wee hours, since by the time I arrived, the room was empty and the warm water merely tepid.

After a few moments exploring, I discovered an adjoining room with clothes hooks and stacks of soft towels. I peeled off Sly's mud-caked outfit, grabbed a towel, and approached the warm pool. I leapt in head-first. Even tepid, it was heaven.

Bracing myself on the far side, I looked back to see a trail of dirt settle to the bottom. That encouraged me to wash in earnest. Although I suspected Hollings of exaggerating about the lice, I scrubbed my scalp three times, just in case.

I paddled to the shallow end and leaned against the edge to relax my aching muscles. I had several moments of pure bliss before my thoughts returned to my parents. No matter how much I wracked my brain, I couldn't figure out any way to help them. Part of me wanted to sneak away, steal a horse, and rescue them myself, but I had no chance of finding them in the swamp. And if I were caught, I'd lose all hope of helping them. Armand was in no shape to intercede for me, and Father Graves had already made clear his thoughts on recruiting Inquisitors to look for them. My only chance was to somehow convince Roman to help me, but how?

Footsteps echoed through the chamber. I hopped out of the pool and grabbed for my towel.

"I was told I might find you here."

"Lord Histlewick," I said with a bow. "I'm glad to see you made it back safe and sound. We were worried sick when you vanished on us."

"Not so worried that you could spare a single man to search for me."

"I apologize for that, My Lord. It was decided that your own men would be up to the task."

Histlewick stepped out from under the arches and eyed me closely. Wrapped in only my towel, I colored under his scrutiny, but held my ground.

"My, how quickly we've gone from wearing their shackles to apologizing on their behalf. If I didn't know better, I might even believe it was heartfelt."

"Was there something you require of me, My Lord?"

"You did me a service once, and I don't forget my debts.

With that in mind, let me ask instead whether there is something you require of me?"

My jaw dropped. Whatever I'd been expecting from the man I'd come to view as "the imposter," it wasn't this. My thoughts went immediately to my parents.

"There is one thing."

For the first time, I saw Histlewick smile—or grimace. With him, it was difficult to tell.

"Name it."

"My parents. They, too, were lost in the swamp. Is there any way to make sure they're all right?"

Histlewick scratched his head and frowned. "I suppose I could arrange for your discreet late-night departure."

"I can't leave like that. They'll hunt me down."

"Apparently they hold you in higher regard than they do me."

"I need to know if they're safe."

Histlewick rubbed his chin. "The problem is I wouldn't recognize your parents if I saw them, and they are unlikely to reveal their identities to strangers. I can provide you with resources, but if you want to know their fate, you'll need to find it out for yourself."

"What kind of resources are we talking?"

"A pretext, perhaps? Say I were to take a shine to you and invite you along on one of my hunts. Once you locate your parents, you could resume your post here, and no one would be the wiser."

"You'd be willing to do that?"

"It seems a minor thing to me. When would you like to go?"

"Right away. They may be dying in that swamp."

"Hmm. It might be difficult to establish a convincing enough friendship in so short a time, but I'll see what I can do. When the time comes, follow my lead."

"I will, My Lord."

Hollings appeared within one of the archways, carrying a stack of neatly folded clothing. He paused as he caught sight of me in my towel. Then he noticed Lord Histlewick standing nearby, and his eyebrow shot upward. "I do hope I'm not interrupting anything."

"Not at all," Histlewick replied. "I was just leaving."

Hollings inclined his head as Histlewick slipped past him, and watched sidelong after him until his footfalls faded.

"I took the liberty of bringing these down for you," he said at last. "Jaccard is convinced something here should fit you adequately until such time as he can tailor to your precise specifications."

"Thank you, sir."

In rapid succession Hollings ushered me from barber to cobbler, and then to hatter. It was the first time I'd ever worn a top hat, and when Hollings presented me with a gentleman's walking stick, I thought I was going to burst with pride.

Hollings' eye was critical, though. After a thorough inspection, he pronounced me "a dreadful-looking cobble job," and urged me to seek out Jaccard as soon as possible for things that might actually fit.

As he showed me to my chamber, I could tell the difference immediately. People we passed in the hallways now eyed me with deference, and perhaps a bit of curiosity. It was a refreshing change from the mix of dread and pity I'd grown accustomed to. The room was miniscule, and although it seemed clean and functional, settling in was not an option. We barely had time to drop off the hat and walking stick if we were going to make a timely appearance at dinner.

Hollings was uncertain as to the precise nature of my role on the staff, but he was taking no chances. He spent the entire trip to the dining room admonishing me to remain firmly in the background unless something specific was requested of me. I was to eat nothing; the help took their dinner only after their betters had finished, and did so in the kitchens, not the dining room. I was to speak only if spoken to, and then to reply only in the briefest possible terms. I was not to make eye contact, and to assist only when it was clear that my assistance was expected and proper.

I nodded as he ticked off each item on his long list. I didn't have the heart to tell him that I had absolutely no idea when, if ever, my assistance at dinner would be expected or proper. Playing the role of Roman's servant was going to be far more challenging than playing Armand's ever was, but it seemed an ideal way to keep a low profile until Histlewick made his move. Until then, keeping my head down was going to be key. No sense getting caught up in something that might spoil Histlewick's preparations. The waiting was torture, but I endured it convinced Histlewick's plan would give me my best shot at rescuing my parents.

Dinner was dazzling. We arrived just as the cuckoo announced the hour. Every chandelier blazed with light, and the table sparkled with numerous candelabra. The delicious scent of roast boar permeated the room, and the fireplace radiated cozy warmth. In this new context, the fearsomeness of the dining-room menagerie dwindled to insignificance, inspiring instead a sense of novelty and wonder.

Once Roman took his place at the table, the other diners followed suit. All of Roman's people except Armand were present—Father Graves, the Ordinal, Darron, Barclay, and even Prentiss. As Hollings and I took up posts against the wall behind Roman, I recognized many faces belonging to Inquisitors from the swamp excursion as well. However, the spot immediately adjacent to the Ordinal, like the one next to Father Graves, remained conspicuously empty, and I found myself wondering whether the two mysterious missing diners might be connected in some way.

After several minutes, the Ordinal picked up his napkin and placed it on his plate. "My apologies, Roman," he said. "I'll go see what's keeping Elyria."

Before Roman could answer, a vision in off-the-shoulder blue velvet swept into the room.

"No need, Father," she said. "I'm here."

Her hair was pulled up on the sides only to tumble down in back in a cascade of golden curls. She flounced expertly into her seat just as Hollings pushed it in for her. Producing a fan in white lace and blue accents, she fluttered it a few times, and then with lively brown eyes peered over it at each of the nearby diners in turn.

"Did I miss anything?"

Hollings had to elbow me before I recovered myself enough to pull my eyes away and close my mouth.

Roman nodded a greeting to the young lady. "Now we're just waiting on one more," he said.

At that point Father Graves cleared his throat and inclined his head in my direction. Roman craned his neck, until at last his gaze met mine.

"Mr. Flinch?" he asked. "Is that really you?"

I was suddenly grateful for Armand's rigorous training. "It is I, sir," I said. "How may I be of service?"

"Well if you wouldn't mind taking your seat, we could finally get this meal under way."

My seat? My heart leapt into my throat as all eyes settled on me. Conversation hushed. *My* seat.

"With pleasure, sir."

As I took my place between Father Graves and Darron, I caught a fleeting glimpse of Hollings' scandalized glare. Normally that would have worried me enough to cause nightmares, but then I noticed the fair Elyria's dark eyes regarding me over her fan, and Hollings' assessment no longer seemed all that important.

CHAPTER TWENTY

OBJECT OF THE PROPOSITION

The Ordinal cleared his throat. "Elyria dear, this is the impressive young man who was so instrumental in the success of our mission to rescue Roman's son."

Shocked, but more than a little gratified by the Ordinal's about-face, I began casting about for a suitably self-effacing response...until it became obvious he was actually referring to Barclay.

Barclay inclined his head to the young lady seated beside him. "Your father is too kind. Any credit for the success of the mission should rest squarely on his shoulders. I was honored to contribute, but in all fairness, my role was merely supportive."

Elyria gave Barclay a sidelong smile. "Why, Mr. Lavicius," she said. "Surely you don't mean to say my father's assessment was inaccurate?"

"Not at all. I freely admit to being every bit as impressive as he says. Indeed, I've never known your father to be inaccurate, except perhaps in his attempts to sing your praises. But even in that he is blameless, since having met you, it is obvious that words alone, regardless of how flattering, are simply not up to the task."

As Barclay blathered on, Hollings' staff began placing fine china plates showcasing Saville's uncanny skill with roast pork. Although I was starving, I barely noticed, intent as I was on trying to come up with something clever to entice Elyria's attention away from Barclay. The pressure, however, proved to be too great—everything that came to mind seemed either unsophisticated or crass.

Unwittingly, Father Graves came to my rescue. "And let's not forget the inspired contributions of young Flinch here, not only in rescuing Armand, but in saving the rest of us from our own folly. I hope you'll all join me in raising a glass in his honor."

The table erupted in a chorus of "Hear, hear!" and I found myself blushing in earnest as Elyria's eyes sought me out once more.

"Well, well, Mr. Flinch," she said. "It seems you've amassed an enthusiastic following. While I don't mean to pry, I am now insanely curious: how ever did you rescue all these men?"

Now I was in a spot. I couldn't imagine Roman would want the actual details of my intervention to be made public, but neither was I eager to minimize my accomplishment if it meant comparing unfavorably to silver-tongued Barclay.

I compromised. "It was nothing, really. Anyone who'd bothered to acquire a detailed working knowledge of the techniques of the enemy could have done it."

"You're being far too modest," Father Graves said. "I…"

The Ordinal cut him off. "Roman, I must protest the turn this conversation is taking. Would you really have us sit idly by while the boy schools us in all the unseemly details of Phrendonic heresy?"

Elyria eyed me with new appreciation. "So he's truly a heretic?"

Roman ignored the question. "I think we should take this opportunity to remember the brave souls who gave their lives for the success of the mission and the honor and glory of their Church." Without waiting for the Ordinal's assent, he stood and launched into a eulogy for the fallen Inquisitors. The rest of the guests fell silent and bowed their heads.

Throughout Roman's speech, I caught Elyria stealing glances at me from beneath her lashes. When at last our eyes met, I risked a conspiratorial smile, which, to my delight, she returned.

By the time the eulogy was over, the delectable aromas emanating from my plate finally captured my attention. Despite being ravenous, I'm proud to say I retained enough presence of mind to emulate the etiquette of my neighbors. Although Barclay and Elyria had resumed an animated dialogue, her eye consistently wandered back in my direction. When it did, I flashed my best subtle smile. Unless I missed my guess, Barclay was taking completely the wrong approach. If even the whiff of heresy couldn't put her off, it was a decent bet the fair Elyria's tastes ran more to mysterious rebels than social climbers. As a result, the more he nattered on, the better I looked by comparison.

Comfortably full, I turned my attention to Darron. He'd been uncharacteristically silent during the meal, and I was hoping that didn't bode ill for his brother.

"How is Armand faring?"

"Slow improvement," he replied. "Although he's by no means out of the woods, there is hope the Ordinal has gotten the infection under control."

Darron's eyes were puffy and his complexion pale. He apparently hadn't slept much.

"Oh, and Mr. Flinch?"

"Yes?"

"Albert explained what you did for my brother. I just wanted to say that I'm sorry I misjudged you, and, well... thank you."

I nodded. "He's lucky to have you pulling for him."

Just then Father Graves tapped my shoulder. "Mr. Flinch, if I could have a moment?"

"Of course, Father."

"Roman has asked me to look into your discovery in the armoire, and I was wondering if I might trouble you to accompany me later this evening. It's turning into quite the little puzzle, and I'd hate to miss anything."

"I'm happy to help."

"What discovery is this?" Elyria asked, interrupting Barclay in mid-sentence. "I just adore a good mystery. Perhaps my insights could prove useful as well."

My heart leapt at the possibility of Elyria accompanying us, until I saw Roman shoot Father Graves a cautionary glance.

Next to him, the Ordinal harrumphed. "This is not the sort of puzzle that's appropriate to the talents of a young lady."

Elyria snapped her fan shut. "If by that you mean it does not involve tracking down an errant count in a cross-stitched sampler, I had already surmised that."

The Ordinal's tone crossed the line from annoyance to anger. "Don't try my patience."

Elyria's laughter shattered the tension. "Oh Father," she said, fluttering her fan once more. "You really must stop taking yourself so seriously. You know I'd never do anything to displease you."

"I know no such thing."

She leaned over to give him a peck on the cheek. "Well then, it's time you learned."

He regarded his daughter for a long moment before finally allowing himself to be mollified.

She summarily changed the subject. "Does anyone know what Saville is planning for dessert? Her confections are always so magnificent that I find myself rushing through my meal in anticipation, and by this point, I'm always dying to find out." With a barely perceptible glance at her father, she added: "Assuming it's not top-secret, of course."

"Elyria!"

A smug little grin danced across her lips. "Just teasing, Father," she said. "Oh, here it comes."

With crisp coordination, two members of Hollings' staff worked their way down the table, one whisking away the old plate while the other replaced it with a warm crock. When mine arrived, it was filled with a rich butterscotch pudding topped by a heaping mound of freshly whipped cream. It was so appealing, I nearly forgot my etiquette—my spoon was already hovering just above the cream before I noticed the others were waiting for everyone to be served. I laid the spoon discreetly aside and checked to be sure Elyria hadn't noticed.

At this point, Hollings leaned forward to whisper something in Roman's ear. I only managed to catch bits and pieces, but the message had to do with the arrival of a carriage from Caprian. Roman wore the grimace of a man who'd just been reminded of something inconvenient. Since his voice carried better than Hollings' did, I was able to make out his response.

"The commons for the moment," he said. "I can't afford to take any more risks right now."

"As you wish," Hollings said.

As Hollings strode away, Roman cast a pensive glance in my direction. I wondered if by "risks" he meant me. And then I remembered he'd recently sent Inquisitors after the others staying at Armand's pub. That had to be it. He had just

consigned Sly, Chef, and maybe even little Lisbet to imprisonment with the heretics in the commons. I shuddered. It was
all my doing. If I hadn't stupidly tried to make a deal with
Joanna, none of this ever would have happened.

When everyone finally started in on their desserts, I didn't
join them—I'd suddenly lost my appetite.

Elyria picked up on it immediately. "What's the matter, Mr.
Flinch? Is the dessert too sweet for your taste?"

The image of Lisbet in shackles and a mask was still fresh
in my mind, but voicing my true concerns was out of the
question. I settled instead on a cryptic response that I thought
would still convey my feelings of deep melancholy.

"On the contrary," I said. "In fact, I find myself wondering
whether after today any dessert shall ever seem sweet again."

Only after the Ordinal choked on his wine did I realize
the statement might be subject to a variety of interpretations.

Elyria raised a delicate eyebrow. "Why, Mr. Flinch," she
said, "I never would have taken you for a flatterer. While I
might normally be concerned about comparisons to the pudding, in this case, it's so exquisite, I must say, I'm touched."

The instant the Ordinal recovered from his spasms, he
turned to Roman.

"We need to talk."

But Roman didn't reply. Instead, he rose to his feet, his
attention fixed at the other end of the room.

"Lord Histlewick," he said. "What an unexpected surprise."

The gloomy Lord stood in the doorway to the kitchens. "I'll
be brief," he said. "I wouldn't want to overstay my welcome."

"Nonsense," Roman said. "Please, won't you join us?"

Darron slid his chair out from the table. "He can have my
place. I should check on Armand anyway."

Darron took his leave as Histlewick made his way toward
the head of the table.

Roman indicated Darron's chair, but Histlewick shook his head. "I won't be here that long."

Roman resumed his seat. "How can we be of assistance?"

"Given the logistical issues associated with such a crowded house, I've decided to move my spring hunt ahead a few weeks. I thought you should know."

"There's no need for that," Roman said. "If there are any specific problems you are having with the staff, I'm sure we can address them to your satisfaction."

"The decision is already made. Besides, the only way to remedy a crowded house is to make it less crowded. Since you are unable to do so, I have taken it upon myself. I trust that I can look forward to a resolution of the issue before I return?"

Roman placed his napkin back in his lap. "We are all grateful for your hospitality, and I'd like nothing better than to finish up our work here as soon as possible. I can, however, make no guarantees."

"Of course not," Histlewick said. "In the meantime, I have a small request."

"Name it."

"It seems my squire has fallen ill and will be unable to accompany me tomorrow."

"Nothing serious, I hope?"

"I expect not, but I suddenly find myself in need of a replacement."

"I'm not certain I am able to help you there. My men and I travel unsquired."

"Oh, I don't need anyone with any particular expertise. In truth, I rather prefer my squires to be a little green. Almost anyone of an appropriate age would do." Here he reached out and gently turned my chin toward him. "Indeed, I expect Mr. Flinch, here, would be perfect."

"Out of the question. I have need of Mr. Flinch."

"It would only be for the duration of the hunt. Surely you can spare him for that long."

"I'm sorry. You're going to have to find someone else."

Histlewick drew the back of his finger along my jawline. "Don't you think Mr. Flinch should have some say in the matter? After all, he may never get another opportunity like this. What say you, Mr. Flinch? Can I interest you in the experience of a lifetime?"

I don't know what I'd been expecting, but this was definitely not what I'd had in mind when Histlewick told me to follow his lead. I hoped Elyria was too naïve to appreciate what Histlewick was suggesting, but the sight of her horrified eyes peering at me over her fan disabused me of that notion. There was a chance this was all part of Histlewick's ploy to help me rescue my parents, but in the end, his performance proved just a little too disturbing—I couldn't bring myself to risk it. I'd figure out another way.

"I'm sorry, My Lord," I said, "but if the Inquisitor General needs me, my primary duty lies with him."

"Well, I guess that settles it," Roman said.

"Let's not be too hasty about this," the Ordinal interrupted. "After all, Histlewick has sacrificed a great deal on our behalf. What kind of guests would we be if we denied him such a simple request?"

"I'm sure we can accommodate the request in other ways," Roman said.

The Ordinal, however, was adamant. "I'm sure we could too—but I see absolutely no reason to do so. The boy goes with Histlewick, and that's my final word on the matter."

CHAPTER TWENTY-ONE

SOUL SEARCHING

The route to the Marstow wing, where the Inquisitor General's team had taken up residence, was less complicated than many in Histlewick manor, but I still had to pay close attention if I ever intended to manage it on my own. On the way, Father Graves informed me that the wing was named for Lady Marstow, who, in return for her substantial dowry, had wedded a Histlewick Lord. Within days of the nuptials, they discovered that they were possessed of temperaments so radically different that even their commonalities were irreconcilable. Since giving up the dowry was out of the question, the Lord banished his Lady to the wing that now bore her name with the intent of encouraging as little contact between the two of them as possible.

Once we were well away from the other diners, Father Graves immediately changed the topic. "Try not to worry," he said. "I have faith that Roman will be able to talk His Ordinence out of this decision. He can be very persuasive when he puts his mind to it."

I nodded. While grateful for the reassurance, I didn't want to encourage any speculation as to why Histlewick had taken such an avid interest in me.

At last, we came to a pointed arch framing a set of double doors, their gleaming surfaces decorated with graceful filigree completely at odds with the solid, functional architecture of the rest of the manor. Father Graves pushed them open to reveal a sitting room dripping in ornamentation. Every available surface sported some manner of scrollwork, ruffle, finial, pattern or tassel, each apparently selected without the slightest regard for the effect as a whole. I was so bewildered by it that Father Graves was all the way across the room before I even noticed.

The bedroom was little different. A soaring brocade canopy suspended above a richly carved head board stood out from the forest of embellishments to provide something of a focus. Beneath it, I spied what appeared to be Lord Histlewick's head poking out from under a rainbow-striped coverlet.

"Has he regained consciousness?" I asked.

Father Graves shook his head. "I don't think there's much hope of that."

"Why not? What's wrong with him?"

He sank wearily into a chair near the bed. "Well, if His Ordinence is to be believed, he's lost his soul."

"Lost? What do you mean?"

"I mean there's nothing physically wrong with him."

"So it's a coma then? Or a brain injury?"

Father Graves shook his head. "It's far more sinister than that. His brain is fine, but the soul that animates it is just… missing. You can imagine this is not the sort of thing that happens by accident."

"Who could even do something like that?"

"That's a very good question. Before their defeat at Exidgeon, the most skilled Chervillian heretics were suspected of such things, but it's been generations since then. Today, any remaining followers of Chervil are scattered, unsophisticated, and for the most part, harmless."

I was leery of asking, but I figured the unspoken question was so obvious that I had little to lose, and might at least get an idea of which way the wind was blowing. "So you think a Phrendonic did it?"

Father Graves sat back in his chair. "I don't know. It's not the sort of thing for which they are generally known. There is, however, at least one notable exception."

"And that is?"

"A woman known to us only as Dreamweaver," he said. "She had a reputation for using methods so extreme that even other Phrendonics shunned them."

"And you think she's responsible?"

He shook his head. "I sincerely doubt it. She was burned at the stake long before either of us was born."

"So why mention her then? Are you implying you think it's possible some other Phrendonic did it?"

"There is that," he said, "but there's an additional connection I find very curious. Do you recall that I told you that the Church once rewarded the Histlewicks for a service rendered in the distant past?"

"Not specifically. What service?"

"It turns out that Hasset Bey, the man who finally brought Dreamweaver to justice, was the son of a Histlewick Lord."

"I don't follow. Stealing Histlewick's soul can't be retribution if she's long dead, and after all these years, who would even remember?"

"Oh, I doubt it's that," Father Graves said. "What worries me more is the possibility that Hasset Bey may have exacted more than merely justice from his prisoner."

"You think he stole her secrets?"

"I know the idea is farfetched, but I'm at a loss to explain our patient's condition with anything that isn't. I was sort of hoping you might be able to come up with something more plausible."

"I still don't understand. If Histlewick possessed the knowledge, why would he become the victim?"

"It's possible that Histlewick wasn't the one who ended up with it. Indeed, Darron's description of the room where you found our patient suggests it could have lain undisturbed for quite some time. Is that a fair assessment?"

"I suppose so," I said. "And, for that matter, who knows how many other forgotten rooms there are in this complex?"

"True. One thing I'm not clear on, though, is why, of all places, the imposter would put you in that room if he knew there was a chance you might find his victim there."

I was saved having to comment by Roman storming in and slamming the door. "If that pompous ass countermands me publicly one more time…"

Father Graves rose to greet him. "I presume this means your discussion with His Ordinence didn't go as well as you'd hoped?"

"What discussion? We got to his apartments and, before I could even broach a subject, he dismissed me as if I were some minor functionary."

"He didn't relent on Histlewick's request?"

"After what happened at dinner, there's not much chance of that."

Father Graves' eyes widened. "But Histlewick's our prime suspect. If he's gotten his hands on Dreamweaver's secrets, you may be sending the lad into mortal danger."

Roman snorted. "Judging by the look in Histlewick's eye, the danger to the lad might be greater if he hasn't."

Father Graves' eyebrows knitted in disapproval. "Need I remind you that we are talking about a young man's soul, here; I hardly think it's a laughing matter."

"Relax, Albert. I have no intention of sending the boy off without some means of protecting himself."

Father Graves waved his hand in the direction of the bed. "Protecting himself? From someone capable of this? What are you going to give him, an army?"

"He does have that watch of his. It's not like it hasn't come in handy in the past."

"Useful perhaps, if Histlewick plans to Sacrifice him, but will it save his soul?"

Roman shrugged. "That question lies much more soundly in your bailiwick than mine. If it makes you feel any better, you could always outfit him with a Profanity or two. It's not like we don't have a few to spare."

"You'd grant him dispensation for that?"

"I don't see why not—provided, of course, that no one else finds out about it."

"That sounds more like a death sentence than a dispensation. Roman, what's gotten into you?"

"I never promised him a picnic. He had fair warning that this position wouldn't be one for the faint of heart. The truth of the matter is, Albert, we need him. Overnight, Histlewick has gone from being a reluctant ally to a completely unknown quantity. As much as I'd prefer to keep the boy here to ensure my own safety, in the short-term that's no longer on the table. In the meantime, if Histlewick really has taken an interest in him, maybe he can get close enough to find out what we're up against."

"For the love of all that's holy, Roman, he's just a boy."

"This 'boy' of yours has already acquired quite a reputation for keeping his head under fire. And you yourself rave about his insights into the workings of your Profanities. All in all, I couldn't have asked for a better candidate for this mission—or can you think of someone more suited?"

Father Graves' frown was tight. At last he shook his head.

"There, you see?"

"You could at least do him the courtesy of asking."

"As you wish." He turned to me. The intensity of his gaze almost took my breath away. "I need you, Mr. Flinch. No one else can do this. Can I count on you?"

The words were simple, but his voice held a subtlety that spoke to the soul. I could feel the ferocity of his dedication and the nakedness of his need. Under other circumstances, I might have been moved to pledge my aid unconditionally, but I had needs of my own.

"And my parents?"

His command wavered momentarily. A counter offer was clearly not something he'd been expecting.

"Very well," he said. "Find out for me what makes Histlewick tick, and I shall grant them clemency."

I tried to keep my voice from cracking as I upped the ante. "That doesn't help them if they never make it out of the swamp, does it?"

He regarded me for a long moment. Cold dread that I'd pushed him too far crept into my heart.

At last Father Graves interceded. "In all fairness, he was forced to abandon them there to save Armand."

Roman raised an eyebrow at Father Graves, and then turned back to me. "All right. I'll send someone to look for them, but at this stage, without knowing their fate, I can't make any guarantees."

"In that case," I said, "I am happy to be of service."

"Glad to have you on board, Mr. Flinch. For future reference, though, you should be aware that I am not accustomed to negotiating with my staff every time a suitable task presents itself."

"I appreciate that, sir, and I'm grateful for your understanding in making an exception in this case."

He favored me then with a sidelong look. "You do have guts, Mr. Flinch. I'll grant you that."

CHAPTER TWENTY-TWO

FLIRTING WITH DISASTER

Shadows from the flickering firelight danced across the shelves of the tiny library. Father Graves sat across a small round table from me, his gloved hand hovering over a number of Profanities. The rest of the collection occupied either meticulously labeled library shelves, or still lay within one of the many crates that had yet to be opened.

"These, at least, are small enough to be unobtrusive," he said. "Any preference?"

I scanned the collection and shrugged. "It might help if I had some idea what they did."

He brightened and dropped a folder stuffed with papers on the table. "Maybe these will help. Mind you, I can't say for certain which schematic refers to which piece, but your luck may be better than mine."

His thirst to possess the knowledge hidden within the sheaf of papers was plain, but there was little hope I'd be able to slake it. Phrendonic schematics were notoriously peculiar to the individual craftsman. Given time and multiple examples, one might be able to glean the meanings for some of the common symbols, but without a key, a single schematic was useless. It was like trying to decode an entire language from a single phrase.

"I don't think there'll be time for that," I said. "I need to be ready to leave by dawn, and it's already getting late."

"Humor me. Take a peek, and see if they might be helpful."

I took the first sheet he offered me. "I guess it can't hurt to glance at them."

I looked up from the schematic to see Father Graves grinning. "Well?"

"This is my father's schematic."

"I thought you might recognize it."

I paged through the others. They, too, were drafted in my father's hand. "Where did you get these?"

"I sent for them. Once Roman told me your true identity, it only seemed prudent. Fortunately, we intercepted the shipment before it left Caprian."

Upon closer inspection, several items on the table now seemed familiar. "So what makes you think these schematics go with these items?"

"Unless I'm mistaken, they all bear your father's mark. If we're lucky, at least some of them should match the documentation."

It took a moment for the full import of his request to sink in—he was asking me to give the Inquisition the key to my father's life's work. If my father wasn't already dead, that would probably seal it. And yet, after everything Father Graves had done for me, how could I deny him, particularly when he was motivated, at least in part, out of concern for my welfare?

"Are you all right?"

"Just tired. It's been a long week."

"Will the schematics help?"

"Perhaps in the long term. It's not always obvious what a

design is supposed to accomplish. With luck, in one night I might be able to match up an item or two with its schematic, but even then, unless the device is unusually simple, I still might not appreciate all its subtleties."

He began placing items back into an empty crate. "Fair enough. It's a shame, though. I was hoping to provide you with something useful."

"I can think of something that might help."

"Not without knowing what it does," he said. "It's too dangerous. You could be killed—or worse."

"Oh, I completely agree. That's why I was going to suggest the kaleidoscope monocle."

Father Graves' forehead creased. "I'm not sure I see the point. If Roman is going to grant dispensation to carry a Profanity, I'm pretty sure he'll want to make it count."

"Think of it this way. Just because it doesn't do anything dramatic doesn't mean it won't be useful. Too many people are aware that I carry something that protected Armand from a Sacrifice. If I am seen wearing that monocle—something that's obviously a Profanity—they'll naturally assume the monocle was what I used. That way, if any heretics out there decide they need to rid me of that capability, there's at least a chance they'll target the wrong thing."

"You know, I think I'm beginning to appreciate what Roman sees in you. It hadn't even occurred to me that the watch could be a target."

"Once word spreads, I think that's inevitable."

He rose to his feet. "An excellent point, and you'd certainly be making clever use of an otherwise useless bauble. Now, let's hope I can figure out where it's gone to."

As Father Graves dug through various crates, I quietly slipped its schematic back into the center of the stack.

"Ah, here it is." He placed the box on the table before me.

He removed his gloves and held the monocle up to the light. Each of its seven wedges was tinted a different color, red through violet.

He must have noticed my shock that he would handle it so carelessly.

"Oh, it's perfectly harmless," he said. "I had a friend who took a particular interest in this item, and over my strenuous objections tried every trick she could think of to get it to do something. If nothing else, her failure at least convinced me that it was safe to handle. Here, try it on for size."

It took me several attempts, but I finally worked out how to keep it in place over one eye. "What do you think?"

He took a long moment to contemplate the effect. Indeed, he took so long I began to feel self-conscious. "You don't like it?"

"It does make a statement. Let's just hope it's not too obtuse for your intended audience to appreciate."

By the time I left Father Graves, I was so tired I lost my way several times trying to find my room. Once I found it, I threw myself down on the lumpy pallet in relief. Any euphoria I might have had from acquiring the monocle was tempered by the guilt engendered by the half-truths I'd been forced to tell. The whole charade left me feeling queasy. Even though I'd resolved to use the watch only for emergencies, I'd come away from the meeting with a need for reassurance so visceral it couldn't be denied.

You never write. You never visit. I bet you're only talking to me now because you want something, right?

"Actually, I have a surprise for you."

Oh—my—word.

"It suits me, don't you think?"

You took it? What if they catch you?

"Actually, they gave it to me. They even gave me dispensation to carry it."

Does that mean you're expected to return it?

"Probably—unless, of course, it happens to get lost or stolen."

Perish the thought. I take it this means they still think it's a kaleidoscope?

A light tap interrupted my response. Fortunately, I hadn't had a chance to do much more than loosen my cravat, for when I opened the door, Elyria stood before me.

"I'm so sorry," she said, craning her neck to peer past me. "I didn't mean to interrupt you and your guest."

Whoa, who's that?

Ignoring the voice in my head, I stepped to one side to allow Elyria an unobstructed view. "Guest?"

Her eyes glinted with suspicion. "I would have sworn I heard conversation."

"You've found me out. I talk to myself when I'm alone. A most ungentlemanly habit, I know, but in my defense, I wasn't expecting visitors at this hour. To what do I owe the pleasure?"

Elyria studied her fan. "To my father."

Who's her father?

"I was under the impression he didn't much like me."

"He doesn't, but that doesn't give him the right to do what he did."

What did he do?

"That may be, but as an Ordinal, he certainly has the power."

Wait, the Ordinal is her father?

"An innocent compliment—that's all it was. You'd think a grown man would understand that just because someone glances in my direction, it doesn't necessarily mean he has untoward designs on my person."

Oh, I don't know…

"It's not your fault."

She looked up from her fan in surprise. "I never said it was. But that doesn't mean I can't do something about it."

"I can take care of myself."

Her fan snapped shut. "Can you, Mr. Flinch? Didn't you see how that vile man looked at you? When you're out in the wilderness alone with him, just how do you think you'll fare?"

"If it comes to that, I'll figure something out."

"And if this last-minute plan of yours should fail, then what? Do you really expect me to live with that kind of guilt?"

"I take it you have a better idea?"

"As a matter of fact I do. I want you to take this with you." From her finger she removed a golden band adorned with a faceted stone of deepest blue.

I made no move to take it. "Does your father know about this?"

"Who do you think I got it from?"

"Wait a minute. Your father gave you a Profanity?"

"In case you haven't noticed, this is dangerous territory for a young lady, and my father is not the sort of man who takes chances. Besides, it's not a Profanity." She pressed a clasp on the side of the ring and the gemstone flipped open to reveal a glistening needle. "In the event of an emergency, one little scratch should suffice."

Better take it. You can't afford to antagonize her.

With exquisite care she pressed the gem closed again and held it out to me. "Go ahead. It's the least I can do."

"Won't that leave you defenseless?"

"I'm unlikely to need it as long as we stay in the manor, and my father won't leave until Father Armand is well again. You should be back long before then. If you're not, I'll simply tell Father I lost this one and he'll get another."

Take it!

I reached out my hand. She placed the ring squarely in the center of my palm and curled my fingers up around it. "There. That wasn't so hard, was it?"

Despite the surreal circumstances, her concern for my welfare touched me. "It's kind of you to care."

Her smile turned suddenly coy. "It's the least I can do after making off with your sweet tooth like that."

We both started at the sound of Hollings clearing his throat. He stood a small distance down the hallway, his arms loaded down with a stack of neatly folded clothing. "At the risk of becoming repetitive," he said. "I do hope I'm not interrupting anything."

"Not at all," Elyria said. "We're finished for the evening, aren't we, Mr. Flinch?"

Without waiting for me to reply, she swept down the corridor past Hollings. When she reached the corner, she paused, turned back toward us, and, donning a mischievous grin, blew me a kiss. With a final wave of her fan, she was gone.

Hollings raised his eyebrow, dumped the clothing in my arms, and shook his head. "That, Mr. Flinch, is precisely why we do not fraternize with our betters."

He left without another word.

I suppose it would be naïvely optimistic to expect that fellow to be discreet about this?

"Let's just say it might behoove me to get an especially early start come the morning."

CHAPTER TWENTY-THREE

A FAIR TRADE

I shivered in the pre-dawn twilight as I waited for Histle-wick to make his appearance. The courtyard seethed with activity. Apparently a hunt required participation from nearly every member of the household staff. Scurrying servants loaded supplies and equipment into Histlewick's carriage, even though it already seemed full to bursting. Proud stallions stamped and snorted nearby, their breath misting. I cringed at their size and spirit, since my duties might actually require me to ride one.

The jacket of my squire's uniform was a perfect fit—so perfect, in fact, that I suspected Hollings' friend Jaccard must have had a hand in it. It was similar to the jackets worn by Histlewick's servants, except that Histlewick's red-wolf emblem was emblazoned across the back. A small Church insignia sewn on the upper left chest served as a reminder of the temporary nature of my stint in Histlewick's employ. Control, it seemed, was something Roman Goodkin relinquished only grudgingly.

The hat was crafted of sturdy black felt, the wide brim pinned up against one side, while the other sported a profusion of red and black plumes. I took to it immediately. Wearing it made me feel like a chivalric emissary from some bygone age—a stretch, I know, but the fantasy was better than the reality.

Histlewick appeared without fanfare, but the servants responded as though trumpets had announced him, falling wordlessly into line at his approach. His stride was confident, and his bearing less grim than I'd ever seen it. He seemed almost eager to be gone. I tried to convince myself he was merely looking forward to the hunt, but I couldn't block out the memory of his predatory expression at dinner. Once his inspection was complete, the servants dispersed and his eye fell on me.

I removed my hat and bowed low. "Squire Flinch reporting for duty, sir. What can I do to help?"

"My people know what they're doing," he said. "Keep out of their way for an hour or so until we're ready to leave. Then, on my signal, mount up. You'll be riding the second in line there, behind my dappled gray."

"Yes sir."

I slapped on my hat and took a seat on one of the courtyard benches in plain sight of the bustling servants. Daring to believe I might actually be on my way to find my parents, I began considering where best to start looking. The obvious choice was the swamp where I'd last seen them. From there, I could attempt to follow them downriver. After all, the location and condition of their boat might prove informative even if they'd abandoned it. If they'd survived long enough to leave the river, my chances of finding them would be pretty slim, but I still had to try.

I suddenly became aware of someone standing near me.

A servant by her outfit. A stranger. Then I caught sight of her golden curls.

I leapt to my feet. "What are you doing here?"

Elyria took a step back, but held my gaze. Even in the dim light I could she'd been crying. "I came to warn you," she said. "When I arrived back at my apartment last night, my father was waiting for me. I've never seen him so angry."

"What did you tell him?"

"I couldn't lie to him. The manservant saw us."

My mouth went dry. "Talking. He only saw us talking."

"My father has been known to make unwarranted assumptions. You should leave right away before he finds you."

"I can't. Histlewick's not ready yet."

The Ordinal's angry voice echoed across the courtyard. "Elyria!"

"Oh no! He can't find us together."

I plopped my hat down over her head. "Here, tuck your hair up. Then, try to make it back to your room."

Tears welled in her eyes once more. "You don't understand…."

There wasn't time to argue. I dove behind a low hedge not a moment too soon. The Ordinal stormed into view, accompanied by two Inquisitors. He crossed the courtyard several times, calling out for his daughter. Fortunately, the hat seemed to throw him off. He never gave Elyria a second glance. Instead of slipping quietly away, however, she took up my spot on the bench and lingered in plain sight. I tried to wave her off several times, but she either didn't see, or deliberately ignored me.

I moved along the hedge, angling to signal her again from a less obvious spot. The instant I stopped, I felt a sharp pain in the back of my skull. Rubbing my head, I turned to search for the cause, but when nothing seemed out of place I resumed trying to catch Elyria's eye. Moments later, a pebble glanced off the top of my head and skittered across the courtyard. This time, I was quick enough to catch a flicker of movement from the roof of a nearby shed.

Lisbet.

Guilt hit me hard. Without explicit evidence that Roman had actually taken them prisoner, I'd been able to justify treating my friends from Armand's pub as a low priority. Now that proof had literally hit me over the head, I was wracked with remorse for failing them. I glanced back to where Elyria sat motionless on the bench, her head bowed. Though I was sympathetic, at this point Lisbet needed me more. Not only that, but if the Ordinal succeeded in finding his daughter, it would be better for us both if I wasn't caught lurking nearby. Cursing my logic, but unable to find a way around it, I abandoned Elyria in favor of Lisbet's shed.

I expected to get a quick summary of Lisbet's situation, and then try to devise some sort of plan. Instead, by the time I made it to the shed, she'd already climbed atop the stone wall that separated the manor from the rest of the village. She beckoned once and then dropped over the edge. I clambered onto the shed and then onto the wall in pursuit, but when I scanned the maze of narrow alleys below, she was already gone.

I paused, reluctant to leave the courtyard, since there was no obvious way to climb the wall from the outside. What if I couldn't find Lisbet again? Looking back, I noticed the Ordinal had stopped his roaming and taken up a position near the manor entrance. He stood watching with arms folded, an Inquisitor on either side.

At that moment, far earlier than expected, Histlewick swung into his saddle and signaled in Elyria's direction. My heart sank at her predicament. When she failed to respond to

Histlewick's summons, our subterfuge with the hat would be exposed. Unfortunately with the Ordinal present, there was nothing I could do. The best she could hope for was that the Ordinal wouldn't connect the hat with me.

To my surprise, Elyria didn't reveal herself. She marched toward Histlewick, all the while keeping the brim of the hat low. Once he saw motion, he turned away without looking back. Then, with a level of expertise I could never have managed, Elyria pulled herself astride the stallion Histlewick had chosen for me. A horn sounded, and Histlewick urged his mount forward.

The hunt was officially underway. Once the overloaded carriage at the rear of the procession disappeared beneath the arch, the Ordinal, no doubt satisfied that I was no longer a threat to his precious daughter, withdrew into the manor.

Even though I was faced with the complication of having to catch up with the hunt, I was grateful for the opportunity it gave me to help Lisbet. After all, if Roman was as desperate for intelligence on Histlewick as he let on, he'd probably be willing to lend me a horse to help gather it. After a quick scan to make sure no one was looking, I leapt over the wall.

The village consisted primarily of narrow alleys separating two-story stone houses and shops. From one of these Lisbet peered out at me with an exasperated expression, but the instant our eyes met, she ducked out of sight again. At that point I gave up on getting close enough to talk, instead focusing on keeping her in sight. Unlike the last time I'd followed her, I avoided squirming through culverts or forcing my way through hedges when a more civilized route was obvious.

Eventually Lisbet left the back alleys in favor of a crumbling stone barn. I tugged on the latch and crept inside. Piles of hay rested against one wall, but it was late in the season, and much of the space lay empty. Square wooden pillars reached to the roof and horizontal support beams criss-crossed the space above me. The far wall framed a rough-hewn sliding door. Through an open window above it, I saw the sky finally beginning to lighten.

Lisbet darted barefoot across one of the support beams toward the window. Refusing to be outdone by a ten-year-old, I scrambled up a ladder, took three steps along one of the narrow beams, and felt my sense of balance evaporate. I could easily have walked the beam had it been sitting on the ground, but my mind rebelled at the thought of crossing it one floor up.

Lisbet frowned and huffed at me. "Come on," she said. "We're almost there."

Determined not to embarrass myself again, I took a step in her direction—and froze.

Lisbet beckoned emphatically. When I still didn't move, she scurried toward me along the beam, grabbed my hand, and tugged. The move caught me off guard. I staggered forward to keep my balance. Desperate to avoid both of us falling, I teetered in lockstep with her to the far wall. Hugging the coarse boards, I waited for my pulse to stop hammering in my ears. Lisbet wasn't the least bit perturbed. Standing on tiptoe, she peered over the windowsill and pointed outside.

"Look," she said. "There."

The view appalled me. Across the broad cobbled street lay Histlewick commons, surrounded by a solid wall of white stone. Over a hundred slack-jawed men, women, and children wandered the pasture. They all wore the same expression my parents had worn when last I'd seen them. More than a dozen Inquisitors patrolled the wall, each armed with sword and crossbow. Immediately across, a wooden gate in the wall provided access to the commons, or would have, had it not been secured with a brass lock and chain.

Lisbet tugged at my sleeve. "No…there."

She pointed toward a familiar silhouette. It was Sly.

"Is Chef down there too?"

Lisbet nodded.

My first reaction was that I should find a way to convince Roman to release them, but I had a feeling I'd used up my last bargaining chip getting him to agree to search for my parents. My next thought was that Armand would probably have more clout than I did, though I'd need to find a way to let Armand know Sly and Chef were prisoners. In the meantime, I needed to find somewhere safe to hide Lisbet.

Off to our right, the gate to the village stood open, likely in anticipation of Histlewick's departure. To our left, the bulk of the village was just beginning to awaken. If I could find an inn, I might be able to buy Lisbet a room until Armand healed enough to retrieve her, but even that might be tricky if Inquisitors were still searching for her.

The nearby blare of Histlewick's horn almost startled me off the beam. I dropped to a crouch then peered cautiously over the sill. Histlewick rode past, right beneath our window. Elyria was next in line, the brim of my plumed hat still pulled low over her face.

What was she doing? Once Histlewick discovered her—and surely he would—he'd send her back to the manor, then come looking for me. After all, the whole point of this hunt was to get me away from the manor to save my parents, wasn't it? Maybe if I called out to Histlewick, I could take back my place in the parade. Maybe I could even prevail upon Elyria to sneak a message back to Armand about Sly and Chef.

Then I saw the Inquisitors patrolling the wall. Lisbet must have escaped from them, and I doubted even Histlewick's objections would prevent them from taking her prisoner again. I couldn't abandon her, and I'd never forgive myself if they recaptured her because of me. I had no choice—I'd have to find another way. Seething with frustration, I held my tongue and watched as the procession continued on toward the main gate.

The Lord sat high in his saddle, masterful and determined. He looked neither left nor right, which perhaps explained why he'd not yet discovered Elyria's subterfuge. He was making a show of ignoring the Inquisitors garrisoned in his commons, and as far as I could tell, they returned the favor. Once he reached the open gate, the horn sounded thrice more, and Histlewick passed out of sight.

Despite Lisbet's insistent tugging, I continued to stare after them, bitter that my search for my parents had been thwarted yet again. I was still watching when the gates closed behind the overloaded carriage. Then my frustration turned suddenly to fear, for at that moment, Joanna emerged from the building nearest the gate, took a deep breath, and stepped into the street.

CHAPTER TWENTY-FOUR

A SERIOUS CASE OF THE VAPORS

She'd shed the hat, and whether by a trick of cosmetics or some Phrendonic art with which I was unfamiliar, at least a score of years as well. Even if I hadn't recognized her profile or her gown, her imperious bearing would have given her away. Still, the transformation was remarkable. Her hair was now black and full where once it had been silver, her step lively where it had been subdued. I warned Lisbet to silence with a finger to my lips, gently nudged her head down out of sight, and crouched beside her. Together we peered over the windowsill.

Joanna strode to the commons gate beneath our window and paused, studying the chain.

The challenge was instantaneous. "You there. Away from that gate."

Joanna faced the Inquisitor with studied nonchalance. "I'm sorry, is there a problem?"

"Be on your way. The commons is forbidden."

"My apologies, I've only recently arrived. I didn't know."

"You know now. Move along."

"Perhaps you can help me. I'm looking for my cousin, but I have no head for maps. Could you take a look?"

The Inquisitor held out his hand. "Let's see it."

She produced the document and stood to one side while he tried to make sense of it. After several moments he scratched his head and opened his mouth to speak, but before any words came out, he toppled face-forward onto the cobbles.

Lisbet clapped her hands over her mouth and turned to me with wild eyes.

Joanna didn't miss a beat. She wailed so convincingly for help, that if I hadn't known better, I'd have sworn she meant it. Within moments, a small knot of Inquisitors formed. Several examined their fallen comrade while the rest listened as she explained how the man had simply collapsed in the street. By now, several of the patrolling Inquisitors had gathered atop the wall, drawn by the commotion. As the panicked men discussed what to do next, Joanna edged outside their little circle.

Lisbet tugged at my sleeve, but I stayed put. Joanna was up to something, and if I was going to report the incident to Roman, I needed to be able to tell him what it was. Yet, nothing about her behavior made any sense to me. Reluctantly, I turned to another resource for assistance.

Addictive, aren't I?

"Yeah, hold me back," I said. "And while you're at it, take a gander down there. I can't seem to get enough of her either."

Dear Lord, is that Joanna?

"Either that, or her daughter borrowed her dress."

What's she doing with all those Inquisitors?

"I was hoping you could tell me."

Can't help you with specifics, but let me ask you this—if it involves Joanna and Inquisitors, are you sure you want to be standing this close?

The flash momentarily blinded me. Judging by the screams,

few if any of the Inquisitors had been spared. When the after-image faded, Joanna was the only person still standing. Inquisitors lay scattered within a scorched circle that encompassed those in the street as well as those who'd been patrolling the wall. Survivors cried out in gut-wrenching agony as they lay feebly batting at flames on their smoldering vestments. Joanna surveyed the carnage with an expression of grim satisfaction—until something caught her eye that made her scowl.

Then I saw it too—the scorched area was not a perfect circle. Where it came closest to the barn, the edge was indented, defining a small, telltale crescent that had escaped the flames.

Joanna's gaze flicked from the scorched cobbles to the barn, and then to our window. For one electric instant our eyes met. I struggled with whether to flee or bluff. Since both options struck me as equally futile, I ended up standing there, gaping. Lisbet's tug on my arm finally snapped me out of it. Before I could react, a crossbow thrummed. Joanna staggered, but did not fall. She whirled to face her assailant, her jaw working to form syllables while the man struggled to reload. With a shock, I recognized Kendall.

Tendrils of white smoke streamed from a wound in Joanna's side. She convulsed, sank to her knees. Smoke billowed from her lips as well. Yet, such was the force of her will that her recitation continued uninterrupted. Kendall could not reload in time, and he knew it. Eyes wide with dread, he ceased his fumbling to stare as Joanna's spell approached completion.

"Do something," I cried.

Sorry, sport, not in range.

I was dimly aware of movement next to me. Something small and round shot out of the window. It arced gracefully, finding its mark on the side of Joanna's head. She blinked at the impact. Her fierce look went slack. The determination etched on her face gave way to anguish. At last, she toppled, erupting in a whirlwind of roiling smoke that scattered her clothes across the cobbles, then simply faded away.

That was Joanna all right. She was never one to make a bland exit.

I jumped, not bothering with the beam. As soon as my feet hit the floor, I heaved open the barn door and rushed to where Kendall was already moving among the fallen, trying to identify those who most needed aid. It was ghastly. Their faces blistering, their hair and eyelashes singed away, they reached toward us blindly, crying for help or weeping in pain. The stench of scorched hair, flesh, and fabric took my breath.

Eleven in all. One had died—he'd had the misfortune of wearing a particularly flammable scarf—but that number was sure to rise. There was little I could do other than reassure them help was coming. My frustration was compounded by the fact that if only I had known—if I'd reacted sooner—I might have been able to use the watch to thwart Joanna's spells.

Lisbet kept her distance. She had good reason to be leery of men in vestments. At one point she dashed over and snatched up something from the cobbles near Joanna's ruined gown. Odd for her to abandon the safety of the barn to retrieve a pebble, but then I'd never understood the motives of women. Maybe the round pebbles she favored were difficult to come by, or perhaps this one had some special significance. Whatever her reasons, by the time additional Inquisitors arrived, she was safely tucked away out of sight once more.

Kendall wasted no time sending to the manor for help, but another of the Inquisitors had already passed away before Father Graves' carriage rolled into view. Ricard steered his team through a small assembly of gawking townsfolk. At Kendall's direction, he pulled to a stop near the most grievously injured. Father Graves and the Ordinal tumbled out. The Ordinal took charge of the triage operation, while Father Graves, journal in hand, extracted Kendall's account of recent events. It wasn't long before I heard my name.

"If it hadn't been for Flinch's quick thinking, I'd have been a goner."

Father Graves eyed me over his spectacles. "Mr. Flinch, could I have a word, please?"

"Yes, Father?"

"What happened here?"

"It was Joanna, sir."

"That it was," Kendall said, nodding. "I recognized her from the swamp."

Father Graves exhaled slowly. "I suspected as much. Where is she now?"

Kendall patted his crossbow. "I'd wager she won't be troubling us again."

Father Graves' eyes narrowed. "What do you mean?"

"I only got one shot, but I made it count."

"She's injured?"

Kendall shook his head. "It wasn't the kind of wound you'd survive. I expect she must have known it too, and Sacrificed herself, like her husband did."

Father Graves glanced anxiously about. "If that's true, then where's the body?"

"The whole gosh-darned thing went up in smoke," Kendall said. "Her dress is all that's left."

Father Graves strode over for a closer look at the scattered garments. "These aren't even singed. What's your take on this, Mr. Flinch?"

I know you're not prone to take advice, but trust me on this—this is one can of worms you do not want to open.

"I don't know," I said. "Even if she'd limited the Sacrifice to encompass only herself, a fire hot enough to destroy her body would almost certainly have burned her clothes as well."

"If it's not a Sacrifice, then what?"

"I can think of only one other possibility."

"Demonology." The taste of the word made him grimace. *I don't know why I even bother.*

Kendall blanched. "Are you saying my bolt may not have done her in after all?"

"I have no idea," Father Graves said. "If she's crossed that line, she's gone well beyond my limited expertise."

"But she saw me," Kendall said. "She knew me, too—I saw it in her eyes."

"Let's not go jumping to conclusions," Father Graves said. "So far we have very little evidence and a whole lot of conjecture. We have plenty to worry about without stirring up a frenzy based on superstitions and half-truths. Until we know for certain, this conversation stays among us, understood?"

Kendall was incredulous. "What if she finds me first? It'd be a little late to start talking then, wouldn't it?"

"Look at it this way," I said. "If she was a demon, and she wanted to kill you, wouldn't you already be dead? Since you're not, that's pretty strong evidence your crossbow actually did the job."

"You think so?"

"I do. I don't know what she was trying to accomplish here, but whatever it was, we interrupted her before she finished. Do you think a demon would allow a simple crossbow to get in the way?"

Father Graves pulled on his white cotton gloves. "Sounds reasonable to me," he said. "Now that that's resolved, I have some evidence to collect. Kendall, would you mind grabbing one of the empty crates on top of the carriage?"

As Kendall headed off, Father Graves turned to me.

"Now, Mr. Flinch, perhaps you'd care to enlighten me as to

how it is you happen to be here rather than on the hunt with Lord Histlewick. You may want to consider this an opportunity to practice your response, since Roman will no doubt be asking the exact same question."

"It was an accident—Histlewick left without me."

Father Graves went down on one knee to examine Joanna's abandoned gown. "He left without his squire? I had no idea His Lordship could be so careless."

"I think he was under the impression I was with him."

"Care to elaborate?"

My collar was growing uncomfortably warm. "Um, I think someone impersonated me."

At this, Father Graves looked up. "So, knowing Histlewick's intentions, you duped someone into taking your place?"

"It wasn't like that at all."

"A word to the wise—when Roman asks these questions, your reasons had best be compelling. There are those who will demand to know why we found you here instead with the hunt, and Roman will need to explain that in a way that leaves no doubt as to your loyalties."

Kendall finally returned and Father Graves fell silent. He carefully lifted the gown for transfer while Kendall held out the crate for him. Just when the silence began to grow awkward, Kendall spoke up. "Father, I apologize for overreacting. I don't know what got into me."

"Think nothing of it. You're not the only one who's unsettled by all this, but I think Mr. Flinch has the right of it—the longer we go without further incident, the greater the likelihood that your crossbow spoke the final word on the subject."

Behind them, the gate to the commons burst into flames. Father Graves swallowed hard and turned slowly to look.

Next to him, the crate slipped out of Kendall's trembling grasp and clattered to the ground. "I'm a dead man," he said.

CHAPTER TWENTY-FIVE

GOD WILL KNOW HIS OWN

Lisbet was a problem. With Roman expecting me to account for my detour from the hunt, there was no way I'd be able to slip away to find lodging for her. With no other ideas and little time to think, the best I could do was buy myself more time. During a particularly chaotic moment that involved the arrival of several commandeered carts, I slipped into the barn.

I didn't see Lisbet, but I knew better than to assume that meant she wasn't present. "Meet me in the manor house court-yard tonight," I said.

Without waiting for an answer, I slipped back outside, hoping no one had noticed my absence. Once the last patient was safely loaded up, the Ordinal commanded several petri-fied Inquisitors to remain behind in case the flames burned through the commons gate. Then on his signal, the grim cara-van wound its way toward the manor.

Once we made the courtyard, Roman was everywhere at once, directing preparations for a makeshift infirmary and solving a myriad of other logistical problems. Father Graves intercepted him at the first opportunity, and motioned me over.

"It was Mrs. Hockery," Father Graves said. "Mr. Flinch witnessed the entire incident."

Suspicion flickered in Roman's eyes. "Witnessed, but did not prevent?"

Father Graves licked his lips. "I wondered about that as well. The evidence suggests that he tried, but was too far away for his efforts to be effective."

"What was he doing there? Wasn't he supposed to be with Histlewick?"

Father Graves glanced my way. "Histlewick apparently left without him. It looks to me like he was trying his best to catch up. By all accounts, His Lordship's hunt had just passed. They probably missed each other by a matter of moments."

"And Hockery just happened to be there?"

"Quite the coincidence. Perhaps she was waiting for him to leave town before she tried anything."

Roman's brow furrowed. "Why would she care about Histlewick's whereabouts?"

"I wasn't referring to Histlewick."

Roman spared me an appraising glance. "You think she viewed the boy as that pivotal?"

"So far, he has been our most effective defense against her."

A smug grin blossomed on Roman's lips. "Until she encountered Kendall and his crossbow."

Father Graves seemed suddenly troubled. "About that...."

Roman held up his hand. "I know that look. I've already had my fair share of bad news today. If you insist on adding to it, at least have the decency to present whatever it is in the most positive possible light."

"In that case, you'll be happy to know all that trouble I

went to collecting and transporting the Profanities may not have been in vain."

"You've finally discovered something useful?"

"Not exactly, but unless I miss my guess, the reasons to keep looking are more pressing than ever."

"If you're referring to Hockery's accomplice…"

"I wasn't, but that's an excellent point, too."

"Then who?"

"Let me put it this way, Mrs. Hockery didn't so much die, as evaporate. By the time I got there, all that was left of her was her gown."

"You aren't suggesting she escaped, are you?"

"I'm suggesting we need to be open to that possibility. Until we know for certain, I strongly recommend that you keep Mr. Flinch with you at all times."

The Ordinal's breathless arrival interrupted the Inquisitor General's reply. "Ah, Roman, there you are. This is more than I can manage on my own—I need skilled help, and I need it now. Send someone into the village. If there are any Sisters of Solace down there, get them up here as soon as possible."

"I'll find someone right away," Roman said.

"Oh, any word on Elyria?"

"Not yet, but the manor's a big place. Let her cool off. Once she gets hungry, she'll come out of hiding."

Darron was the next to vie for Roman's attention. "Father, we have a situation developing down by the commons. Another gate has gone up in flames."

Roman winced at the news. "Use some of the commandeered carts to make sure those gates stay blocked. Station more men there—do whatever it takes. We can't risk a single escape."

"We've already blocked them with carts, but they're not very effective without guards. The problem is, with all the injuries, we're running low on men. If any more gates go down, I don't know how we're going to manage."

"I'll send to the Holy City for more men."

"That could take weeks. We don't have weeks."

"I'll send to Caprian then."

"That's still three to four days, minimum."

"All right, see what you can recruit from the village."

"Are you sure that's a good idea? The villagers have made no secret of their outrage at the use of their commons as a prison."

"Darron, I can't be everywhere at once. Assess the situation, solve the problem."

"Problem-solving takes resources."

At that point Prentiss made an entrance on horseback, swinging out of the saddle next to Darron. "The situation continues to worsen, sir," he said. "Shortly after you left, flames engulfed a third gate."

Roman's frown deepened. "At this rate, how much longer can you keep the prisoners contained?"

"The rest of the day, easily," Darron said. "Probably even well into the night. After that, the men will need to rest—that's when we're going to feel the pinch. I suppose we could try recruiting villagers and pairing them with Inquisitors to keep them honest."

"Do it," Roman said. "Prentiss, in the meantime, do you think you'd be able to oversee keeping the prisoners compliant? Our current expert was among the injured."

Prentiss bowed. "It's an honor to serve, sir."

"I have to get back to my patients," the Ordinal said. "Until I get some Sisters up here, I'm going to need Hollings and the staff—cutting bandages, seeing to patients' basic necessities, that sort of thing."

Roman nodded. "By all means."

In the wink of an eye, our little group dwindled to just Roman, Father Graves, and me.

Roman put his hand on Father Graves' shoulder. "Albert, I need to know what I'm up against—I need a way to fight back."

Father Graves shook his head. "I'll check my sources, but I'm not hopeful. All the reliable information I have concerning demons wouldn't fill a small pamphlet."

"The Profanities, then. Surely there must be something there we can use."

"I'll do my best."

Father Graves hurried off toward the Marstow wing, leaving me alone with Roman.

"She must have been Evoked," I said.

"What?"

"Joanna. She must have Evoked a body and found a way to transfer her soul into it. That would explain how she could evaporate like that. But when the body goes away, what happens to her soul? Wouldn't that kill her?"

"Albert seems unwilling to assume that."

"But even if her soul somehow survived, how much of a threat could she pose in that state?"

"Unlike my predecessor, I'm not willing to underestimate a heretic of Hockery's caliber. If she has the wherewithal to engage in such advanced demonology, we must presume she has the means to Evoke again."

I made a mental tally of all the spells required for such a feat. Yes, it would be complicated, but no more complicated than the pocket watch. Still, I had my doubts. If she had that capability, what was she waiting for?

Then it occurred to me all those spells ought to be detectable. Based on my tally, almost all of the monocle's wedges should color in response. In theory, if Joanna was still a threat,

I'd be able to tell if she got close. In practice, the situation wasn't quite so straightforward—all the wedges were already colored from detecting spells on the watch. So, to find anything with the monocle, I'd first need to ditch the watch. But that meant giving up the watch's protection against Joanna's Sacrifices. I wouldn't have dreamed of giving up the watch's protection, except that if I used the monocle to help find and eliminate Joanna as a threat, Roman wouldn't need me anymore. Maybe then I could convince him to let me search for my parents. The problem was, if she found us first, without the watch we wouldn't stand a chance.

Wracking my brain for a solution, I tagged along behind Roman as he toured the manor lobby, which the Ordinal had appropriated as a makeshift infirmary. Within the gold-flecked marble fireplace, a black cauldron from the kitchens hung steaming. Nearby tables were stacked with rolls of muslin, gingham and gauze that Hollings, Saville and several others were tearing into strips. Cots and pallets littered the polished granite floor, their miserable inhabitants writhing and moaning. The patients' suffering took a toll on Roman, and by the time he turned his attention back to the courtyard, his jaw was taut, his face pale and drawn.

At noon, we paid Father Graves a visit. He'd made little progress—he simply didn't have enough information to draw reliable conclusions about Joanna's status.

Roman's expression darkened. "And the Profanities?"

Father Graves shook his head.

"What about the schematics?"

He shrugged. "I can't read them."

"Even with Mr. Flinch's help?"

Father Graves folded his arms in front of him. "In case you haven't noticed, Mr. Flinch is otherwise occupied."

Roman's frown deepened even further. "It's pointless to protect me if I'm to be the only survivor. The value of a shield is determined in no small measure by the strength of the weapon in the other hand. Albert, I need that weapon."

"The situation is likely not as desperate as you make out. In all probability, Joanna Hockery died this morning. I only voiced those suspicions out of an abundance of caution."

"In which case, there's no reason Mr. Flinch can't stay here with you to puzzle over schematics."

"On the other hand, the commons gates only ignited after she'd supposedly been killed."

"True, but she could have cast those spells in advance, like she did with the Sacrifice on Armand's things."

Father Graves scratched his chin. "You have a point, but if she really is dead, your need for deciphering these schematics becomes far less pressing. In that case, it makes more sense for Mr. Flinch to remain with you."

I tried to suggest it would make more sense for me to catch up with Lord Histlewick, but Roman held up his hand and cocked his head, listening. Only then did I hear the cries.

Father Graves let fall the schematic he'd been studying. "Where's that coming from?"

Roman's jaw dropped. "The courtyard."

The three of us raced through the convoluted bowels of the manor. When we finally reached the exit, a knee-high layer of thick coffee-colored smoke blanketed the courtyard. Flames spouted from the bed of a sturdy wagon standing just inside the gate. Inquisitors and servants alike scrambled to contain the blaze, their efforts confounded by billowing sickly-sweet fumes as well as by the panicked rampage of a runaway draft horse.

I recognized Prentiss among those gathered about the wagon. Instead of aiding those who were ineffectually hurling water from buckets, he'd recruited an Inquisitor, and together they strained to shove the wagon out through the gate. He called out for everyone else to stay back, but his words went unheeded, lost amidst the cries of the others. Meanwhile, Darron tried to contain the terrified animal by herding it into a corner.

Roman waded out toward the wagon, the dense vapors swirling about his knees. Ignoring Prentiss's warning, he grabbed hold of the hitching pole. With his added strength, the wagon finally began to creak backward.

Despite Darron's attempts to calm it, the horse was still wild, rearing and kicking at random. He had managed, however, to shepherd it into a boxwood-lined corner. Capitalizing on the close quarters, he lunged for the reins. The horse snorted and shied away, backing into the hedge to avoid him. A shrill shriek split the air. The boxwoods erupted, and I caught a momentary glint of sunlight off Lisbet's filthy blonde mop before she dashed out of sight once more.

Startled, the horse reared and lashed out. Darron threw himself back to avoid its flailing hooves. I heard a thud as he hit the cobbles, but I couldn't tell if he was hurt. All that remained to mark where he'd fallen was a fading eddy in the vapors.

By now the wagon had built enough momentum to take it through the gate. Once outside, the slope of the hill carried it away from the manor and into the village, trailing a noisome caramel-hued plume behind it. The horse launched itself across the courtyard and out through the gate after it.

Roman coughed and tried to fan away the vapors. "What is this stuff?"

"It's the drug we use on the prisoners," Prentiss replied. "When the gate near the storage shed caught fire, we thought it best to move our supply to the manor. We weren't expecting an attack on the wagon."

"The drug?" Roman asked. "How much do we have left?"

Prentiss swallowed. "That was all of it, sir."

"But we have over a hundred prisoners down there."

"I am aware."

"Can we substitute something else?"

Prentiss pondered for a few seconds and shook his head. "I'm sorry, sir. Even if we could identify a replacement drug, I don't see how there'd be time to acquire sufficient quantities."

"What about masks?"

"At best, there are enough for only a small fraction of the prisoners."

The pounding of approaching hooves sent the two of them scurrying, but it was Barclay's gelding that burst through the gate. Barclay reined in the mount. "I've just come from the commons," he said. "We need more men."

Roman eyed Barclay incredulously. "Darron told me we had enough to last us. Has something else happened?"

"Desertion, sir. Darron and Prentiss hadn't been gone five minutes when a whole group of men abandoned their posts."

"What's going on down there?"

"It's the demon. They're convinced that you're powerless against it, and that it's just a matter of time before it strikes again. They don't want to end up like the others."

Roman's eyes narrowed. "I don't care how you do it, but get those men back to their posts. If those prisoners escape, they'll only swell the ranks of our enemies. Take Darron with you."

The situation had just gone from bad to worse. Escaped Phrendonic prisoners would increase Roman's fear of being Sacrificed regardless of whether Joanna survived. If I didn't do something fast, I'd never convince him to let me leave—I might as well give up all hope of rescuing my parents. What could I even say that would distract him from such dire circumstances? Nothing sprang immediately to mind, but I was determined to find something.

Prentiss scowled in puzzlement as he scanned the courtyard. "Where is Darron, anyway?"

Father Graves called out as he waded through the vapors. "He's over here somewhere, but I can't seem to find him."

"He's not submerged in that, is he?" Prentiss asked.

Father Graves nodded. "Only since the horse left, though. Ah, here he is."

Roman sprinted to the spot. Dropping to one knee, he lifted Darron by the shoulders to raise his head out of the fumes. Even from where I stood, his unnatural pallor was obvious. I'd never get Roman's attention now.

"I'll get the Ordinal," Father Graves said, dashing off across the courtyard.

Roman struggled for several long minutes to rouse his son, but Darron didn't respond. "He's not hurt. Why won't he wake up?"

"It's probably the drug, sir," Prentiss said.

"How long will he be like this?"

"I can't say. The dosage is critical. If he took in too much..."

"Begging your pardon, sir," Barclay said, "but without Darron's clout, I seriously doubt any of the deserters are going to reconsider."

Prentiss rubbed his chin thoughtfully. "It wouldn't matter anyway. Once the drug wears off, there's no way they'd be able to stand against that many heretics."

Two somber Inquisitors approached. One of them spoke up. "The Ordinal requested we bring him."

Drained of all expression, Roman watched as they carried away his son.

"Sir?" Barclay asked. "What do you want us to do?"

Roman didn't answer immediately. He stood unmoving, staring vacantly into the distance. After a long moment, he bowed his head. "When they write of me, they will say I was undone by the hubris of good intention, that I lacked the foresight to recognize a cause that was truly lost. They'll be wrong. My downfall was appreciating too late that this was a war on two fronts."

"I'm sorry, sir," Barclay said. "Did you want me to pursue the deserters without Darron's help?"

Roman shook his head. "No, Prentiss is right. Absent the drug, there's no point."

"We can't just let the prisoners escape," Barclay said. "Without the drug, we'll be defenseless."

Roman nodded. "I can't argue with that either."

"So that's it? We're just going to cut our losses and run?"

"I'm afraid our responsibility to our injured makes that option untenable as well."

Barclay shifted nervously. "I have some experience with these heretics, sir. If they come for us in force, the manor won't offer much protection. You aren't suggesting we surrender, are you?"

Prentiss fixed Roman with a sidelong look. "There is one other possibility," he said. "We could make it so that the prisoners aren't able to escape."

Roman's face was ashen. "If they'd only given me some time to work with, I might have found a way to spare them, but they've left me no choice."

"You aren't serious," Barclay said. "You can't be."

He started to say something else, but Prentiss cut him off. "You go see to your son, sir," he said. "We'll take care of this."

Roman nodded. "I appreciate that," he said. "I owe you."

CHAPTER TWENTY-SIX

THE ESSENTIAL CHARM
OF A PRISM BREAK

My mind racing, I ducked back inside the manor and slammed the door behind me. My first impulse was to plead with Roman, to beg him to reconsider. The problem was, if he didn't, I'd have no other recourse. If Roman was capable of this, I doubted even Father Graves could reach him. And there was Lisbet to consider. If she were captured, would Roman's orders apply to her, too? If she stayed in the courtyard, it was just a matter of time before she was discovered. And what about Sly and Chef? As much as I wanted to run off to rejoin Histlewick's hunt, I couldn't leave knowing what Roman had in store for them. I hoped my parents would forgive the delay, but I had to do something.

I cracked the door. To my relief, Barclay and Prentiss were no longer in sight. Trusting that those who were left in the courtyard had gotten used to seeing me in Roman's company, I stepped outside and headed over toward the hedge where I'd last seen Lisbet.

"You can come out now," I said.

A subtle movement. She peered back at me from the top of the shed. I'd never have spotted her if I hadn't seen her there once before.

"Hurry," I said. "We don't have much time."

She eyed me dubiously.

"Are you coming or not?"

Silence.

"Well, I'm going. If you're coming, you'd better come now."

Turning, I marched deliberately back toward the door. By the time I got there, I could hear bare feet padding along behind me. I bit off several nails waiting for her to work up the courage to follow me inside. She jumped when I shoved the door closed behind her. I tried to look confident, but I'm sure I was every bit as nervous as she was. Fortunately, I managed to recall the route back to the Marstow wing. It would have been a terrible time to get lost.

Once we made it to the sitting room, Lisbet's eyes went wide with delight. She dashed from one gewgaw to the next, variously petting the tassels, and gazing up at the glass finials in wonder.

"Wait here," I said. "I'll be right back." I took a few steps and turned back. "And don't touch anything."

Her hand froze in mid-reach. She stuck her tongue out at me and plopped down in the middle of an oval braided rug. She pulled from her pocket a small, rose-tinted bottle.

"What's that?"

"Nothing," she said. "Bugs and things." She held it out to me. "Wanna see?"

The thing was crusted with grime. Since she clearly hadn't lifted it from the manor, I had no desire to see more. "Fine,"

I said. "Play with that, then, but make sure that stopper stays on, all right?"

She nodded and went back to staring through the glass.

It felt risky leaving her behind, but I had several doors to check, and if I ran into someone, I didn't want to be in the position of having to explain her presence. As it turned out, I was overcautious—the first few rooms were empty. Presumably everyone had been called away to help with the injured. Behind the fifth door, I found the person I was seeking.

Armand lay atop a paisley coverlet, his heavily bandaged knee resting on satin pillows. His face was thinner than I remembered, and he lacked color. He set aside his book and looked my way. He did not smile.

"This is an unexpected surprise," he said.

"I have nowhere else to turn."

"You can keep right on turning, Mr. Flinch. I have little patience for those who repay kindness with deception."

"In my defense, I did risk my life to save yours."

He grimaced, and adjusted his leg on the pillow. "True," he said, "but if you'd just leveled with me from the beginning, how many more lives might have been saved?"

"In case you haven't noticed, your father heads up the Inquisition. Let's talk for a moment about the lives they've destroyed, shall we?"

"That's unfair," Armand shot back. "He's only taken the position because he believes he can temper the excesses of his predecessors. He's trying to save lives, not destroy them."

"He's sure got a strange way of going about it."

"What do you mean?"

"He just ordered the execution of everyone imprisoned in the commons. Barclay and Prentiss are on their way there now to carry it out."

Armand blinked at me in shock. "That's preposterous."

"Sly and Chef will be relieved to hear that," I said. "But you'd better tell them soon if you're going to—otherwise you'll be saying it to their corpses."

"What do they have to do with this?"

"Your father hasn't told you, has he?"

"I have no idea what you're talking about."

"While you were out, he raided your charity—Sly and Chef are among the droolers roaming the commons."

"Now I know you're lying," he said. "My father and I have an agreement...."

"Don't take my word for it," I said. I turned and called down the hallway. "Lisbet, can you come here?"

She bounded over. When she caught sight of Armand, she squealed and ran to him instead.

"Take good care of her," I said, turning to leave. "After today, she probably won't have anyone else."

"Where are you going?"

"I'm going to find someone who can help."

Armand's voice echoed behind me. "Wait," he cried. "Come back."

Almost everything I'd done since Joanna had waylaid our carriage, I'd done to either help my parents or repay Armand for his kindness. I could accept Roman being suspicious, or even Darron for that matter, but for Armand to doubt me—to eye me as if I'd just stabbed him in the back—that was more than I could take. Despite all that, I nearly turned back when he called, but pride got the better of me. I couldn't bear for him to see me cry.

By the time I made it back to my room, I'd found a shoulder to cry on.

If I were you, I'd find myself a horse and put as much distance between me and this place as I possibly could.

"What about Chef and Sly? I can't just leave them."

I hardly think it's in your best interests to join them.

"There must be something I can do."

I don't see what. The Ordinal is the only one in the manor who outranks Roman, and I somehow don't expect he'd be sympathetic.

"If only Lord Histlewick were here…"

If Histlewick had the power to defy Roman, there wouldn't have been prisoners in his commons to begin with.

"There must be someone who can help me."

At this point, I can't think of anyone who would even want to help you, much less have the power to do so. Your best bet is to get out of town.

"That's it," I cried. "You're a genius."

Quite so, but frankly it doesn't take a genius to figure out what your next move ought to be.

I snapped the watch shut and slipped it under the mattress.

Wait, what are you doing?

"I'm going to find someone who might actually want to help."

Without me?

"Sorry, my friend, but your presence renders the monocle useless, and to have any chance at all, I expect I'm going to need it."

Are you out of your mind? You'll be defenseless.

I headed out into the hall and closed the door behind me. "Good to know you care."

But it could be years before anyone finds me here.

"Guess you'd better wish me luck, then."

Don't be a fool. There's got to be another—

The instant I was out of range of the pocket watch, the monocle lost all but two of its colors—only the red and green wedges remained. That was a huge relief. It not only confirmed that the watch had been interfering, it also suggested that the monocle was working according to its schematics. Now all I had to do was put it to good use.

My best chance of doing that was to find Ramos, Joanna's accomplice. My impression was that he was only helping her reluctantly. Now that she was out of the picture, maybe I could convince him to help me instead. The trick, of course, was finding him. The monocle could help, but only if I had something to look for. When I remembered Joanna's charm bracelet, everything fell into place. Since we didn't find it with Joanna's clothes, it was a pretty good bet Ramos ended up with it.

The manor was eerily empty as I made my way back down to the courtyard. Once I noticed someone had closed the court-yard gate, I headed for Lisbet's shed instead. Getting over the wall wasn't a problem. The two Inquisitors they'd spared to guard the gate were there to keep dangerous heretics out, not to keep the servants in. I was prowling the village streets in no time.

Nothing moved in the vicinity of the manor. Indeed, the remains of the cart still burned unattended where they had come to rest against a smithy. Scorch marks marred the smithy's white stone wall, but the smoke had been mostly dispersed by a determined spring breeze. Only once I was well into the village did I finally see activity, but those few who were outside spoke in whispers and went silent if I got close.

I gave the commons a wide berth. The less reason I gave Barclay and Prentiss to think about me, the better I liked it. Since my search would begin near the village gate with the building from which Joanna had emerged, I'd have to reach it by circling around. Somewhere along the way, the monocle went completely transparent. I took that to mean the spells that enabled communication with the watch had finally run their course.

I approached the building from the back, trying my best to stay hidden. Noting the shutters on the windows were closed, I scooted closer, shielding myself briefly behind a well-used privy. From there I made a dash for the exterior wall. Crouching down between a cracked butter churn and a dented wash tub, I had a closer look at the monocle. It was still transparent. That was a disappointment. Unless I was wrong about the monocle or the bracelet, it looked like Ramos wasn't in.

I climbed the rotting wooden stoop and forced myself to knock. There was no answer. After knocking a second time, I tried the door. It creaked inward on rusted hinges. The room was dreary and cramped. Cast iron pans and implements dangled from racks affixed to the chimney. Although there was no fire, smoke still rose from the coals.

I poked my head in for a better look. "Is anybody here?"

After several moments of silence, I stepped inside.

A table and several rough-hewn chairs stood across from me. A burlap sack lay across one of the chairs, and a tankard rested on the tabletop. A quick inspection of the sack revealed it was empty, although as I put it down, something tiny dropped from it—a single burgundy bead. The tankard was unlike any of the crude ceramic mugs that adorned the shelves, and it still had ale in it. There was no sign of a keg anywhere in the room, which led me to believe the tankard had come from somewhere else, an inn, perhaps. That made sense. Joanna was not someone I could easily envision tolerating squalor unnecessarily. After one more sweep for anything out of the ordinary, I ducked out the way I'd come in.

Given its isolation I was surprised that the village even had an inn, but a conversation with an old woman in light blue homespun set me straight. She looked up from clipping asparagus shoots in her garden long enough to give me directions, along with an answer to my implied question.

"Wherever there're menfolk, you'll always find liquor," she said, "and no woman worth her salt is gonna put up with a man who liquors it up at home." She straightened up and squinted at me. "You one of the Lord's men, then?"

"Yes, ma'am."

"Which family?"

"I'm sorry, I don't follow."

"There ain't but three families the Lord picks his new folk from—been that way for generations. You don't have the looks of any of 'em."

"I'm from out of town."

The old woman screwed up her wrinkles into a suspicious frown. "Thought as much. First there was all that hoo-rah with the commons, and now this. Things is changin' too fast for my likin', and I'll wager not for the better."

Uncomfortable with where the conversation was headed, I thanked her for the directions and sped off toward the inn. I found it at the end of a cul-de-sac nestled up against the west wall of the village. As I set foot on the inn's ramshackle porch, the monocle suddenly blazed with color—all seven wedges, red through violet. I stepped inside with renewed confidence that I'd come to the right place.

The inn was more crowded than I'd expected for a late afternoon. Three men sat at one of the tables, nursing tankards like the one I'd found back at the house. Two more men occupied stools up against bar, chatting with the innkeeper. The door slammed closed behind me, and conversation ceased. All eyes were on me as I made my way up to the bar.

"I'd like a room, please."

The grey-haired innkeeper didn't put down the glass he was drying. "No offense, laddie, but we'll just wait for your parents' say-so before we start making any decisions."

I reached into my pocket and scattered coin across the bar. "It'll just be for me," I said.

The innkeeper's eyes widened, prompting me to wonder just how badly I'd overpaid him. "As you wish, sir." He set down the glass and with a deft hand, scooped up the coins. "Right this way."

He led me up a narrow stairwell and down a dark corridor. "Here ya be," he said, opening a door. "Will ya be needin' anything else?"

"This should do for now."

He nodded. "As you say, sir. You want that I should look after your horse?"

"That won't be necessary."

"If there's anything else you need—"

"I'll be sure to let you know."

The room was barely bigger than my room at the manor, and considerably less clean. I went to pour myself some water from the bowl and pitcher, only to discover a pair of lace undergarments stuffed inside. Deciding I wasn't thirsty anyway, I waited for the stairs to stop creaking, and then cracked the door and peered out.

I tried the room across the hall first, but it was empty, as were the next two. In the third, though, I hit the jackpot—the coat rack boasted a burgundy hat adorned with a peacock feather.

"Ramos?" I said softly. "Are you in here?"

I stopped short—someone was concealed beneath the bed-clothes.

"Ramos, is that you?"

When I finally worked up the courage to lift back the sheets, my heart nearly stopped. It seemed Joanna wasn't dead after all.

CHAPTER TWENTY-SEVEN

ÒRESS FOR SUCCESS

But neither was Joanna precisely alive. She looked almost peaceful, her breathing shallow but regular, her silver hair splayed across the pillow. Her cameo rested on the nightstand. The charm bracelet still graced her wrist. Of Ramos, there was no sign. Had he turned on her? Somehow that didn't seem likely. But if not Ramos, who?

I didn't have time to puzzle it out. The longer I waited, the greater the risk Prentiss and Barclay would carry out their orders before I could stop them. Without Ramos, my plan was a shambles, and now I had no way of finding him. Visions of Sly and Chef slaughtered like cattle made me reckless. If I couldn't get Ramos, Joanna would have to do.

At first I'd been petrified she'd awaken. Fighting down that fear, I gently shook her. "Mrs. Hockery," I said, "wake up."

When that didn't work, I shook her more firmly. There was still no response.

I didn't understand it. Even when he'd been Slept by Joanna back in the swamp, Kendall had shown some signs of life. In Joanna, I detected no eye movement, no twitching, nothing. She was every bit as limp as Histlewick's double had been when I'd stuffed him into the wardrobe.

Histlewick—what had Father Graves said about him? His soul was missing? It seemed Joanna's was missing too. Wherever it had gone after she'd evaporated, it hadn't returned here. But why leave all her jewelry behind? Unless...

Unless she intended the condition to be temporary. That made perfect sense. With an Evoked body Joanna could brave a risky situation without fear of dying. If the body were destroyed, she would need either the capacity to re-Evoke, or failing that, an accomplice to collect up her soul and reassemble her. In Ramos, she had that. And once he did, there was nothing to prevent her from creating another demon to wreak more havoc. As long as she and Ramos continued to work as a team, she literally couldn't lose.

I couldn't stand by and let that happen—too many innocent people's lives were at stake. I cast about for a weapon, and then thought better of it. I'd never be able to force myself to deliver the blow anyway. I'd have to settle for keeping her away from Ramos. I threw open the shutters to see whether I could get her out through the window. It was a two-story drop straight down. I'd have to hide her instead.

First I removed her bracelet and slipped it into my pocket. I didn't know whether Ramos would be able to use it to track her the way I had, but I wasn't taking any chances. Next I laid a blanket by the bed and piled pillows on top of it. The pillows muffled the sound of her feet hitting the floor as I dragged her out of bed. The blanket made for smooth sliding across the hardwood. From there, it was a simple matter to drag her down the hallway to my own room, where I was able to arrange her sitting up in an armoire, much as I had once done with Histlewick.

Next, I needed to get out of there. If Ramos found me at the inn, all my efforts would be wasted. The monocle also went in my pocket. No need to draw undue attention at this point, particularly since it was useless in the presence of the bracelet.

On my way out, I tossed more coins on the bar.

"I'll be in and out during the next week," I said. "I'd appreciate it if I'm not disturbed."

The innkeeper swept up the coins. "As you wish, sir."

I was halfway to the exit, my head swirling with half-formed ideas for new plans, when a chair slid out from one of the tables directly in my path. I pulled up short as a man rose out of the chair. My head tilted backward as I tracked his progress. Standing, he was fully twice my height. His thinning hair was gathered at the nape of his neck with a leather cord. Dense muttonchops clung to his cheeks like a pair of plump rats. His forearms were thicker than my thighs.

"Nice coat ya got there," he said.

"Thanks," I said. "Lord Histlewick gave it to me."

His friends at the table exchanged nervous glances.

"Did he now? If ya don't mind my askin', why would he be doin' that?"

"I received it when he took me on as his squire."

"Yeah? Well, I heard tell he already had a squire. What happened to him?"

"That's a tale that would take some time to tell."

"We got time, and seein' as how Cory's my cousin'n all, I got more than a passin' interest."

"In that case, let me buy you gentlemen a round of ale and we'll talk about it." I held out my hand. "The name's Flinch."

The man brightened at that and shook my hand, nearly crushing it. I struggled to maintain a smile as I blinked back tears. "That'd be right kind of ya," he said. "I'm Buck, and this here's Denner and that there's Wollens."

I pulled up a chair. Now that Buck had released his grip on my hand and taken his seat, I breathed a bit more easily.

"It's like this, gentlemen," I said. "Lord Histlewick has decided it's high time the Church moves its prison out of his commons and makes way for the village to put their livestock back where they belong."

Denner's jaw dropped so low I could see his tonsils. "His Lordship's going to take on the Church?"

I lowered my voice, and the men leaned in closer. "That's where things get complicated. Lord Histlewick doesn't want it to look like the Church folk are anything other than his good buddies, so he decides that the best thing for everyone is if all this happens while he's out of town."

Buck was suddenly eager to contribute to the conversation. "So that's why he took off on his hunt so early?"

I nodded. "Nothing much gets past you, does it, Buck?"

He leaned back, a thumb hooked in each suspender as a broad smile blossomed between his muttonchops. "You got that right."

At this point the innkeeper delivered the drinks. I tipped him another coin.

"Wait a minute," Denner said. "If His Lordship's gone, how's all this supposed to happen? Someone's gotta be in charge of it, right?"

"That's right," I said, "but it can't be someone from around here. It has to be someone who's free to disappear once everything's over with, but with enough of a connection to His Lordship so that people know it's for real."

Buck leaned forward. "Are ya talking 'bout someone like His Lordship's squire, maybe?"

"Buck, you are one quick study," I said. "No offense to your cousin, but now I think you can see why His Lordship decided he wasn't right for this job. But don't you worry, he'll be right back squiring as usual as soon as there's an opening."

Wollens squinted at me past a nose so hooked I felt like I was talking to a hawk. "Seems to me a plan like that is apt to make the Church hoppin' mad," he said. "Even if they don't take it out on His Lordship, they could make things mighty rough for the rest of us."

"His Lordship's got that part figured out, too" I replied. "He's going to blame it all on the heretics. That's another reason he needed someone who's not from around here to get things moving. If the Church insists on punishing the village, he'll offer to do it for them, and then just not do it. He thinks once they're gone, they won't pay this place much mind anymore."

Wollens still wasn't convinced. "We've been putting up with this for months and His Lordship stood by and did nothing. Why now? What makes this any more important today than it was yesterday?"

I took a long slow drink of my ale before I had an answer. I set the tankard down on the table and looked at each man in turn. "Because, gentlemen, yesterday, they weren't talking about making the prison permanent."

All three men started talking at once. I let them vent their outrage for several minutes before pounding my tankard on the table to regain their attention.

"It's true," I said. "Lord Histlewick's original strategy of being helpful backfired. Things went so smoothly that now the Church is looking to turn not just the commons, but this entire village, into a prison camp for heretics. I just hope I can drum up enough support to keep that from happening. I'd hate to have to look His Lordship in the eye and tell him I failed."

"You tell me what you need," Buck said. "Me and the boys'll make sure you get it."

By the time the next round of drinks arrived, I'd deputized Buck and outlined a plan whereby he and his friends were to recruit as many villagers as they could to mass at the commons. Once we had enough people, I would try to convince any Inquisitors who remained to throw down their weapons and leave. Without guards, I figured we stood a fair chance of moving the prisoners outside the village before Prentiss and Barclay could carry out Roman's order.

After toasts to both their bravery and their loyalty, I finally managed to escape the inn, thankful that Ramos hadn't walked in on us during the show. I ran most of the way back to the commons, making straight for the barn, since I wanted to see without being seen. I slipped inside and scrambled up the ladder.

Across the road, as before, slack-jawed prisoners still wandered the grounds. The three gates I could see had been reduced to slabs of smoking charcoal. Overturned wagons made for imperfect substitutes, each paired with a single Inquisitor to ensure those imperfections were not exploited. Only two Inquisitors still walked the wall.

I dared to be optimistic. If Buck and his friends could gather even a small crowd, this plan might actually work. As I pondered our next move, the appearance of another set of vestments on the far side of the commons drew my eye. The Inquisitor shoved two hapless prisoners before him, herding them up the hill toward a large shed jammed up against the wall of the compound. I broke out in a cold sweat at the thought of what likely awaited them there. In a panic, I scanned for Chef and Sly, praying they were still outside.

I was interrupted by laughter—actually more of a subtle chuckle, coming from behind me.

I whirled to see Ramos leaning casually against the post that held the ladder. He looked up at me, arms folded. "Well,

well, well, it's Mr. Theratigan—now this is an unexpected surprise."

"Am I glad to see you," I said.

"And I'm glad to see you, too," he replied, "although I expect for different reasons. Let's start with yours, shall we?"

"They're planning to kill the prisoners. I need your help to stop them."

"Very clever," he said. "A compelling story, plausibly constructed from current events, with the added benefit of an emotional appeal that plays directly off my own recent imprisonment. If I hadn't already been aware of your working relationship with the Inquisitor General, I might even have fallen for it."

"I'm telling the truth."

"It's not the truth of your story so much as your loyalties that worry me," he said. "I'd like to propose a test. I want you to return to the manor, retrieve Joanna's gown, and bring it back down here to me. If you manage that without tipping off any of your ecclesiastical compatriots, I might be willing to consider hearing you out."

"That doesn't make any sense," I said. "If you're so afraid my loyalties lie with the Inquisition, why wouldn't I bring back Inquisitors instead?"

"Well, apart from ruining any chance of rescuing your precious prisoners, if you did that, I'd be far less inclined to remove the Sacrifice. Oh, and if you're thinking that pocket watch can save you like it saved your friend Armand, think again. I've taken that into account. Now if I were you, I'd get started. You don't have much time."

CHAPTER TWENTY-EIGHT

NOT A MOMENT OF TRUTH

Iran. Visions of wailing Inquisitors drove me onward. My
side throbbed, my lungs heaved, and still the village flew
past me. All the way I cursed myself for having left the
watch behind. Even if Ramos had been telling the truth about
finding a way around its protections, at least I would have had
some idea how much time I had left.

I threw myself at the courtyard gate, pounding its oaken
timbers with both fists. My panic didn't help my cause. One of
the guards climbed onto the wall and I could see him scanning
the village behind me for signs of what I was fleeing. After
an eternity, the gate finally creaked open. I slipped inside and
sprinted directly for the little portico that led to the Marstow
wing. I burst into Father Graves' library, not expecting him
to be there. He looked up from a table of scattered schematics in surprise.

"Where have you been?" he asked. "You know full well
that Roman's at risk whenever you're not with him."

"I've been Sacrificed."

Father Graves leapt to his feet, nearly overturning the table. "Dear Lord, how long ago?"

"I'm not sure."

"How do you know?"

"Ramos did it. He told me."

"Wouldn't the watch have protected you?"

"I didn't have it with me."

"Why on earth not?"

"I don't have time to explain. I need Joanna's dress. He says he'll remove the Sacrifice if I take it to him."

"I'll get it. In the meantime, you head back out to the courtyard. If time runs out while you're still in the manor...."

"I'll wait outside," I said. "Please hurry."

Waiting in the courtyard, I started wondering why Ramos would care so much about Joanna's garments. If they were really that important, why would he be willing to risk losing them if by some stroke of bad luck, I was a little late making it back? For that matter, how could he know he'd circumvented the watch's protections and yet not seem to realize that I didn't have the watch with me? Unless....

I reached into my pocket, drew out Joanna's bracelet, and hid it in the hedge. Then, wearing the multicolored monocle, I put some distance between myself and the bracelet. The colors faded to full transparency—there were no spells in range. There was only one reasonable explanation. Ramos was bluffing.

I palmed the monocle just as Father Graves burst out onto the portico, the crate tucked beneath his arm. I dashed toward him, but he held up his hand

"Stay back," he said. "We can't risk the manor." He brought the crate to me instead.

The guilt made me squirm, but I couldn't tell him—he'd want to know how I knew.

"Take it," he cried. "Go!"

I grabbed and ran. He called out for the Inquisitors to open the gate, and I flew through without slowing my pace. Only after I was out of sight of the manor did I slow down to consider my position. Ramos had tricked me into believing I was going to die if I didn't do what he wanted, but when I'd first met him, he'd seemed a decent sort. Either I'd completely misjudged him or he was desperate. I decided to go all in on the latter.

Spying a thick vine clinging to the stone of a nearby wall, I wedged the crate in behind it, careful to make sure it was concealed beneath the leaves. Once satisfied it was stable, I hoofed it back to the barn. To my dismay, it was empty.

"Ramos," I called out. "I'm back."

Echos.

Scanning the rafters and looking for disturbances in the hay, I called out again. "I want to make a deal."

Behind me, the hinges creaked. I turned.

"No dress, very little time left, and no watch to protect you," Ramos said. "Forgive me for saying so, but your hand is looking a little weak at the moment."

"I have the dress. Help me save the prisoners, and I'll take you to it."

"I have a better idea. Bring the dress to me, and maybe you won't burn to death."

"No deal. Either you agree to help me, or I'm walking out that door."

"That's suicide."

"You better hope it isn't, or you'll never see that dress again."

We stood there staring across the barn at each other for a long time. At last Ramos looked away. "Clearly, I'm not cut out for this line of work," he said. "Just so you know, when

I agreed to help Joanna, it was to rescue her husband. When that fell through, rescuing the prisoners seemed a logical extension, but I had no idea she was going to Sacrifice those Inquisitors."

"There's nothing you can do for those Inquisitors," I said, "but you can still help me save the prisoners."

"What do you want me to do?"

"I'm gathering townsfolk to confront the remaining Inquisitors. Follow behind us, and if the Inquisitors give us trouble, put them to sleep."

"How many?"

"As many as give us trouble."

"I'm almost tapped out," he said. "When it comes to this sort of thing, I'm no Joanna, and I already spent much of the morning starting fires. I could do two, maybe three at the outside."

I started up the ladder. "We'll have to make it work."

A long pause. "We'd stand a better chance if we had Joanna helping us."

"That's right," I said, inching my way across the beam. "A better chance of killing more people—hasn't she already caused enough damage?"

Ramos stiffened. "She wasn't the one who started this."

"It's not about that," I said. "She's too unpredictable— there's no telling who she's going to Sacrifice next."

Ramos refused to concede the point. "There's a fair chance I can manage her temper, but no chance at all that I can match her skills."

A glance confirmed the commons now held half the prisoners it had held that morning. As I watched, an Inquisitor ushered two more into the shed.

"We're running out of time," I said.

"I'm not asking for my sake. I'm thinking of Ilse and the boys. How do you suppose they'd fare without me? Haven't they suffered enough?"

"I'm sorry—it's too risky."

"It's too risky not to," he countered. "Don't you see? Rescuing the prisoners has been her plan all along. She'll want to help. Look, I'll make sure she behaves. If she tries anything you don't approve—anything at all—I'll Sleep her myself."

"If you two would prefer to use your own plan to save the prisoners, be my guest, but you'd better be quick about it, or there might not be anyone left to save."

"We can't. Not without the dress."

"Why do we always keep coming back to that?"

"Because I fear Joanna may still be in it."

"Ah, so that's why it's so bloody precious."

"Please," he said. "Get me the dress. I'll do as you ask."

Another look out the window confirmed there were still not enough townsfolk to make an impressive display. "All right," I said, "but if we find she's there, she stays there until after we rescue the prisoners, understood?"

I hopped down off the beam. "This way."

It was a risk, but his help might mean the difference between success and failure—better for him to be grateful rather than grudging about it.

I pulled the crate from behind the vine with a flourish and lifted off the lid to reveal Joanna's gown. "Here you go," I said.

He balanced the open crate in one hand and fished a lady's compact from his pocket with the other. "Just a second," he said, working the catch with his thumb.

"Hold it right there," I said. "What's that supposed to be?"

He ignored my question and gazed into the mirror. After a moment his brow furrowed. He snapped the compact closed and returned it to his pocket. "She's not here," he said. "They found it, didn't they?"

"I don't know what you're talking about."

"Never mind. A deal's a deal. You're certain you want to attempt this without Joanna?"

"Unless she's waiting around the corner," I said, "I don't think we have a choice."

When Buck spotted me, he was so eager to report he nearly bowled me over. The move so startled Ramos that I had to shake my head to interrupt his mnemonics.

"There ya are," Buck said. "Once I told folks His Lordship needed help clearing the commons, it got 'em all riled. Some of the older folk were none too happy, but most of the rest of them were of a mind that it was 'bout time somethin' got done. They're comin' out to help."

"How many?" I asked. "More than twenty?"

Buck blushed beet red. "I don't rightly know," he said. "The boys are still at it, so there'll be more than there are, mark my word."

As it turned out, there were now over thirty villagers milling about near the barn—more than enough to attract the Inquisitors' attention.

"Buck, go tell your friends I'll be there shortly," I said. "I'm going to try something. Ramos, you stay back out of sight, but keep an eye out for trouble."

Ramos nodded, and Buck lumbered off toward the gathering crowd. I strode toward the two Inquisitors who were eyeing the crowd from the wall, my heart thrumming. As I got closer, I recognized one of the Inquisitors—he'd been at the dinner in the manor. I crossed my fingers that he remembered.

"There's an emergency up at the manor," I said. "The Inquisitor General wants all Inquisitors to report to him there right away."

"What kind of emergency?" the Inquisitor asked.

"He didn't specify."

"What about the prisoners? Shouldn't at least a few of us stay? It's looking like these villagers may be up to no good."

"Let me put it this way," I said. "If he wasn't truly desperate, do you really think he would have sent me to deliver the message?"

The Inquisitor glanced back into the commons, and then turned to his partner. "You go ahead," he said. "After I tell the others, I'll be right behind you."

He sped off along the wall, while his partner hopped down next to me and held out his crossbow. "Here, take this," he said. "Keep an eye on the compound. If either the villagers or the prisoners get out of line, report it right away. Don't use this unless it's life or death—you'll only get one shot."

I accepted with a solemn nod. He patted me on the shoulder and jogged off toward the manor. Before he was even out of sight, I was already sprinting toward Buck. There was no time to lose. In less than twenty minutes, Roman would know the prisoners had been left unguarded.

CHAPTER TWENTY-NINE

TURNABOUT IS FOUL PLAY

The original plan had been to escort the prisoners outside the village to give them a chance to recover from the drug. Once Roman learned about the escape, however, even his diminished forces could make short work of any prisoners roaming out in the open like that. I had little choice but to rely on Buck's expertise.

"We need a place to hide the prisoners," I said. "Someplace nearby, but where they won't be found for at least several hours. Any suggestions?"

Buck scratched a muttonchop with a sausage-sized finger. "What about yonder barn?"

"Too close," I said, "and too dangerous. If the Inquisitors discover the prisoners there, they'd be trapped."

"There's the weald to the north of the village" he said.

"How far?"

"A good long walk."

"Not close enough."

His eyes lit with sudden inspiration. "How about the catacombs?"

"Where are they?"

"The other side of town."

"Will they hold everyone?"

"And then some."

"It'll have to do," I said.

"What's our next move?"

"The Inquisitors should be gone by now. I'll go first. As we come across prisoners, have your friends lead them to these catacombs of yours. If all goes well, we can try to smuggle them out to the weald after nightfall. Got it?"

As Buck relayed the message, I strode over to the cart that blocked the entrance to the commons and gave it a shove. It didn't budge. I was still struggling with it when Buck arrived.

"Here," he said, "let me get that for ya."

With one hand, he lifted the front of the cart and moved it aside.

I nodded my thanks and pushed on through the gate. Of the original hundred, only twenty prisoners still wandered the walled pasture, all of them teens or children. Not a single Inquisitor remained in sight. I pressed on toward the shed, praying we'd reach the others in time. On the way we found Sly seated in a small patch of tall grass, staring. I pulled him to his feet, brushed him off, and delivered him to the care of one of the village women. I managed it all without receiving so much as a glimmer of recognition. Haggard and expressionless, he was almost unrecognizable, but I had no doubt it was Sly—he was wearing my old clothes.

Crossbow at the ready, I approached the shed. Situated up against the wall of the commons, it was a low dirt-floored building with a wide sliding door. The structure sported five windows, but they were small and set high. Standing to one side, I motioned to Buck to open the door.

The pungent smell of pine hit me like a wall. Although

I could hear movement in the darkness, my eye was drawn to tiny glowing lights atop a small table—fireplace embers stacked within a glass chimney taken from a lantern and set on a silver tray. As I watched, a string dangling from the rafters above the tray moved, losing slack. For a moment I was puzzled, but then I placed the smell—it was gin.

"Buck, stop!" Tossing aside the crossbow, I dove for the door, trying to keep it from sliding open any farther, but I was too late—the string pulled taut. The chimney catapulted off the tray and crashed to the floor. Scattered coals ignited the vapors. The whole building sighed as an inferno erupted within it, its tiny windows bursting outward in sprays of vicious shards. I rolled out of the doorway as flames washed over me. Buck slammed the door closed again, tucked me under one arm, and ran.

I struggled to get free. "Put me down!" I cried, "Chef's in there!"

I doubt he even heard me. The wails of trapped prisoners pursued us down the hill, back out the gate and for quite some distance after that. He didn't stop until we'd reached the inn. He was shaking and covered in sweat.

"Demon's work, and no mistake," he said, gasping for breath. "I ain't never seen a fire take off like that."

A chilling thought occurred to me. What if Father Graves had lied to me about my parents? What if they had been in the shed with the others?

I'd have to force myself to stop thinking like that, or I'd fall apart. There was no evidence he'd ever misled me, so I decided simply to trust him until there was. Still, it was all I could do to not be sick.

"Yeah, it was demons, all right," I said. "Where's Ramos?"

"The stranger with the box? I dunno."

"What about Sly?"

"If you mean your prisoner friend, he should be at the catacombs soon."

I admit I wasn't just concerned about Sly—I was overwhelmed by the need to feel like I'd done at least something right. "Can you take me to him?"

"Sure thing. You able to walk?"

I hadn't even considered that. My right hand was tender and turning red, and my hair and clothes were singed, but that was about the extent of the damage. If Buck hadn't acted so quickly, it could have been much worse.

The walk was longer than I'd expected. Buck could see I was suffering and tried his best to distract me. How I envied him. He could move on unaffected by what he'd witnessed, secure in the belief that a demon was to blame for it all. I knew better. Sure, we'd been set up, but I could have chosen not to get involved. If I hadn't done anything, maybe Roman would have changed his mind. Maybe Armand would have found a way to rescue the prisoners.

I could almost feel Chef cuffing me on the back of the head, telling me well-mannered people mind their own business. Never again would I see him dance at the prospect of a working stove, or taste his amazing porridge. I could now understand how Roman must have felt standing over his fallen son, knowing, at least in part, his own actions were to blame. But I was not Roman, and I vowed then and there I never would be.

We headed steadily downhill, curving around until we found ourselves approaching the manor. I hadn't before appreciated that its north and east sides overlooked steep cliffs. To some extent that may have been the natural lay of the land, but to me, the area had more the feel of an ancient quarry. At last we reached a gate in a shoulder-high wooden fence that spanned the road before us. A warped section of plank nailed to the gate read "Keep Out," the faded letters barely visible. Undeterred, Buck lifted the latch and held the gate open for me.

He caught my look. "My family's land," he said, puffing out his chest, "by grant of His Lordship."

"I can think of no one more deserving."

"We Cahills have been guarding His Lordship's wolves for generations, though I s'pose you know all about that, bein' that you're his squire and all."

I didn't, of course, but seeing as how I was stepping onto their land, I had a sudden urge to find out. "How many generations has it been, now?"

Buck sputtered. "A whole lot," he said, "and that's a fact."

"I suppose there's quite a lot to learn."

"You got that right, though the ban makes it a whole lot easier than it would be."

I chose my words carefully. "How did you manage before the ban?"

"It's always been, leastwise as long as we've been keepin' wolves. Still, folks didn't always pay it enough mind, 'specially when their animals were at stake and it was just a fine. Gramps says folks started takin' it serious once His Lordship upped the sentence to death for hurtin' a wolf. It got better still once we started usin' the commons to keep the livestock safe."

"No wonder people were upset when the Church took over the commons."

Buck nodded. "Folk don't like standin' by helpless when their animals are gettin' dragged off into the night. They can try to scare 'em off of course, but the wolves round here don't scare so easy as once they did. Nowadays, if you're not careful, ya might find it's you what's gettin' dragged off."

The road beyond the gate leveled out for a bit. We passed an ancient yew, its vast limbs splayed out in unlikely directions.

Past the yew stood a large old house, presumably cobbled together from quarried stone. The dark thatch of its roof stood out in stark contrast against the creamy hues of the cliff behind it. A wooden porch had been slapped across the front of the building as an afterthought. The old floorboards creaked in time with a rocking chair inhabited by a tiny woman in brown homespun. Her knitting needles clacked in counterpoint to the steady rhythm of the chair.

"Buckley Hobart Cahill, I got a bone to pick with you," she said. "I hear tell it was your bright idea to toss those poor li'l babes into those musty old catacombs. I swear, if that head of yours didn't have a mouth for eatin', it'd be no use to you at all."

It didn't seem fair to let Buck take the blame. "I'm afraid that was my doing," I said.

The needles stopped as she pulled her eyes off the knitting to appraise me.

"Flora Sue," Buck said, "this here's Mr. Flinch. He's helpin' His Lordship with a plan to get the Church out of our commons."

"I trust this plan has more sense to it than the one for storing babes in caves?"

I stuttered a little at that, but Buck rescued me. "We was right in the middle of it when a meddlesome demon sticks his nose in and burns down the old farrier's shed. I ain't never seen the likes of it."

"Don't you go gettin' yourself caught up with no demons," Flora Sue said. "We got more than enough to worry 'bout round here without that yet."

"She has a point," I said. "Maybe we should spend some time coming up with a better place to hide the prisoners."

"We're one step ahead of you," Flora Sue said. "We already divvied up the young'uns among us womenfolk to care for. Once we were done with that, there was only a few left we thought was old enough they could go to the catacombs. Gwen's got her eye on 'em for the moment, but I wouldn't wanna go and keep her waitin'."

Buck climbed the steps and planted a kiss on the side of Flora Sue's cheek. "I don't know how I ever got so lucky as to get hitched up with you, Flora Sue Cahill. You're my own personal miracle, you are."

Flora Sue flushed a little. "Buck, you big lummox, not in front of the company. As long as we're talkin' miracles, for once, how's about you be back from your gallivantin' in time for dinner?"

"Cross my heart," he said.

"It was nice to meet ya, Mr. Flinch," she said.

I bowed. "It was my pleasure."

After the house, the road sloped downward. There was no longer any doubt we were in a quarry. The rock dropped off in uneven steps, many taller than I was—some taller even than Buck. We descended first one ramp and then the next as we wound our way deeper. Sleek swallows rolled and swooped about the cliff face beneath the manor. Here and there, deep shadows hinted at openings that might be more than mere depressions.

I pointed them out to Buck. "So, are those the catacombs?"

"Nah, we're not there yet," Buck said. "Most of them there holes are just small caves cut out of the rock that don't go nowhere."

"But the catacombs do, I take it?"

"They sure do. Ain't no one alive, exceptin' maybe His Lordship, who's been through 'em all. Gramps says when he was a lad, some of his cousins went in explorin' and never came out again. More'n likely got lost and couldn't find their way back. Lookin' back on it, I s'pose it wasn't the best idea I coulda come up with."

"Well I think it was a pretty good idea," I said. "At the time we were expecting lots more prisoners, and we had no idea they'd be mostly children."

"That's kind of ya to say," he said. "I'm guessin' I wouldn't have thought of it at all if I hadn't seen His Lordship doin' the same thing. I s'pose I should have thought it through. Just cuz His Lordship does it, doesn't mean I ought to."

"Wait, are you saying Lord Histlewick is also hiding prisoners in these catacombs?"

"It's all right," he said. "We ain't usin' the same branch."

"How many of these prisoners were there? Were they also taken from the commons?"

"Just a man and a woman. He brought 'em through here in the wee hours just the other night. I expect he musta brought 'em through the swamp, cuz the carriage was covered in that moss stuff."

"Once we've checked on Sly, do you think you could show me this other branch?"

"Sure thing," he said. "You thinkin' there might be cause to favor one branch over the other?"

"Buck, my friend, I think that's very likely indeed."

CHAPTER THIRTY

UNDERGROUND GUARDIAN

The path was longer than it looked. Since the ramps were carved in the face of each step, any downward progress could be made only at right angles to the direct route. The farther down we went, the higher the manor-topped cliff loomed. Buck took it in stride, whistling a tune I'm sure I would have recognized if he hadn't been utterly tone-deaf.

"Almost there," he said.

"That's the third time you've said that."

"Yeah, but this time I mean it."

"You didn't before?"

He flashed me a sheepish grin. "No offense, but you was lookin' like you could use a little pick-me-up."

A long, low howl reverberated up the canyon. Others joined in, creating a frenzied fugue of lupine voices that chilled me to my marrow. I cast about in a frantic search for shelter, visions of Bessie's mutilated carcass dancing before my eyes, but there was nothing. Stranded in a rocky maze of planes and angles, we stood helpless. Exposed.

After several moments of sheer panic, it finally dawned on me that Buck was watching me, his eyes bright with amusement.

I could feel my cheeks flush. "I suppose you're going to tell me I'm overreacting."

"I don't rightly know, but if you're worryin' 'bout them wolves gettin' to you, you hadn't oughta be. They lair below the last step, and the last step ain't got a ramp—it's just a big old wall. They couldn't make it up here if they wanted to."

I struggled for a way to save face. "But something's got to be stirring them up, right? What if I'm worried about that?"

Buck grinned. "Nothin' much gets past you either, does it?"

I was mortified. In retrospect I couldn't believe how callous I'd been at our first meeting. "Buck, I—"

He interrupted me, pointing. "There it comes now."

At the very bottom of the man-made canyon a familiar carriage drew into sight from around the cliff. One by one the wolves showed themselves. Three or four cavorted at the base of the cliff, looking for all the world like expectant puppies awaiting the arrival of their master. I threw myself down at the edge of our current step to get out of sight and motioned for Buck to do the same.

"That's Lord Histlewick's carriage," I said. "What's he doing here?"

"I dunno," he said. "Could be His Lordship's already brought down a boar or some such, and fancied makin' a wolf treat out of it."

The carriage pulled up in the midst of the wolves, who circled it excitedly. Presently, Histlewick himself climbed out. He spent several minutes patting up the wolves until at last they lost interest and wandered out of the sun to lie down. Only then did he return to the carriage. He held out his hand to assist a second passenger, whom I might have suspected was just another one of his servants, if it hadn't been for the hat—a hat with red and black plumes. *My* hat.

"Looks like he's found himself another prisoner," Buck said.

"Prisoner? Are you sure?"

"Well, it don't look like he's fixin' to feed him to the wolves, but I s'pose ya never know."

"Are you saying that's a possibility?"

"I ain't never seen him do it, but that don't mean he never would."

"He wouldn't dare. She's the Ordinal's daughter."

"I ain't never asked a pig 'bout its next of kin before I ate it."

Had that been Histlewick's intention, there was precious little we could have done about it from where we stood. Fortunately, it wasn't. As Histlewick shepherded Elyria into a passage at the base of the cliff, it occurred to me that perhaps Buck had just been trying to get a rise out of me. Yet, when I looked him in the eye, I saw not the slightest trace of guile.

"That's where he took the others, too," Buck said.

"Why there, as opposed to the catacombs we're headed for?"

"The wolves."

"Are they that aggressive?"

"It's not just that. It's death to hurt a wolf. A guy'd have to be queer in the head to go down there and risk a death sentence just for the honor of defendin' himself."

"There must be exceptions. What if you didn't know?"

Buck shook his head. "His Lordship is deadly serious 'bout his wolves."

I shuddered as I recalled how we'd lost Bessie. What if I'd shot that wolf? For a change, I felt fortunate for my lack of skill with a crossbow.

Buck pointed to a fold in the rock on the next step down. "In case you was wonderin', that's where we're headed."

The entrance to the catacombs was small enough that Buck had to turn sideways to slip inside, but it opened out to a sizable cavern. A high irregular ceiling testified to the cave's natural origin, but the floor was smooth and clear of debris. Red and white gingham curtains cloaked cubbies in the walls, and I could make out the bottoms of crates and barrels beneath the hems. To one side, several rows of coat racks had been affixed to the white chalk wall, though they held nothing at the moment except a pair of lanterns that supplemented what little sunlight filtered through the cave mouth. Wool blankets spread across the floor served as makeshift pallets for the three prisoners, Sly among them. Each was bound about the waist by a length of coarse hemp tied to a heavy barrel.

Atop the barrel, a woman in a simple dress fashioned from the same checkered fabric as the curtains sat tatting lace. Her dark hair, which she wore mounded in precise layers on the crown of her head, conspired with half-moon spectacles to provide the illusion of height and an air of sophistication completely at odds with the picnic pattern of her clothing.

Buck bounded forward. "Miss Gwen!" His bear hug lifted her clean off the barrel.

"Buckley Cahill, you put me down this instant."

Once her feet were safely on the floor, she laid her lace across the barrel and inspected it for damage.

"I can't thank you enough for helpin' out like this," Buck said, looking a little awkward from the reproof.

She smoothed her dress and patted her hair before replying.

"Now then," she said. "This has all happened just a little too quickly for me to absorb properly. Why don't we sit down like civilized people while you tell me how you arrived at the conclusion that drafty catacombs are a suitable place for harboring small children."

Buck turned to me, pride evident in his eyes. "That's Miss Gwen," he said. "She's got honest-to-goodness book learnin'."

"On second thought," Gwen said, extending a hand, "perhaps it would be best to begin with proper introductions. I am Miss Gwendolyn Hutchins. And you are?"

Buck jumped in. "This here's His Lordship's new squire, Mr. Flinch. He's helpin' His Lordship clear out the commons, but it's all sorta hush-hush, and that's why we needed someplace those Church folks would have a hard time findin', even if it was a little drafty."

I shook the lady's hand and smiled. Then I knelt for a closer look at Sly. He lay on his side, his staring interrupted only by an occasional long slow blink. "Are they hurt?"

"Not obviously," she said, "but they still seem to be suffering the effects of whatever drug they were administered. I had to restrain them to keep them from wandering off. You're free to take the restraints with you if you need them."

"That's very kind," I said, "but once they recover, we won't need them."

"Once they recover? You aren't planning for that to occur here, are you?"

"I don't think we have much choice."

"You speak as if staying were an option. I assure you it is not. These catacombs are closed to outsiders. Buck overstepped when he offered them. I don't know what he was thinking."

"Well, he is His Lordship's squire," Buck said.

"That may be," Gwen said, waving her hand at the prisoners, "but they are not. I can't allow them to awaken here."

"I'm sure Buck meant no disrespect," I said.

"I'll deal with Buck presently. In the meantime, I need for you to take these people elsewhere."

"Forgive me," I said, "but I don't see how that's possible while they're like this. In any event, if you're really worried about keeping these caves a secret, we shouldn't move anyone before it's good and dark outside. If we're spotted, the Church will swarm the place with Inquisitors looking for other escaped prisoners."

Gwen blanched. "All right, nightfall then—but not a moment longer."

I nodded, eager to seem agreeable. "And while we wait, I was hoping I could impose on your generous nature for one more small favor. Buck said he'd show me the other branch of these caves, but for that we need someone to stay behind to keep an eye on these three."

Gwen's shock was palpable. "Buck said what?"

"Where has the time got to?" Buck asked, backing toward the cave mouth. "I'd love to help, I surely would, but I promised the missus I'd be home for dinner, and I'm thinkin' I might already be late."

"Stop right there, mister."

"But Flora Sue—"

"Flora Sue is the least of your worries right now. You march yourself right back in here and take a seat. First, you're going to explain to me what led you to concoct this ridiculous plan of yours, and then we're going to have a little chat about responsibility and the importance of following rules."

Sulking, Buck ambled over and sat cross-legged on the blanket next to Sly. "We just needed to clear out the commons," he said, "and it ain't my plan anyways, it's His Lordship's."

"I suppose it was his plan to show Mr. Flinch His Lordship's branch of the catacombs as well?"

"That wasn't my doing," Buck said. "His Lordship already showed him the entrance. I was just gonna take him down for a closer look."

Gwen arched an eyebrow at me. "So, Mr. Flinch. Perhaps you'd care to explain how Lord Histlewick came to place such faith in an outsider. If it's true, such behavior on His Lordship's part would be unprecedented in all the time we've been keeping track."

"I don't think he intended to show me," I said. "On the way down here, Buck and I happened to see him hustle a young lady out of his carriage and into a tunnel down by the wolves. I was more than a little concerned, since she did not appear to be a willing participant."

Gwen's eyes narrowed. "A young lady, you say? Are you certain?"

"I am," I said. "The young lady and I are friendly acquaintances."

"Who is this young lady?"

"She's an Ordinal's daughter, and he dotes on her. Once he discovers she's missing, he'll take this whole town apart until he finds her. Stone by stone, if necessary."

"What makes you think she's missing?"

"If the objective had been a poignant reunion with her father, they wouldn't have had to slink around back, would they?"

I paused to let Gwen digest that point. Her pensive scowl told me something about it wasn't sitting well.

"Buck," she said at last. "Go outside and check on that carriage. Oh, and try to stay out of sight, won't you?"

Buck jumped to his feet. "Sure thing."

"Mr. Flinch, could I trouble you to keep an eye on these three while I run a quick errand?"

"Certainly."

I'd expected her to follow Buck outside, but to my surprise, she grabbed a lantern and headed deeper into the cave. After several minutes, the faint squeal of ancient hinges echoed through the chamber.

Buck rushed back in. "His Lordship's leavin,'" he said. "Where's Miss Gwen?"

"She'll be right back. Did the young lady leave with him?"

"Nope," he said. "He came out alone."

The hinges groaned again, followed by a deep metallic thud that I could feel in the bottoms of my feet. Gwen appeared then, carrying a ring of large keys.

"His Lordship left," Buck said.

"So I heard."

"What are the keys for?" he asked.

"Knowledge," she said. "When one's way of life is threatened, I find it prudent to avoid making decisions in a vacuum. Mr. Flinch, are you still interested in a tour of His Lordship's catacombs?"

"I sure am."

"Good. I think it is high time this lady friend of yours and I had a little chat."

CHAPTER THIRTY-ONE

CREATURE OF HABIT

Gwen sent Buck back up the hill to get Flora Sue. If all three of us were going, someone had to keep an eye on Sly and the others. While he was gone, I danced around the topic of the keys, but Gwen was not inclined to share. Buck and Flora Sue returned with extra lanterns, oil, water, and some hardtack. Flora Sue said little, but I could tell by the set of her jaw that she did not approve of her husband's latest venture.

The moment she was satisfied everything was in order, Gwen set off, cutting short Buck and Flora Sue's lingering farewell embrace. The catacombs were a curious mix of natural cavern and carved tunnel. The carved tunnels were easy to spot. In cross section they resembled gothic windows, flat at the floor, with vertical walls that curved gently to a point in the middle of the ceiling. As we progressed, we passed a multitude of side passages, as well as the occasional iron-bound door. All the doors and many of the passages were chiseled with inscriptions in a language I didn't recognize. Early on, Gwen passed the inscriptions by without a second glance, but the farther we descended, the more she studied them, and the more anxious I became. The stifling silence of the catacombs was getting to me, and if I were to lose track of Gwen, I could end up wandering for days and never make it back to the surface.

At one point I pushed on a door to see if I could get a glimpse of what lay beyond. Cool dry tunnels like these would be perfect for aging wine, and I was curious to know whether the locals had come to the same conclusion. The door didn't budge, and the attempt earned me a sharp rebuke from our guide. I did not risk displeasing her a second time.

At long last we arrived at a passage barred by a cast-iron gate. Gwen picked through the keys on her ring until she found one that suited her.

"This gate marks the entrance to passages Lord Histlewick claims as his exclusive domain. Knowing that, Mr. Flinch, are you still prepared to proceed?"

"I will if you will."

It was simple fact. Finding my way back alone wasn't an option, and if Histlewick caught us, I figured there was at least a chance I could use my status as squire to exculpate me. Regardless, I could hardly turn my back on my parents now.

"So be it." She inserted the key into the lock, and the gate creaked open. Once we were all through, she locked it behind us.

The passages on this side of the gate lacked inscriptions, and Gwen began referring to some sort of map. Of the three of us, the trek was toughest on Buck, who was forced to stoop most of the way, and yet he whistled merrily through it all. While I would normally have found such artless attempts to carry a tune annoying, in this context they inspired me.

Beyond the gate, our progress slowed considerably—either the map was spotty on important details, or Gwen's map skills left much to be desired. We wormed our way steadily upward, slogging through slanted tunnels and trudging up treacherous stairways. It wasn't long before I began looking forward to each of Gwen's frequent pauses as an opportunity to catch my breath. At last we entered a stretch of corridors with flat ceilings and fresher air. These passages felt familiar, and yet I was still befuddled by the maze.

"How, in all these tunnels, are you going to find where she's being held?" I asked.

Gwen flashed a knowing smile. "Men are creatures of habit," she said. "To answer that question, one need only ask where he's kept such prisoners in the past."

Then it dawned on me. "You're talking about the library room?"

She looked up from her map in surprise. "You've seen it?"

"Once, briefly, but it looked like it hadn't been used by anyone for ages."

"I expect it hasn't."

"Then how could it have become a habit?"

"Habit is a beast of many faces. There are those things you repeat so often you no longer think about them, and there are those that take so much thought the first time that when faced with a similar situation, you don't want to repeat the process."

"So he's done this before?"

"Once," she said. "To the lady for whom he designed the room."

"That makes no sense. Why go to such lengths to decorate a prison cell?"

"Why put honey on a bear trap?"

"You don't think the room's being tucked away underground like this would be a clue that something was amiss?"

"The efficacy of the bait depends on the nature of the prey. To a young lady seeking asylum, a well-appointed subterranean apartment might seem like just the thing."

Or to a young lady fleeing her father's wrath, I thought. "What happened to this prisoner after he captured her? Did he turn her over to the Inquisition for a reward?"

"Goodness, no," Gwen said. "It would have taken far more than His Lordship's ill-conceived prison room to subdue this prisoner. He was lucky to escape with his life."

"Really? Who was she?"

"The accounts refer to her only as the Mistress. His Lordship learned too late she was not someone to be trifled with."

"So you never met her?"

Gwen chuckled. "Met her? Heavens no. This all happened long before I was born. Ah, here we are."

Indeed, the prison-room door now stood before us. Buck held up his lantern for a closer look. Meanwhile, Gwen rummaged through her keys until she found a match for the lock, but as she went for the keyhole, I grabbed her hand. When she raised a quizzical eyebrow, I tried knocking instead.

The answering voice was unmistakably Elyria's. "Who is it?"

"It's me, Flinch," I said. "Open up."

"Flinch?" she cried. "Go away, you'll spoil everything."

"Is anyone else in there with you?"

"Of course not, now go away."

"Just open the door and let me see that you're all right," I said. "After that, if you still want me to go, I will."

"Promise?"

"Cross my heart."

"Oh, all right."

The door rattled a little. Then it rattled a little more violently.

"It's stuck," she said.

"Did you have any problems getting in before?"

"No," she called back. "It was fine on the way in."

"Let me try from this side."

The door still didn't budge.

"Nope. No luck."

"That bastard! He locked me in."

Gwen eyed me with new appreciation. "Well played, Mr. Flinch. It seems barging in could have been a bit awkward. Shall I try the key now?"

I nodded, and she inserted it into the lock. Though she struggled with it for some time, it simply would not turn.

"Wrong key?" I asked.

Gwen shook her head. "He must have changed the lock."

The door shook again. "Mr. Flinch, are you there?"

"I'm here."

"You've got to help me."

"I'm working on it." I turned to Buck. "What about the hinge pins?"

He held up the lantern to the door. "Flat at both ends," he said. "We'd need to cut through 'em, and for that, we'd be needin' tools."

"And the door itself?"

"If I had a sledge, maybe. That's one thick door."

I wracked my brain for alternatives, but nothing came. Yet, I knew there had to be a way in, because someone, most likely Darron, had retrieved Histlewick's twin from the armoire inside this very room while the rest of us were in the swamp trading hostages.

"Did Histlewick say when he'd be back?" I asked.

"He didn't," Elyria said, "but unless he intends to starve me, it won't be long."

"Why did you let him bring you here in the first place?"

"He offered to help me. Fool that I was, I believed him."

"Help you? In what way?"

"This morning Father threatened to betroth me to Barclay whether I would have it or no. When Histlewick's hunt made it outside the walls, I tried to flee, but Lord Histlewick overtook me. When he heard my plight, he offered to hide me until the danger had passed. He can be very persuasive when he puts his mind to it. Besides, the idea of facing that swamp alone..."

"I understand," I said.

Gwen stepped up to the door. "His Lordship was at all times a gentleman?"

"Who's that?" Elyria asked.

"Her name's Gwen," I said. "She's helping."

"He was, Gwen," Elyria said, "at least until he locked the door without telling me."

"Thank goodness," Gwen said, stepping back once more. "Then his secret's still safe. Still, he's playing a dangerous game. I don't like it one bit."

"What secret?" I asked.

Gwen looked at me askance. "The same secret he shares with all his squires before taking them on."

"Oh, of course," I said, "that secret. Sorry, I wasn't thinking."

"I think we've done all we can for the moment," Gwen said. "We should head back. We don't want to be found here."

"Wait a minute," I said. "We can't just leave her here."

"I don't like it any better than you do," Gwen said. "It's nothing short of lunacy for His Lordship to tempt fate like this, but right now, I don't see any alternative, and getting caught would only make things worse."

"Elyria," I called out. "We don't have a way through the door right now. We're going to get help."

"Please hurry," Elyria called back. "And Flinch?"

"Yes?"

"Whatever you do, don't tell my father."

CHAPTER THIRTY-TWO

TRIALS AND TRIBULATIONS

On the return trip, I argued we should search for Histlewick's other prisoners. I even tried begging, but Gwen steadfastly refused, adamant that roaming the caverns was too dangerous. After a while, I fell silent as I pondered ways to convince her to help me. Failing that, I even considered pilfering Gwen's keys, but without a guide, I'd have been hopelessly lost. Still, if I couldn't find a way to sway Gwen, it's not like I had a choice.

By the time we made it back, night had fallen and the cavern was awash with the warm glow of lanterns. Flora Sue nearly bowled me over in her haste to welcome back her husband. Gwen and I had the decency to look away, but I still saw enough to make my ears burn.

"Careful there, mate. Get any closer to that and you'll have to brag your first time was by proxy."

"Sly! You're awake."

"I'm told I have you to thank for that."

"I had a lot of help," I said.

"What have you done with Chef and Lisbet? You know they were taken too, right?"

"Lisbet's with Armand."

"And Chef?"

I started tearing up and had to turn away.

Sly's voice caught. "Oh no...."

"They'd rounded all the adults into the shed," I said. "Trapped it to go up in flames when the door opened. I didn't know...couldn't have known."

"And they had a demon helpin' 'em," Buck said. "No lie."

"All right gentlemen," Gwen said, "enough chit-chat. It's well past sundown, and it's been a trying day. Time to move out."

"Move out where?" Sly asked.

"I can take 'em out to the weald," Buck said.

"Is there a cabin there or someplace they could stay until the situation calms down?"

Buck scratched his belly as he considered. "Not as far as I know," he said. "Maybe some blinds or tree stands."

"That's not going to work. Isn't there anyone who lives out that way who would be willing to take them in for a day or two?"

Buck shook his head. "Most folks wanna live inside the walls. Since we got forced outta the commons, some folks go out to tend the livestock at night, but they use tents, and they stay closer to home than the weald."

"I suppose a cozy room in a quaint inn is out of the question?" Sly asked.

The other two prisoners, a boy and a girl in their early teens, wandered over to flank Sly. Still groggy from the drug, they stood wide-eyed and bewildered as we discussed their fate. Their forlorn faces finally got the better of Buck.

"If it's only a day or so, maybe they could stay with me and Flora Sue," he said.

Flora Sue was clearly less than enthusiastic. "Well, I s'pose they could stay in the root cellar. It might take a while for someone to find 'em there."

"Perfect," Gwen said. "You folks go on ahead. I'll tidy up here and follow along in a bit."

We shuffled single-file out of the cave. Buck and Flora Sue led the way, and I brought up the rear, ready to assist if anyone stumbled. I probably wasn't any better off than the others, preoccupied as I was with trying to puzzle out how I could help Elyria without involving her father. If they knew, Roman or Father Graves were almost certain to tell him. Was there any way I could convince them not to? A part of me was grateful for the distraction—it kept me from dwelling on Chef.

I held my breath when we came to the first ramp, but Sly and the others climbed without difficulty. I yawned as we approached the second ramp. By this point I was so tired that even the prospect of sharing a bed with parsnips and rutabagas was palatable. Indeed, I must have been nodding off, because when our little column of refugees stopped abruptly, I collided with Sly. He steadied me and pointed upward.

A dark figure stood at the top of the next ramp, the glow from his lantern casting sinister shadows across his face. He smiled then, but it only made him seem more malevolent. It took me a moment to realize it was Prentiss.

"Mr. Flinch, I'm so relieved to find you here," he said. "After all, it's always such a disappointment when a villain escapes justice." He beckoned, and four Inquisitors peered over the rocky edge. As one, they aimed their crossbows directly at me.

They shackled our hands and feet and chained us to each

other in a line. Once Prentiss was satisfied we were helpless, he approached me and held out his hand.

"I'll take that pocket watch of yours," he said. "I do hope you understand—it's against policy to allow prisoners to carry Profanities."

"I don't have it."

"Surely you don't expect me to take your word for that."

I didn't grace him with a reply.

"Search him," he said.

The searching Inquisitor barely glanced at either Elyria's ring or the monocle. "It's not on him," he said.

"Search the others, then."

Of course, they came up empty.

"All right, you've had your fun, Mr. Flinch. Where is it?"

"Why should you care as long as I'm not carrying it?" I asked. "Or does your interest in the device extend beyond the usual policy concerns?"

I held his gaze for a long time, but his cool, sardonic smile never wavered. At last, he turned and stalked up the ramp. "Take them to the manor," he said, without looking back. "If they attempt to escape, execute them."

Once we were close to the manor's front gate, they separated me from the others and pulled a mask over my face. When they tugged my chain, I stumbled forward into the courtyard. The challenge of breathing kept me from focusing on where we went from there. Nevertheless, when the mask finally came off, it was clear from the room's décor that I was somewhere in the Marstow wing—my shackles were now linked to the solid timbers of a candy-striped canopy bed. Smirking just out of reach, Prentiss directed the Inquisitors to wait for him outside.

"Here's how this is going to work," he said. "You're going to tell me where you hid the watch, and I'll testify that you acted alone when you killed all those poor defenseless people."

"You're bluffing," I said. "Roman isn't going to stand idly by while I take the blame for your crimes."

"Perhaps you're right. Perhaps he'll even come clean about his own complicity in the deed. After all, what self-respecting politician wouldn't jump at the chance to confess to genocide? Why settle for a front-row seat at the gallows when you can engage the hangman's services directly?"

"He's the Inquisitor General. He's going to have considerably more options than those."

Prentiss licked his lips. "That depends on how I testify, doesn't it?"

"It's your word against mine."

"And Barclay's," Prentiss said. "You remember him, don't you? He's the man responsible for capturing Marshall Hockery, the leader of those pesky heretics. In the eyes of many, that makes him a hero."

"If that's true, he's got way too much going for him to risk it all perjuring himself over a Profanity."

"A Profanity that blocks Sacrifices?" Prentiss asked. "For someone who spends considerable time undercover among heretics, could there be a more potent incentive?"

For that, I had no answer.

Prentiss reached for the door and paused. "Clearly you need some time to think this over. I'll check back in the morning." He took the lantern with him.

I can't say I slept much, but at least the bed was soft.

He was back with the dawn. "Your decision, Mr. Flinch? How will your friend Buck fare in today's proceedings?"

Somewhere in all that tossing and turning, I'd realized my answer wasn't going to make the slightest bit of difference. There was no greater threat to Prentiss's plans than the truth, and since, like me, Buck had been present when the fire started, there was no way Prentiss could allow him to live.

"I've decided to spare your conscience," I said. "Extortion rarely paves the straightest path to truth."

"Suit yourself," he said. "The watch can't have gone far."

I took some small satisfaction in knowing my decision mattered more to him than he let on—he slammed the door on the way out.

Several hours later, the Inquisitors came for me. When the mask came off, I found myself in a cavernous room with vaulted ceilings. The dank smell of mold and wood rot made it difficult to breathe. I was chained to a heavy table—one of several scattered about the space. Once a servant's workroom, it now held racks of dust-laden wine bottles. Someone had kindled a fire in the fireplace, and two Inquisitors basked in its glow, shuffling papers and murmuring to each other. Two more guarded the doorway. Another sat off to one side, scrawling notes on a stack of parchment.

The man nearest the fire smoothed his mustache with his thumb as he appraised me. His doughy face was not exactly welcoming, but neither did I detect any particular malice.

"Why don't we get started," he said. "I am Senior Inquisitor Rainstock. Could you please state your name for the record?"

I considered refusing to reply, but I still knew too little about what was happening to risk that. "My name is Thoren Theratigan, sir."

"Thoren, he said, "these proceedings involve a very serious matter. It's important you tell me the truth. Do you understand?"

"Yes, sir."

"You've been accused of heresy murder. Do you know what that means?"

"Someone's saying I killed people with magic?"

Rainstock turned to the man with the parchment. "Let the record reflect the accused understands the charges levied against him."

I had a feeling I knew, but I asked anyway. "Who's accusing me?"

"Now Thoren," Rainstock said, "this tribunal is more concerned about the truth of the allegations than the identities of the accusers, so let me ask you this instead—are they true?"

"They are not true, sir."

"You're certain?" he asked. "I caution you that there's a great deal riding on your answer. A confession early on could result in a more lenient sentence."

"I said they're not true."

Rainstock winced, but didn't argue the point further. "Very well," he said. "Let the hearing begin."

CHAPTER THIRTY-THREE

LEGALLY BOUND

"Mr. Theratigan, once again for the record, is there anyone who bears you any ill will, whose testimony might therefore be suspect?"

What was I supposed to say? That Prentiss had accused me to get my pocket watch, which, by the way, also happens to be a Profanity? That the Ordinal hated me because I'd once had the temerity to chat with his daughter? Or maybe I should accuse the Inquisitor General of wanting to be rid of me because I'd seen him order the execution of the very same prisoners I now stood accused of killing? Only now did I fully appreciate the clever design of Prentiss' trap. Struggling only dug the jaws in deeper.

"Mr. Theratigan, your answer, please."

A knock at the door took the pressure off, at least for the moment. Rainstock's eyes darted toward the guards flanking the door. "Could you deal with that?"

The door burst open before the guards could react, and Father Graves poked his head in. "What do you know, Lisbet? Hollings was right—there is something odd going on down here." Lisbet clung to the doorframe with trembling fingers and peered in at the Inquisitors with wide eyes.

Rainstock smiled through gritted teeth. "If you don't mind, Father, this is a closed session."

Father Graves stepped inside. "Oh, I don't mind. I am curious, though. With all the injured people who require tending, and all the defenses that need bolstering, don't you think you could find more productive uses for your time than sitting in meetings?"

"I don't expect this to take long, and even if it does, I'm sure you'll agree identifying the heretic responsible for our recent tragedies is of paramount importance."

"Oh, so that's what this is about. I must say I'm impressed you were able to collect all the necessary evidence so quickly. Last I checked, the ashes were still smoldering."

"Witness testimony is best served warm."

"Testimony can be biased, fabricated, or mistaken. That's what makes physical evidence so crucial."

"Your opinions on the merits of physical evidence are well known, Father. Now, if you'll excuse us…"

During the exchange, Father Graves had wandered farther into the room. When I looked up from my chains, and finally caught his eye, he rounded on Rainstock. "What's the meaning of this?"

"I've already told you. We're trying this suspect for heresy murder. I'm not going to ask again. If you continue to interrupt these proceedings, I'll have the guards escort you out."

"You do realize this suspect is Roman's manservant. When he finds out what you're doing, he's going to be livid."

A crooked smile tugged at the corner of Rainstock's mouth. "Oh, I sincerely doubt that, Father," he said, holding up an official-looking document. "You'll note the order bears the Inquisitor General's personal seal."

Father Graves stopped cold. His voice dropped to a whisper. "Why didn't he tell me?"

"Try not to take it so hard. After all, he probably thought you had your hands full tending the injured and collecting evidence."

"He's distraught about his son. He probably didn't even know what he was signing."

"Then by all means, go to him. Find out what he was thinking. Maybe then we can finally set about the business of extracting a confession."

"You can't proceed if the authorization is in doubt."

"It looks legitimate to me. Are you willing to testify under oath that the authorization was fraudulently obtained?"

"Damn it, Rainstock. You know I can't do that until I talk to him."

"You'd best hurry along then. If, in the meantime, we get that confession, we'll let you know. After all, we wouldn't want you to waste any of that precious time of yours on a moot point. Guards, could you please help Father Graves find the exit."

Father Graves didn't take his eyes off Rainstock as the guards reached for him. "Lay so much as a finger on me, gentlemen, and I'll see to it Roman slaps you in chains."

The guards paused in mid-reach.

Rainstock snorted. "And just how long do you expect that ploy is going to work? I'm well within my authority, and you know it. You have no business here."

"Who's representing the lad?"

"What?"

"He's entitled to an advocate. Who's defending him?"

"Oh that," Rainstock said. "We offered the job to the requisite three Inquisitors, but upon hearing the evidence, they each declined, as is their right."

"Then I'll do it."

"Don't be a fool. The evidence is overwhelming. Persisting in the face of it could be interpreted as complicity."

"I'll take that risk."

Rainstock stroked his mustache. "I suppose it would lend a certain legitimacy to the verdict. Very well. Assuming he'll have you, I'll allow it."

"I'll have him, sir," I said.

"In that case," Rainstock said, "let's continue these proceedings where we left off."

Father Graves held up his hand. "If I could beg the tribunal's indulgence for one moment?"

"What is it now?"

He stepped into the hallway and took Lisbet's hand. "Uncle Albert has to stay here and do some work. Can you find your way back to Uncle Armand on your own?"

She nodded up at him with big serious eyes.

"Off with you then."

He was sending a message. When she showed up alone, Armand was sure to know there'd been trouble. I doubted even he could fix this mess, but a glimmer of hope beats no hope at all.

She whirled to leave, but the way was blocked. "Don't you worry, Father," Prentiss said. "I'd be happy to look after the girl for you."

"I wouldn't want to impose," Father Graves said.

"Nonsense, Father. Your generosity in taking the lad's part inspires me. It's the least I can do."

"I appreciate the thought, but it's really not necessary. I'm sure she can find her way back on her own, and Armand isn't doing anything else anyway. He'll be happy to look after her."

"Oh, I insist. Rambling ruins like these are never truly safe, particularly for one so young."

I couldn't take it anymore. "Run, Lisbet," I cried. "Don't let him get you."

That was all it took. Like lightning, she ducked under Prentiss' arm, but he was quicker—grabbing her by the back of the collar. She struggled to free herself, but to no avail.

"What are you doing?" Father Graves demanded. "Release her at once."

Prentiss glanced at Father Graves for only a moment, but it was enough. Lisbet stomped on his foot hard, and then with all her might, she launched her rose-tinted bottle at his head. It struck him above the right eye, bounced off, and smashed against the floor in an explosion of skittering spiders, beetles, and bright shiny objects. In the confusion, she twisted out of his grasp and flew down the hallway. Limping and rubbing his bruised forehead, Prentiss took off after her.

"Prentiss, leave the girl be," Father Graves shouted after them.

"Order," Rainstock cried. "I will have order. Close that door this instant."

The guards leapt to comply. Father Graves ducked inside in the nick of time.

"And you, Mr. Theratigan. Any more outbursts from you, and you'll be watching these proceedings through a mask. Do I make myself clear?"

"Yes, sir. Sorry, sir."

Father Graves dragged a chair over to my table and took a seat as Rainstock resumed his line of questioning.

"Now, do you wish to list anyone who might have reason to perjure themselves against you, or don't you?"

Father Graves jumped up. "To address that question, we'll need a detailed accounting of the charges. We'll also need time to prepare a defense. I move for a six-month postponement."

Rainstock exhaled slowly. "Father Graves, let me remind you that you're here to help the lad with his defense, not delay the proceedings. Motion denied."

"Three months, then."

Rainstock thrummed his fingers on his table. "Denied. Care to try again?"

"At least let me see the charges."

"Oh, very well. The Secretary will provide counsel with the list of charges."

The scrawny little note taker rummaged through his pages and held one out. Father Graves sank into his seat next to me as he scanned the document.

"He'll never catch her," I whispered. "She'll be fine."

Father Graves didn't look up from the list. "I know," he said. "It's you I'm worried about. How do you get yourself into these things?"

"Wrong place at the wrong time. When Darron fell, right after you left to get the Ordinal, I saw Roman order Prentiss and Barclay to execute the prisoners."

"Even if that were true, it wouldn't explain why several witnesses place you at the scene just as the Sacrifice went off."

"I was trying to save them. And it wasn't a Sacrifice. Prentiss must have seen me coming. He poured gin everywhere and rigged it to ignite when the shed door opened."

"Hmm, that would explain the absence of a circular scorch mark."

"So you believe me?"

"I believe there was no Sacrifice," he said. "That Roman would have ordered such an execution is a little tougher for me to swallow. Is it possible you misheard?"

"I wish I had."

"We'll sort that out later. In the meantime, we need to get

these proceedings suspended until we can figure out what's going on."

"Can you do that?"

"Watch me." He cleared his throat and rose to his feet. "Am I reading these correctly?" he asked. "Are you accusing the lad of Sacrificing all those prisoners?"

"You saw the shed yourself," Rainstock said. "Is there any doubt?"

"Let's see if I follow the reasoning. It had to be a Sacrifice, right? Only a Sacrifice could have covered enough area to cause so much of the building to ignite at once. How big is a Sacrifice anyway?"

"I imagine they can vary," Rainstock said. "What's your point?"

"In theory, perhaps they can, but do they?"

The drumming of Rainstock's fingers on the table echoed through the chamber. "Relevance, Father?"

"Bear with me. Prior to the incident with the prisoners, there have been four Sacrifices associated with the events at Histlewick Manor. The first was responsible for the deaths of the previous Inquisitor General and Marshall Hockery. The second killed an Inquisitor in the swamp, and if not for Mr. Theratigan's intervention would also have killed the Ordinal and me. The third, also in the swamp, was centered on Armand's possessions, and, once again, resulted in no injuries thanks to the efforts of Mr. Theratigan. The fourth occurred down by the city gates, and caused several more deaths, as well as many grievous injuries."

"Your point?"

"The point is, I examined all four of those incidents, and in each case, the diameter of the Sacrifice, as measured from the scorch marks left behind, was a full sixty feet."

"We get it," Rainstock said. "Sacrifices are huge. That's why it's obvious a Sacrifice was used on the shed as well. Otherwise the whole thing wouldn't have gone up in flames so quickly."

"There's only one problem with that theory. At its widest point, the shed measured forty feet across. Had it been Sacrificed, scorch marks should extend well beyond the foundation. I examined that site as well. There were no such marks. The evidence is far more consistent with use of flammable vapors than a Sacrifice."

"Multiple witnesses reported seeing the lad fleeing the scene immediately after the fire broke out," Rainstock said. "Not only that, but with the exception of the first, he was present at every other Sacrifice you mentioned."

"The other incidents are irrelevant," Father Graves said. "As I read this document, he's charged only with heresy murder for the deaths of the prisoners in the shed."

"What?" Rainstock snatched up his copy of the charges and started scanning.

"In the future I suggest you draft your charges with more care. I move to suspend these proceedings until the crime scene can be properly investigated."

"What difference does it make how he did it? All those prisoners are still dead."

"It makes all the difference. Once you establish there was no Sacrifice, you lose jurisdiction. Your heresy-murder charge defaults to simple murder, and unlike heresy murder, regardless of how heinous, simple murder is a matter for secular courts. Histlewick might decide to pursue the charge, but you could not."

Rainstock continued to stroke his mustache.

Father Graves took a step forward. "Hal, I know you're outraged, but you mustn't give into it. If anything, the seriousness of this offense merits an even higher standard of care than usual. You have a sterling reputation as an able and fair-minded jurist—don't jeopardize that with an ill-advised rush to justice in what could be the most visible case of your career."

"I suppose a more thorough examination of the scene couldn't hurt."

"Now you're talking."

At that instant, my eardrums popped, and the door shuddered. A shrill hiss from the hallway assailed us, a sibilant crescendo that lasted just long enough to set our teeth on edge. It gave way to absolute silence. I wondered for a second if I'd gone deaf. Then I realized I'd forgotten to breathe.

Father Graves clutched my shoulder. "That's not what I think it is, is it?"

"She's back," I said.

CHAPTER THIRTY-FOUR

FORCE MAJEURE

Rainstock whirled on the guards. "Whatever that was, I don't want to hear it repeated. Understood?"

"We'll see to it, sir."

Father Graves pulled them up short. "Don't touch that door."

Rainstock sputtered with indignation. "Contradict me again, Father, and I promise you there will be consequences."

"Open that door, and you'll kill us all. Joanna Hockery's out there. You remember her, right? She's the heretic who's actually responsible for those Sacrifices you were trying to pin on the boy."

"Hockery? I thought she was dead."

"The evidence suggests otherwise, doesn't it?"

"What's she doing here?"

"I don't know, but I certainly don't advise asking directly."

While Father Graves was distracted, I risked a peek at the monocle. At first it blazed with colors but as I went to slip it back into my pocket, it faded again.

"So we're trapped here," Rainstock said.

Father Graves nodded. "At least until we come up with a plan. I don't suppose we have any crossbows?"

Rainstock nodded toward the guards. "They have swords. Will they suffice?"

"Possibly. She'd have to be close to the door to see inside. It depends on whether she's hunting for specific targets or is aiming to eliminate everyone in her path. Any ideas, Mr. Flinch? You know her better than we do."

"Let me talk to her," I said. "If she recognizes me, maybe she'll allow me to relay her demands. She's done it before."

"Out of the question," Rainstock said. "For all we know, the two of you are working together."

"Nonsense," Father Graves said. "If that were true, he would have let us all perish in the swamp."

"So you're saying you think it's a good idea?"

"Of course not," Father Grave said. "It's too dangerous. She might act before she realizes who he is."

"I mean apart from the danger to him. You don't think he'd sell us out?"

"I don't. He once told Roman he'd sooner be punished as a heretic than give up the ability to prevent the Sacrifice of an innocent person."

"I don't suppose you have a better suggestion?"

Father Graves shrugged. "Not at the moment."

"We can't afford to wait," Rainstock said. "There's only one way out of this room. If she torches the manor, we'll be trapped." He eyed the guards and tilted his head in my direction. "Unchain him."

"Don't be ridiculous," Father Graves said. "If she Sacrifices him in the doorway, it'll kill us all."

"Weren't you listening? A Sacrifice anywhere in the manor could kill us all. If we can find out what she wants, at least we stand some chance of appeasing her."

"If you want to interrogate her, you do it. Don't send a boy to do a job you're too afraid to handle yourself."

I tugged Father Graves' sleeve. "Our chances are better if I do it," I said. "She's a little touchy around Inquisitors."

"There, you see?" Rainstock said. "He wants to do it."

Father Graves' furrowed his brow at me. "There's a lot at stake. Are you sure you can handle it?"

I stood and held out my manacled hands to the guards. "Watch me."

Once the chains were removed, I threw open the door, and poked my head into the hallway.

"Well?" Rainstock asked.

"We're too late. She's already gone."

"Quickly," Rainstock said, "everyone out. Deathtrap manor here could go up in flames at any moment. Guards, you go first. Head for the nearest exit. If you happen across Hockery, cut her down where she stands."

"What about everybody else?" Father Graves asked. "Don't you think they should be warned?"

I held up my hand. "I'll do it."

"Not alone, you won't," Father Graves said. "I'm coming with you."

"There," Rainstock said. "Problem solved."

For a short while, Father Graves and I followed Rainstock and his men, but they peeled off as we approached the door to the Marstow wing. We saw no sign of Joanna.

A moment later, Father Graves skidded to a stop. "Do you have the watch?"

"Not with me."

"Get it. Meet me in Roman's chambers."

The corridors were empty as I sprinted back to my room—a welcome relief, given that Joanna and Prentiss were both still on the loose. I found the watch where I'd left it.

I'd given you up for dead.

"Joanna's in the manor."

So I was almost right.

"We're worried she's after the Inquisitor General again. Can you protect him?"

From a determined assault? No.

"But you blocked those other Sacrifices."

She wasn't expecting that. Now that she knows, she can adapt.

"What am I supposed to do? They're expecting me to protect him."

If I were you, I'd be sure to do that from a nice, safe distance—say, from the next town over.

"They're depending on me. I can't just abandon them."

If you keep coddling them, they'll never become self-sufficient.

"If I don't, they'll be dead."

Let that be their first lesson. Never pick a fight with a bully who's three times your size.

"Are you going to help me, or not?"

I've already given you my best advice. As usual, you're going to ignore it.

"You've crossed her before—if your advice is so good, why didn't you take it yourself?"

Running away isn't my strong suit.

"Assume I can't run either. How can I win?"

To the extent you have any chance at all, tactics, I suppose.

"What do you mean?"

Anything she expects, she'll prepare for. Make sure whatever your plan turns out to be, she's not expecting it.

"That's the best you've got?"

I'm a watch, not a crystal ball.

I snapped the watch closed and stuffed it into my pocket. In a few short seconds, it had shriveled from an iron-clad defense into an insignificant diversion. Maybe Joanna didn't realize that yet, but I doubted it—after all, she'd given it to me in the first place. I decided to head back to Roman's chambers by way of the kitchen. I was defenseless, but I didn't have to be blind as well.

Saville was likely still helping out in the infirmary, since the kitchen was empty. I rummaged through the pantry until I found an empty bail-top pickle jar. I flipped up the wire closure to release the lid, then wrapped the watch in a towel and stuffed it inside.

Hold on there. What do you think you're do—

The lid snapped down with a satisfying click. I checked the monocle to be on the safe side, and, as I expected, only the red and green wedges were showing. It was detecting the lingering spells from the watch, but not the watch itself. I popped the monocle into place over my eye and set off for the Marstow wing.

I was lucky. I saw no new colors for the entire trek back—Joanna must have fled the area. I slipped the monocle into my pocket with the jar before knocking on Roman's door.

Roman's chambers occupied by far the largest open space I'd seen in the Marstow wing. Spiral pinwheels and garish hypnotic patterns dominated the décor. Draperies, throw pillows, arrases—none were spared. Even the dome of the ceiling held a pattern that pranked my eye, whirling more wildly the longer I stared at it. I grabbed for the doorframe to steady myself.

"It's disconcerting at first," Father Graves said, "but you get used to it."

He was seated at the foot of a sprawling walnut desk. Roman stood on the far side, gazing out a window.

"How's Darron?" I asked.

Father Graves answered. "The Ordinal is optimistic, but there's been little visible change since yesterday. We're doing everything we can. Come, have a seat, but first, close and lock that door."

"Oh, sorry. I wasn't thinking."

"Roman has something he'd like to say to you."

As I sat, Roman turned to face me. He bore little resemblance to the man he'd been the morning before. His were the sunken eyes of a tortured soul.

"Tell me. What happened at the farrier's shed?"

"Uh, Roman," Father Graves said. "That's not what we discussed."

Roman held up his hand, and Father Graves fell grudgingly silent.

"It happened like this," I said. "I'd gathered townsfolk to rescue the prisoners. I know it went against your order, and I'm sorry for that, but I didn't think you'd have ordered it if you'd been yourself."

"Go on."

"When we started opening the door, I was overwhelmed by the strong scent of pine. At first I didn't connect it, but then I saw the coals in the glass chimney, and it clicked. Someone had gathered the prisoners in the shed and then covered everything with gin. I was too slow, though. I couldn't stop the door before it set off the trap and scattered the coals. The whole shed went up at once."

"Who was responsible?"

"I didn't see anyone, so I can't say for certain."

Father Graves shifted in his seat. "Roman, we've been through this. The evidence is more consistent with the boy's story. Can we move on now? Joanna Hockery could strike at any moment."

"I needed to hear it from him. If I'd waited—"

A fanfare of trumpets cut him off.

Roman whirled and gawked out at the courtyard. "Histlewick? Good Lord, what's he doing back?"

Father Graves joined him at the window. "It was probably the smoke plume from the fire. It had to have been visible for miles."

"Which means, he's on his way here. Could the man's timing be any worse?"

Father Graves shook his head. "I don't see how."

CHAPTER THIRTY-FIVE

LOW TOLERANCE

istlewick's arrival immediately brought Elyria to mind. Should I tell Roman that Histlewick held her captive? There was little doubt if I did, Roman would inform her father immediately. Could I justify disregarding her request if I did it for her own good? After all, if she'd decided she'd rather be Histlewick's prisoner than Barclay's wife, who was I to gainsay her? My head kept urging me to have Roman rescue her, but my heart wouldn't let me say the words.

While I dithered, Roman faced Father Graves. "This is it, then—your last chance. You're sure you won't reconsider?"

Father Graves' brow furrowed. "You seem to think I came to this decision lightly."

"Not at all, but even careful consideration doesn't always beget the soundest strategy—believe me, I know."

"Roman, don't do this. It's beneath you."

Roman shook his head. "Too much depends on this. It's not a question of your authority—you know that. It's that your faith in me, though it is among those things I treasure most in this world, is misplaced. I am a failure and a fraud. How many more must suffer before you see the truth?"

"Your truth is no different from anyone else's. You fall, you stand up again. You fail, you make amends and move on. It's not complicated, but it's not always easy, either. I don't base my faith in you on a belief you'll succeed at everything you try. Instead, for everything you try, I expect you'll do your best, and usually, that's pretty damned good. In my judgment, your leadership is our best hope for making it through this. And, like it or not, as your confessor, your penance is my decision to make. That means there'll be no resignation anytime soon. Deal with it."

The two men locked eyes for several tense heartbeats. At last, Roman bowed his head. "Oh very well," he said. "By your grace, and upon my soul, it shall be done."

"It's about time. Now, who's it going to be first, Histlewick or Hockery?"

"Histlewick's tantrums are annoying, but hardly life-threatening. Hockery's our main concern right now. Have you found me that weapon yet?"

Father Graves produced a jewelry box. "I have found something," he said. "It's not precisely a weapon, but you may find it useful." He lifted the lid to reveal a sinuous golden gecko with glittering peridot eyes, nestled in a web of fine gold filigree.

"What is it?"

"It's called an interceptor. I haven't been able to interpret all of the schematics yet, but the title says it all. References associate the term with a number of different Profanities—all of which performed the same function."

"Which is?"

Father Graves cleared his throat. "This may get a bit technical."

"Make it quick. We can't assume Hockery's sitting on her hands."

"So, a subset of Phrendonic spells—specifically those that achieve particularly energetic effects—require additional energy to work."

"You're referring to Sacrifices?"

"Among others, yes. The energy is typically supplied by an additional spell, termed a Charge. If the energy requirement is particularly intense, the Charge is used up instantaneously, as in a Sacrifice. Otherwise, a single Charge can keep a spell running for about an hour or so. If you want the spell to keep running longer, you need more Charges, but a spell can't accept a new Charge until just before the old one runs out. Make sense?"

"Keep going. I'll stop you if I get lost."

"When multiple spells are present, you need a way to determine which of them gets the Charge. To do that, Charge-requiring spells all have a characteristic called Tolerance. Charges are like water. They fill the overlapping spell with the lowest tolerance first, and they never fill a spell that has a higher tolerance than the Charge—they don't flow uphill."

"All right, you lost me. Can you just tell me what it does, without the mumbo jumbo?"

"It's very simple. An interceptor uses a harmless spell with an extremely low Tolerance to subvert and dissipate an incoming Charge instantaneously. This particular interceptor has the additional benefit of attuning to the bearer automatically."

Roman shot me a wide-eyed look.

"He means to say as long as you wear it, Joanna's Sacrifices won't work on you."

"Thank you," he said. "That, I understand."

Father Graves held up a cautionary finger. "Keep in mind this is different from Flinch's watch. It will only counter

Sacrifices cast directly on your person, not those on your clothes or on others nearby. And it won't protect you from spells that don't require Charges."

Roman lifted the gecko from the box and laid it across his wrist. "All right, where's the clasp?"

Father Graves chuckled. "It's not a bracelet."

"Then how am I supposed to wear it?"

"It's an ear cuff. You wrap it around your ear."

Roman ceased his fiddling to gape at Father Graves in horror. "Good Lord, man. I'm the Inquisitor General. I can't wander around with sparkly lizards dangling from my ear lobes."

Father Graves did a poor job of suppressing his smirk. "It needs to touch your skin to work. I suppose when we have more time, we can rig it up with a chain and hang it around your neck, but until then…"

With ill grace, Roman permitted Father Graves to position the gecko for him. "I'd better not find out you had another one of these things that's a ring or a bracelet or something."

Father Graves shot me a sly wink. "Don't worry, you won't." His smile faded when a knock rattled the door.

Roman didn't bat an eye. "Who is it?" he called out.

"Hollings, sir. Lord Histlewick requests an audience."

Roman strode over and opened the door. "Tell him to wait for me in the courtyard. Warn him that I may be a while."

"His Lordship does not seem inclined to wait."

"Impress upon him the character-affirming benefits of patience."

"I shall do my best."

"Oh, and Hollings?"

"Yes, sir?"

"I'm evacuating the manor."

"The entire manor?"

"Everything except the infirmary. Ask the Ordinal to place Inquisitors at each of the entrances."

"As you wish, sir."

Roman locked the door again, and took a seat behind the desk. "Albert, can I count on you to help Armand make his way to the infirmary?"

"That may not be necessary. He's getting pretty good with the crutches."

"You forget—Hockery knows him. If he runs across her on the way out, the crutches are unlikely to be much help."

"If we run into Hockery, I'm unlikely to be much help either."

"How about we prop you up with a crutch of a different sort?" He reached beneath the desk to retrieve a crossbow crafted of dark wood, its polished surface adorned with silver accents.

Father Graves eyed it dubiously. "You do realize I'm not exactly a sharpshooter, right?"

"She doesn't know that. At least this way she'll think twice before picking a fight—her last fight featuring a crossbow didn't go so well for her."

"If I'm helping Armand, where will you be?"

"Someone's got to go through and clear the place. Flinch and I are the only ones with any defenses at all."

"Oh, no, you don't. If you insist on trying to take the easy way out, you'll be taking me with you."

"Albert, simmer down." Roman reached beneath the desk and pulled out a mate to the first crossbow. "I'm depressed, not suicidal. I'd have preferred a weapon more tailored to the situation, but in its absence, this will have to do. Fortunately, I am a sharpshooter."

"I don't like it. All she'd have to do is get the drop on you by a few minutes."

"You have a better suggestion?"

"Yes. Join us in the evacuation."

"Let her escape? When we have her cornered? How could I face all those men in the infirmary if I did that?"

"Alive."

"For how long? It doesn't look like Mrs. Hockery intends to abandon her vendetta anytime soon. I'm not going to spend the rest of my life looking over my shoulder—not when I can end this here and now."

"But—"

"Albert, enough. Take the crossbow. We need to get moving."

Grudgingly, Father Graves picked up the weapon.

"Come on. We'll take you as far as Armand's room. You have the watch, Mr. Flinch?"

I nodded, patting the jar in my pocket. I didn't like the idea of losing what little warning the monocle might give us, but unless I wanted to reveal its secret, I couldn't use it anyway. As Roman fiddled with the lock, I quietly flicked the release on the jar lid.

The hallway was empty, and moments later, we found ourselves outside Armand's door.

Roman slapped Father Graves on the shoulder. "All right, old man. I'll see you outside."

"Don't you want to speak with Armand before you go?"

He shook his head. "I'd sooner wait. I want to be able to hold my head up when I do."

Father Graves nodded. "I understand. See you outside."

We stopped first at Father Graves' apartments. I threw open the door and ducked out of the way. Crossbow at the ready, Roman stepped inside. A quick inspection revealed no sign of Joanna. Most of the Profanities had now been catalogued, and a sheaf of schematics littered the library table. Topmost was the schematic for Roman's gecko. While Roman searched, I inspected the page for anything that Father Graves might have missed, but it read exactly as he'd surmised.

Satisfied we were alone, Roman paused to glance over my shoulder. "While you're at it, check whether there's anything else in that pile we might be able to use. I love the guy, but Albert's overblown aversion to risk is driving me crazy."

"How much time do we have?"

"Ten minutes."

"I couldn't get through even one of these in ten minutes."

"I encourage you to try. Both our lives may depend on it."

"In that case, we should focus on the wands. They're more likely—"

His raised hand cut me off. "Did you hear that?"

I shook my head.

Silently, he stalked over to the door and held his ear against it. "There's someone out there."

CHAPTER THIRTY-SIX

ONE STEP BEHIND

Roman raised the crossbow and nodded. I flung wide the door.

Histlewick stared back at us, stunned.

Exasperated, Roman lowered the weapon. "Histlewick, what are you doing here? I specifically asked you to wait for me in the courtyard."

"While you evacuate my manor. Yes, I heard. Funny, I'd have thought you'd have been at least curious to hear my opinion on the matter. You know, since I'm Lord and all."

"Normally I'd have consulted you, but this is an emergency. Joanna Hockery is loose somewhere in the manor."

"I'd think the appropriate response would be to call in more Inquisitors to apprehend her. What do you hope to gain by giving her the run of the place?"

"I take it you haven't been to the infirmary."

"We don't have an infirmary."

"You do now—your lobby. It's filled with Inquisitors who crossed Joanna Hockery."

"Only Inquisitors?"

"So far."

"Then isn't it fair to assume only Inquisitors are at risk?"

"She favors burning them. A fire would threaten the entire manor."

"In that case, the solution isn't to evacuate the manor, it's for you to take your Inquisitors and evacuate my town. This charade has gone on long enough. First it was my ballroom, then, my farrier's shed. Now, you tell me it could be the entire manor. You have no right to risk me and mine in the name of this petty crusade of yours."

Roman heaved a world-weary sigh. "You know I'd like nothing better to entertain your long list of grievances, but in case you haven't noticed, right now, I'm in the middle of something important. I invite you to visit just as soon as this crisis is over, but until then, I'm busy."

Histlewick nearly burst with indignation. "I don't suppose it's occurred to you that since you're her primary target, your presence here is the manor's single greatest threat. Until you're gone, no one here is safe."

"And if we fail to bring Joanna Hockery to justice, it emboldens every heretic out there to use lethal force. If that happens, sir, no one anywhere is safe. Now, stand aside. I have a job to do."

Histlewick didn't budge, but Roman brushed past him anyway and stalked off down the corridor. I slipped out too, gave His Lordship a helpless little shrug, and scurried to catch up.

"Better do it quickly, then," Histlewick called after us. "Because I expect His Ordinance is going to see things differently."

Histlewick wasn't just blowing smoke. With Elyria as his hostage, he wouldn't have any trouble forcing the Ordinal to cooperate. The whole dynamic had just changed—Roman had to be told. I waited until we were just out of earshot.

"He's right, you know. The Ordinal's going to do whatever he asks."

Roman kicked open a door and aimed the crossbow inside. "The Ordinal's no fool. He's seen first-hand what one rogue heretic can do. He'll understand better than anyone the need to end this threat here and now."

"Histlewick won't bother trying logic—he's holding Elyria hostage."

"What? Why didn't you tell me?"

"I've been little distracted."

"Right. Sorry about that. Prentiss swore he and Barclay hadn't started that fire, and that you were spotted leaving the scene just as it started. I allowed him to convince me you were trying to keep the prisoners from incriminating anyone else. I should have known better, but the temptation to absolve myself clouded my thinking. Thank heavens Albert intervened."

"What happened to Buck, Sly and the others?"

"Who?"

"Prentiss took other prisoners too. They were trying to help me."

"He failed to mention that. We'll get to the bottom of it once this crisis is over. Right now I need to know the situation with Elyria."

"He's keeping her in the same room where I found the other Histlewick. I've been meaning to ask you, how did you get past the locks to retrieve him?"

"Histlewick was off on the hostage exchange at the time. I had Darron sneak into his rooms to get the keys. He already knew what they looked like, so that part was easy. The hard part was finding his way through those passages. I hope your memory is better than his."

"We're going down there?"

"Unless we want Histlewick calling the shots, I don't see an alternative. Come on."

Word of the evacuation had spread through the Marstow wing, and we encountered no stragglers on the way out. The rest of the manor, however, was a different story. Apparently Histlewick's servants were reluctant to abandon their posts without his say-so. Fortunately, all reluctance faded when the Inquisitor General delivered the order personally.

A pile of bed linens littering the hallway ahead brought Roman up short. He signaled for me to stay back, and brought the crossbow to bear as he approached a nearby door standing slightly ajar. He kicked it in and charged into the room.

There were no more sounds for what seemed like forever. At last, Roman poked his head out. "Mr. Flinch, what do you make of this?"

A young woman lay sprawled across the floor, naked. She was still breathing, and there was no sign of injury. Beneath her lids, her eyes moved, but when I tried to rouse her, she didn't respond.

"She's been Slept," I said. "She'll be fine, but it may be a while before she wakes."

Roman covered the woman with a blanket. "Hockery's work, no doubt. She could still be nearby. Keep your eyes peeled."

Histlewick's apartments were nestled in the heart of the sprawling complex. Great iron-bound doors stood before us like stalwart sentinels in unyielding defense of His Lordship's private sanctum. The air was leaden, on the edge of musty, and though neatly swept, the hallways felt drowsy with age. The brooding silence that had descended in the wake of the evacuation only seemed to amplify the senile whispers of creaking timbers and crumbling stone.

"How do we get past them?" I asked.

"Simple," Roman said. He gave the doors a little shove, and they swung smoothly inward. "You forget—this is his home."

Alert for the slightest hint of movement, Roman stepped inside. I followed and nudged the doors closed behind us. Here and there, shafts of sunlight from skylights pierced the windowless gloom, creating dazzling islands that seemed to float amidst a sea of shadows. We found ourselves in a spacious anteroom connected to an even larger bed chamber by an archway crafted of the local stone.

As we moved farther in, a bed came into view, so vast it made its bearskin coverlet seem tiny. Above it loomed a ponderous headboard of rustic beams emblazoned with the red-wolf insignia of family Bey. Multi-tiered wagon-wheel chandeliers modified from the original candles to use oil were among the room's few concessions to modernization. Wardrobes, dressers, tables, chairs—all were well over a hundred years old.

I wandered the room in awe. It was a case-study in the stereotypically male. I'd never before realized how most rooms strike a balance between masculine and feminine elements until seeing one so utterly lacking half the equation. The Marstow wing, even at its most disconcerting, struck a better balance than this. Every line of every element was either strictly functional or somehow a testament to male prowess. It was at once fascinating and repugnant—I couldn't look away.

"Found them," Roman said, holding up a ring of keys. "Let's get out of here."

"Hold on, what's this?"

While most of the room was meticulously ordered, a black cowhide rug lay with one edge folded over on itself.

"We're not here to sightsee."

Ignoring Roman, I tossed back the rug. A trapdoor lay beneath.

"What do you suppose Histlewick keeps in his cellar?" I asked.

"A shortcut?"

"If it is, it'd be a shame to miss it."

Roman took aim with the crossbow. "All right, open it."

I tugged on the iron ring. The ancient hinges groaned, but provided little resistance. Beneath, a ladder descended into darkness. I knelt and put my head through the opening. "Looks more like a hallway than a cellar."

Roman grabbed a lamp from the nightstand and lit it. "You take this," he said. "I'll go first."

The instant his feet hit the floor, he reached up for the light. "Your turn."

Once I'd made it down, he handed back the lamp and readied his weapon. "All right," he said. "Lead on."

"Which way?"

"Don't look at me. You're the expert."

I tried mentally superimposing my meager knowledge of the passages over what I knew of the layout of the manor. The only thing it got me was a headache.

"We don't have all day."

"All right, let's try this way."

The passage dead-ended thirty feet later.

Roman snorted. "At least that narrows our options."

We soon arrived at the intersection of two corridors. I held the lantern high and scanned each direction for the slightest hint of anything familiar.

"No offense," Roman said, "but I think this may have been a bad idea. We don't even know if we're on right level."

"Wait, what's that?"

Something was leaning against the wall of one of the passages.

"That's it," I cried, "only someone's removed the door."

"Stop right there," Roman said. I froze as he squeezed past me. He aimed the crossbow through the open doorway and peered inside. "All right, it's clear."

I had to see for myself. The room was much as I'd left it, with most of the furniture piled against the far wall. The armoire that had once held the duplicate Histlewick now stood open and empty.

"Assuming Elyria was ever even here, apparently someone else got to her first."

I stooped to pick up something lying next to the sofa. "Oh, she was here, all right."

"What makes you so sure?"

"This." With a flick of my wrist, I splayed the bone ribs to reveal a dainty white fan with blue accents.

"In that case, the only question left is who. It wasn't Histlewick—he had the key."

"Joanna?"

Roman paled as the possibility sank in. "Quickly, back upstairs. We need to move."

"Where are we going?"

"The manor lobby."

"You think the Ordinal's in danger?"

"Not just him. Everyone's gathered there—Darron, Armand, Albert—everyone. And they're completely defenseless."

CHAPTER THIRTY-SEVEN

NOT JUST ANOTHER PRETTY FACE

Roman raced through the manor like a man possessed. It was a good thing he knew where he was going, because it wasn't long before I was hopelessly lost. We passed through a long-abandoned annex, its once-opulent salons and antechambers shedding cobweb-laden mahogany panels like so much withered bark. From such poignant vestiges I finally began to appreciate the grandeur that Histlewick manor had once embodied, and the enormity of its decline.

At the end of a particularly dark passage, we discovered a glowing marble statuette.

"What do you make of this, Mr. Flinch?"

"Joanna again," I said. "She used it to light her way, and discarded it when she didn't need it anymore. No need to attract unnecessary attention."

Roman nodded and pushed on.

We burst out at last into blinding sunshine, startling the door guard so severely he nearly let fly with his crossbow. Ignoring the man's apologies, Roman sprinted across the courtyard for the lobby. He took the stairs three at a time. It was all I could do to keep up.

The crash of the lobby doors slamming open reverberated through the chamber. The echoes gave way to eerie silence. All eyes were on Roman, who stood framed by the doorway, weapon in hand.

"Where is she?"

The Ordinal rose from a bench where he'd been seated next to Histlewick. "If you're referring to my daughter, I still have no idea. We need to institute a search while we still have Inquisitors left to do it."

"I was referring to Joanna Hockery. She hasn't contacted you yet?"

"Why would she contact me?"

"That's the way these things work. Last time we had a hostage situation, she sent a note. This time I'm betting she'll do it in person."

"What are you talking about? Hockery was killed yesterday morning outside the manor. Elyria was last seen inside the manor. We had a little tiff, she got indignant, and she's now hiding somewhere to punish me. There's no reason to suspect Hockery had anything to do with it."

Standing behind Roman I could only see a fraction of the lobby, though it was obvious the whole room seethed with people. Joanna might very well be lurking among them, and they'd never know.

I ducked around Roman and headed inside for a better look. The Ordinal's patients occupied most of the wing to the right of the grand stairway. Evacuation refugees congregated on the left. The stairs led up a full floor through a broad arch to another chamber shrouded in shadow. Once-luxurious second-floor balconies presided over the ends of each wing. The place would be a nightmare to secure.

Meanwhile, Histlewick cozied up behind the Ordinal. "You see my point, Your Ordinence? Your Inquisitor General is on the verge of hysterics, most of your Inquisitors have deserted or are lying here grievously wounded, and all your prisoners are dead. I've already offered additional carriages to transport your patients. What could you possibly hope to gain by staying?"

"Hockery's loose in the manor," Roman said. "We can't leave while she's still a threat."

Histlewick leaned closer until he was practically whispering into the Ordinal's ear. "Sad. We see here the feeble ranting of a man desperate to salvage the tiniest modicum of success from an ongoing campaign of abject failures. Joanna Hockery died yesterday at dawn. Don't take my word for it—you're surrounded by witnesses."

"She's back." Roman said. "Albert saw the signs earlier, and we've since seen additional evidence to confirm it."

"It doesn't matter," the Ordinal said. "None of it does. I'm not leaving without Elyria."

At that moment, Elyria nudged Roman aside and strode past him into the lobby. "In that case, Father, you're going be here a very long time."

I held out her fan as she passed. She took it from my hand with a nod, and snapped it open.

Histlewick paled and took a step back, but the Ordinal was unimpressed. "Does this mean we're finished with our little tantrum?"

"Don't be silly. Tantrums are for little girls, not affianced young ladies."

"So you've finally come to your senses. Barclay will be delighted to hear it."

"Oh, yes. Barclay. Um, I don't seem to recall anyone by that name on the guest list. I do hope he doesn't take it the wrong way, but we had to draw a line somewhere, and he didn't make the cut."

The Ordinal snorted. "You found someone better than Barclay, did you? And it only took you a day? Of course, with all the eligible bachelors in a thriving metropolis like Histlewick Downs, it's a wonder it took you so long. Don't leave me hanging. Pray, tell me. Who's the lucky man?"

Elyria gazed off into the distance and sighed. "He's everything a woman could wish for. Handsome, young, smart, and caring too. And not the type of caring that's concerned only with money or status or power." She meandered over to me, transferred the black and red feathered hat to my head, and patted it into place. "No, he actually cares about me—my needs, my hopes, my dreams. When I'm upset, he comforts me. When I'm in trouble, he rushes to my aid. In short, he's unlike you in almost every conceivable way."

She smiled then, collapsed the fan, and used it to gently nudge my gaping jaw closed.

The Ordinal gave no ground. "There's just one little problem with these plans of yours. In case you weren't aware, Mr. Flinch stands accused of heresy murder. Once his guilt is established, it may be quite some time before he's available to comfort you again. Are you sure you wouldn't like to reconsider?"

"What?" She whirled on me. "Is this true?"

I'd had no idea my feeble attempts to help her had made such an impression. I didn't know what to say. I ended up nodding and mumbling something incoherent.

She turned to glare at her father. "You did this deliberately, didn't you?"

"Actually, I had nothing to do with it."

"Of course you didn't. As usual, things have simply fallen your way by random chance. All right, you win. If I promise to give up all romantic designs on Mr. Flinch, would you at least be willing to pardon him?"

"Only the Primal can pardon, but if you swear you'll give up this preposterous notion of marrying Mr. Flinch, I might be able to prevail upon Roman to drop the charges."

She turned to me, tears glistening. "I can't let them destroy you," she said. "Please find it in your heart to forgive me."

The Ordinal's smile was predatory. "Do we have a deal?"

Elyria pulled out a kerchief and dabbed her eyes. "Oh, very well, I swear."

The Ordinal raised his eyebrows at Roman. "Well?"

"Consider it done," Roman said.

Elyria shot me a quick wink from behind her fan, and then threw her arms around her father. "I take it all back. You're the best father ever. Anyway, now that Mr. Flinch is safe, I'd like to introduce my fiancé."

"You just agreed to give up this Flinch nonsense. My patience has limits."

"Oh, I was never interested in Mr. Flinch," she said. "He's nice enough and all, but he's a bit beneath my station, don't you think?" She turned toward the doorway and beckoned. "Reggie, dear, could you come in here?"

"Elyria, be reasonable. If Mr. Flinch doesn't meet your criteria, what makes you think any of the locals will?"

"Oh, he's not local. His full name is Reginald Audley Silverstoke, and he's the Eighth Count of Chatterton."

Roman stepped aside as Elyria's betrothed made his entrance. My jaw fell open again. I hadn't expected to recognize him.

"Elyria, please," he said. "I really prefer to be called Sly."

The Ordinal's eyes narrowed. "Wait a minute. Didn't Chatterton have a problem with heresy recently?"

"That was all a fabrication," Sly said. "My father had a

bit of a falling out with the Archbishop. Next thing we knew, we were overrun by Inquisitors. My parents were killed in the fighting. I only survived because Chef disguised me and claimed me as one of his staff."

"So," Elyria cut in, "all you'd have to do is clear up the misunderstanding with the Archbishop, and Reggie and I could live happily ever after."

The Ordinal eyed Sly and rubbed his chin. "You know," he said, "if what you say is true, this little plan of yours might actually be worth looking into."

I had to hand it to Elyria. Beneath the fluff and curls she had a keen strategic mind. She must have offered Sly a deal—she would convince her father to recover Sly's family's holdings, and in return he would rescue her from the impending marriage to Barclay. In the midst of all that, she'd also managed to get the charges against me dropped. A tidy bit of work.

Roman could contain himself no longer. "This is all very touching, but in case you've forgotten, there's a madwoman on the loose whose favorite pastimes include Sacrificing Inquisitors. Has it occurred to any of you what might happen if she should come across this many people gathered in one place?"

But Elyria wasn't finished. "Oh, if you don't mind, I have just one more thing. Lord Histlewick kidnapped me. If it hadn't been for Reggie and his friends, I'd still be wasting away in that dreadful cellar room."

Sly's ears colored. "Elyria, please. Call me Sly."

"What?" the Ordinal cried. "What's the meaning of this?" He turned to confront Histlewick, but the Lord had edged away during Elyria's performance, and now stood surrounded by members of his own household.

"Isn't it obvious?" Histlewick said. "This is another little fiction manufactured to tug daddy's heartstrings and make him dance. I wonder what she wants this time?"

The Ordinal raised an eyebrow at his daughter. "Elyria?"

The fan fluttered in her hand. "You've already given me everything a girl could possibly want. I only included that extra bit of information as a bonus. Do with it what you will. I couldn't care less."

"That doesn't sound like a ploy to me," the Ordinal said. "Roman, what's your take?

Roman's eyes darted to Histlewick. "Elyria, would you mind telling me how were you freed?"

"Would I mind?" she asked. "I'd sing it from the rooftops if I could. My brave and noble fiancé mounted a daring expedition through the deep dark maze of ancient tunnels that lie beneath this manor to rescue me. Once they found me, he devised a means of cutting through the hinges to remove the door. So, you see, despite Lord Histlewick's unseemly behavior, I can't help but be a tad grateful. After all, it was he who brought us together."

Roman met the Ordinal's gaze and nodded. "She's telling the truth. Flinch and I just came from there—the hinges had been cut. I'd presumed Hockery must have done it, but it seems Reggie, here, got to her first."

At the mention of his name, Sly put his palm to his face and shook his head.

The Ordinal glanced over at Histlewick. "I suppose this means we'll have to take His Lordship into custody, doesn't it?"

Roman nodded. "Sure looks that way."

"This is ridiculous," Histlewick cried. "What reason would I have for taking the girl hostage?"

"You've been pretty determined to get us to leave," Roman said. "Maybe you hoped to use her as added incentive."

"Open your eyes. There are compelling reasons for that everywhere you look. I shouldn't need anything else."

Roman ignored his protests. "Guards," he said. "Take him."

As Inquisitors converged, Histlewick gave a sign, and several of his own men drew steel. "Call them off," he said, "or this is going to get ugly."

Roman held up his hand, and the Inquisitors froze in place. "You can't win this, Histlewick. Don't make things worse for yourself."

"I'd have thought the same thing about Joanna Hockery, but thanks to her, I have at least as many men here as you do. Let's be adult about this and call it a draw, shall we? I go on about my business, you go on your merry way, and everybody's happy. Surely that's more civilized than the alternative."

Roman appeared to be considering the offer when the gecko dangling from his ear emitted a brilliant flash of light, and all hell broke loose.

CHAPTER THIRTY-EIGHT

Child's Play

The entire room gasped. A few patted their clothes quizzically, as though puzzled they hadn't burst into flames. Startled Inquisitors drew blades of their own and rushed at Histlewick. Steel rang on steel as his own men closed in defense.

Roman sprang into action, pushing those near him toward the exit. "Everybody out. Get out while you still can."

"You first," the Ordinal cried. "She's targeting you."

Roman patted his ear. "I'm protected. I'm going after her. Now go!"

The Ordinal stood his ground. "You're not in this alone. I'm going with you."

Sly grabbed Elyria's hand and tugged her away from her father toward the doorway. By now, many in the panicked crowd had gotten the same idea. I was forced to dodge aside to avoid being trampled.

Safely hidden behind a man-sized urn, I looked out on the carnage. Both the Inquisitors and Histlewick's men had already suffered casualties. Histlewick backed away as the fighting became more heated. Father Graves interposed himself between the Lord and the patients, his crossbow trembling in his hands.

"Make them stop."

Histlewick whirled. Seeing the weapon aimed at his chest, he slowly held up his hands. "How do you propose I do that?"

In the chamber beyond the left balcony something flickered, a paler shadow in the darkness.

"She's there," I cried, pointing. "On the balcony."

The golden gecko flashed once more. For only a second, Father Graves winced and turned away. By the time he stopped blinking, Histlewick was no longer in his sights.

Roman raised his own crossbow toward the balcony and took aim. Before he could squeeze off the shot, Histlewick was at his back, pressing a knife to his throat. The bolt went wide.

"Throw down your weapons," Histlewick cried, "or your Inquisitor General's a dead man."

The swordfight raged on, unabated.

Histlewick waited several tense moments before withdrawing the knife and stepping away from Roman. "I've never before seen men with such deep and abiding concern for their leader. You must be so very proud."

Roman immediately set about reloading the crossbow. "Damn it, Histlewick, you spoiled my shot."

Histlewick snorted in reply. "Take it up with the good Father," he said. "I was only following orders."

"I don't believe this." Roman held up the crossbow for a closer look as the trigger mechanism crumbled and fell to dust. At the same time, the ongoing combat fell eerily silent, and Father Graves cried out as his crossbow discharged and shot the floor, the bolt shattering against the granite.

I heard creaking above me. The thick chains supporting the

chamber's massive chandeliers had begun to flake and thin. "Look out!" I cried.

The first fell among the erstwhile swordsmen, who were too astounded by the disintegration of their blades to appreciate the danger. The second narrowly missed Roman and Histlewick, but struck the Ordinal full on.

Elyria's screams ripped through the chamber. Pulling away from Sly, she raced to where her father lay pinned.

I had to do something. If I didn't, everyone in that room was going to die. I snatched the watch from the jar in my pocket. "How do I stop her?"

Stop Joanna on the warpath? Your guess is as good as mine.

"You did it once."

Get her to hold the watch in her bare hand, and I could do it again, but she'll never fall for that a second time.

Histlewick addressed the shadow lurking beyond the balcony. "Joanna, you've made your point. End this nonsense now, before you destroy the entire manor."

Beside him, Roman crumpled in the midst of straining to shove the chandelier off the fallen Ordinal.

"Joanna!" Histlewick roared. "Enough is enough."

The shadow came forward at last. It was unmistakably Joanna—the young version, with a smooth face, and a mane of dark hair flying wild. She was dressed much as was Elyria, in the plain uniform of one of Histlewick's servants."

"You're a little late, milord. The time to say enough was when the Inquisition sought to use this place as a staging area for their atrocities. When you failed to say it then, you lost any right to say it now. As a result, your precious manor is complicit—it too, must be cleansed."

"Need I remind you we have a deal?"

"Had a deal," Joanna corrected. "You had one simple task, and you couldn't manage even that."

"You're as much to blame for that as I am. Even if I'd gotten the watch, as long as you were missing, there was no way for me to get it to you."

"Circumstances have changed. Feel free to blame me if it makes you feel better. Best do it quickly though—you haven't got much time left. In fact, none of you do."

"I saved your life."

"You act like that was some sort of favor."

"Maybe I'll just take it back, then."

Stooping, he snatched the gecko from Roman's ear. Then, grabbing Elyria by the arm, he spun her around to face him. He gazed longingly into her grief-stricken eyes for one breathless heartbeat. Then he leaned in, slowly, tenderly, until their lips met. It lasted only an instant before she pulled away in shock, but it was enough. A euphoric smile blossomed across his face, and he opened his eyes and sighed. The smile then gave way to a shudder. He popped the gecko into his mouth just as a wave of change rippled through his body.

Elyria's shock turned to terror as the wolf shook off Histlewick's clothing, but it didn't advance on her. Instead, it turned and bounded across the chamber toward the stairs.

Now that's not something you see every day.

"Can he defeat her?"

I have no idea.

"Can you help him?"

Not from this distance, and, by the way, if she completes that spell, it probably wouldn't matter if I could.

Joanna, however, was up on the balcony and I was nowhere near her. Even with the watch I was helpless, just like I'd been when she'd tried to attack Kendall at the barn—and then it came back to me.

"Lisbet," I cried. "Stop her."

The pebble was in the air before I'd even finished saying the words, soaring in a languid arc across the chamber. It struck Joanna square on the chin.

She squawked in pain. "Why, you filthy little monster."

I made a mad dash for the stairs, hoping to get there before she had time to cast again. Fortunately, Father Graves came to the rescue, embracing Lisbet's example.

"Don't just stand there," he cried. "Throw things!"

Within moments, a barrage of random objects began raining down on the balcony—ceramic cups, coins, even bits and pieces from the fallen chandeliers. By the time I made it up the stairs, Joanna had been forced to withdraw.

The stairway opened into a vast space. Massive pieces of furniture lined the room, draped in tarps. The air carried the acrid tang of smoke with a sickening undercurrent of something far worse—something I forced myself not to think about. Instead, I focused on keeping the wolf in sight and pushed on.

Once inside the next room, the wolf darted past a casual arrangement of chairs and fancy sofas toward Joanna's balcony. She couldn't be far now. There was only one problem—a closed door barred his way. Undeterred, he increased his speed, springing at the last minute with bone-crushing force.

The door held.

The wolf scrambled to his feet. He tried pawing at the knob, but his claws couldn't get a purchase on the brass. At last, he sat back on his haunches facing the door. Then he looked back over his shoulder at me, panting. Waiting.

"Do you think it's safe?"

No.

"I'm going to do it anyway."

I figured.

I edged up to the door, turned the knob, and snatched back my hand as the wolf barreled through.

He skidded to a stop in the middle of the next room. We'd arrived at the right place—the balcony was on our left—but Joanna was nowhere in evidence. The wolf began pacing back and forth, sniffing as he went.

"I don't understand. Why can't he catch her scent?"

If she's recently Evoked, she probably doesn't have one.

All at once the wolf erupted in a cyclone of black smoke with enough force that I had to raise my arm to shield my face from flying debris.

"What just happened?"

Dispels don't take Charges.

You mean she Dispelled him?

It's an occupational hazard for Evoked daemons.

"So he's dead, then?"

That depends on his particular schematic.

"Could we do the same to Joanna?"

Sadly, Dispels are not a part of my repertoire.

The smoke cleared to reveal Joanna standing nearby.

"Oh, the irony," she said. "Histlewick inadvertently kept his part of the bargain after all." She held out her hand. "The watch, if you please."

I would have been eager to comply, except for one thing. She'd covered her palm with a kerchief. The watch wouldn't be able to work its magic through it.

"But I need it for protection."

"If you don't hand it over this instant, you're probably right."

When I'd run up the stairway, I'd done so intending to help Histlewick, not to take on Joanna by myself. Even with the watch I was overmatched, and I knew it. I reached reluctantly into the jar in my pocket, but as I did so, a last desperate gambit took shape in my mind. Drawing forth the watch, I held it out to her, but as she reached for it, I wound up my arm and launched it out over the balcony.

"What are you doing?" she cried. She rushed toward the balcony, trying to keep her eye on where it fell, but the instant she became visible to those below, she was met once more by a volley of random objects. When she drew back, I was waiting for her. I plunged the needle of Elyria's ring deep into her arm. She cried out in pain and backhanded me across the face. Staggered by the blow, I lost my footing and toppled over backward.

Joanna ripped back her sleeve to assess the wound. "What's gotten into you?"

"It's poisoned. You have only moments to live."

That'll never work. She'll just dispel herself to eliminate the poison and then come right back again. Why don't you ask me these things before you try them?

Joanna loomed over me. "Out of deference to my daughter, I've been more than patient with you, but poisoning me crosses the line. I'm going to count to ten, and if you're still here when I'm done, you'll have chosen the target for my next Sacrifice."

When she began muttering something, I scurried out the door and yanked it closed. Then, forcing myself to ignore both my hammering pulse and the need to draw in air in great gulps, I leaned back against the door—and waited.

Have you lost your mind? Get out of there.

"Don't you get it? We need Joanna dispelled. We can't do it, but she can—and Elyria's poison is the perfect incentive. The instant she does, I'll be waiting for her."

Weren't you listening? Her schematic clearly allows her to re-Evoke. So what if she dispels herself? She's just going to come right back.

"Not if I can help it."

My patience was rewarded by the sibilant whoosh of another terrific burst of air. The force of it rattled the door, even with my weight against it. The instant it stopped, I rushed back into the room.

Joanna's clothes lay strewn across the floor. I went for the blouse first, shaking it as I scooped it up.

A piece of metal the size of a button dropped to the floor, where it lay glinting in the dim light. It was a gold charm in the shape of a cameo—a mate to those on Joanna's bracelet. No doubt this was what Ramos had been seeking the last time Joanna disappeared. He'd had no way of knowing Lisbet had beaten him to it. She'd also beaten me to a solution for dealing with it.

I pulled out the pickle jar, dropped the charm into it, and sealed the lid.

You know, that just might work—oh, hello, who are you?

Sardonic laughter filled my mind. Then, as quickly as it had started, it was cut short.

"Are you still there?" I asked. "Hello?"

Despite the clamor from the room below, in that moment, all I heard was silence.

CHAPTER THIRTY-NINE

CRIME AND PUNISHMENT

I approached the balcony with my hands in the air. "It's me, Flinch."

"Friendly target," Father Graves cried. "Cease fire."

I dodged a shoe and a hair brush before everyone finally got the message.

With the projectile threat under control, Father Graves turned his attention back to me. "What's happening up there?"

How could I explain? I gazed out over a field of terrified eyes staring up at me. They didn't need a detailed account of what had happened. They needed hope.

"Joanna's…gone."

"What do you mean, gone?"

By the same token, it probably wouldn't be a good idea for them to know I was carrying her with me in my pocket.

"She fled. We're all safe, at least for the time being."

"And the wolf?"

"He's gone too.

"Praise and glory."

Scattered voices echoed Father Graves' refrain.

As soon as I'd said the words, guilt at the deception began to gnaw at me. I couldn't tell them exactly what happened, but neither did I want them thinking Joanna might come back at any moment. I ended up blurting something I probably shouldn't have.

"You need never fear Joanna Hockery again. Now that I know her secret, I swear to you, I'll find a way to bring her to justice."

If I'd been expecting applause, I'd have been sorely disappointed.

"Mr. Flinch," Father Graves said. "We could use a hand down here."

"I'll be right there."

While retracing my steps, a sparkle from the litter-strewn floor caught my eye. Against all odds, the gecko had survived. I tucked it away in my pocket. No doubt Father Graves would want it back.

The rest of the day was a blur. Between tasks, I searched a little for the watch, but I couldn't find it. Father Graves said he'd seen something shoot out over the balcony, but had lost track of it when Joanna had shown her face immediately afterward. No one else seemed to know anything about what happened to it, and with everything else going on, I didn't have time to investigate further. I did make time for a couple quick errands, though, including retrieving Joanna's bracelet from the hedge. The last thing I needed was for Lisbet to happen across that.

Four of the swordsmen had died—two from weapon wounds, and two who'd been crushed by the chandelier. Six more had serious injuries, including the Ordinal, who hovered on the brink of death. It had taken three strong men to lift the chandelier from him. He now occupied a prominent spot in the infirmary he'd once managed, Elyria a constant presence at his side.

Father Graves and Barclay did their best to get the situation under control until Roman awoke and took over, but none of them could match the Ordinal's healing skills. Roman wasted no time dispatching Ricard to the Holy City and Kendall to Caprian for help, but it would take days to arrive. Hollings and Saville pitched in like before, as did the enigmatic Jaccard, who busied himself crafting slings. Of Prentiss, there was no sign. Sly, Lisbet and I helped out as best we could, but for several patients, we were fighting a losing battle.

I took Sly aside. "You didn't happen across other prisoners in the catacombs, did you?"

Sly shook his head. "We weren't really looking for anyone else."

"Do you have any idea what happened to Buck and Flora Sue?"

"It was the oddest thing, mate. They let us all go. Maybe without the commons they didn't have anywhere to hold us, or maybe you were the only one they really wanted. Either way, it occurred to me a grateful Ordinal might be able to pull a few strings on your behalf. I got Buck to ask Gwen to make a trip back through those tunnels to rescue his daughter. Elyria and I got to talking on the way back, one thing led to another, and, well, you see how things ended up."

"Where is he now?"

"Buck? Outside, probably. He and some friends were going to wait there in case we had any trouble. I guess I sort of forgot."

"See if you can find him. Tell him to ask Gwen to come, and have her bring anyone with any skill at healing. We need help."

An hour and a half later, Gwen appeared on the doorstep

accompanied by five ladies in homespun. Each carried a small satchel.

Hollings introduced her to Roman from across the chamber. "A Miss Gwendolyn Hutchins to see you, sir."

"Who's that?"

"She would appear to be one of the locals. She says she's here to—and I quote—help."

"Tell her we're busy."

"Oh, don't do that," I said.

Hollings ogled me in disbelief.

Roman's response was more pragmatic. "Tell me."

"I asked them to come," I said. "I know they seem unsophisticated, but they're about as close to the land as you can get. For them, injuries are a way of life."

He considered for only a moment. "Hollings, show them in. Barclay, keep an eye on them—make sure they don't start applying leeches. Mr. Flinch, I'd like a word with you. Albert, you too."

A few minutes later the three of us were back on Joanna's balcony. "All right, Mr. Flinch. I need to know what happened up here."

Father Graves flipped open his journal and stood with pen poised in patient anticipation.

My mouth went dry. Something about turning Joanna over to the Church felt like betrayal. They had started it, after all. True, Joanna's indifference to the safety of innocent people made her no saint, but in that, the Church was hardly above reproach. In fact, in terms of sheer magnitude of suffering, the Church was far worse. My parents, if I could ever find them, would be the first to attest to that. But what else could I do?

I held the jar aloft and rattled its charm around inside it. "She's not coming back," I said. "She can't. She's in here."

Roman and Father Graves exchanged dubious glances.

Father Graves spoke first. "Perhaps it would be more useful to take this one step at a time."

"There aren't all that many steps. The wolf barged in after Joanna, she dispelled him, and then she dispelled herself. I picked up her trinket and put it in the jar. End of story."

Roman's brow furrowed. "The wolf?"

Father Graves looked up from his writing. "That would be Histlewick," he said. "It seems he was also a demon."

"Do you have a jar for him too?"

The sarcastic note in Roman's voice rubbed me the wrong way. "I don't know if he's associated with an item or not," I said. "I suppose that would depend on his schematic." I waved my hand over a floor cluttered with all manner of small objects. "By all means, feel free to look."

Gwen's prim voice echoed across the room. "I believe the question was metaphorical," she said. Still clad in red and white gingham, she picked her way toward us through the debris. "At least I hope it was, because then I should like to hear the answer as well. Is His Lordship truly gone?"

"May I present Gwendolyn Hutchins," I said. "She's a person of some stature among the townsfolk."

"Pleased to make your acquaintance," Roman said. "While I am grateful for your assistance with our patients, I do hope you understand—this meeting is private."

"It shouldn't be," I said. He was treating her the same way I'd treated Buck when we'd first met.

Roman blinked in surprise. "Again, you contradict me?"

"Hear me out. Gwen was instrumental in rescuing Elyria from Histlewick's prison. In spite of the callous disregard the Church has shown this village, she found it in her heart to help us. What happened here affects her at least as much as it affects you, if not more. I think she's earned the right to stay."

Roman looked to Father Graves for support, but he merely stared back, his eyebrows raised in an expectant expression—the sort a father gives a misbehaving child who's just been told to apologize.

"Well, if he does come back," Roman said, "it won't be for long. The Church tends to frown on demons, particularly those who masquerade as nobility."

"It wasn't a masquerade," Gwen said.

"What do you mean?"

"The demon is the rightful Lord. The condition was forced upon him."

"Even if that's true, I don't see how it would matter."

"Let me ask this," Gwen said. "What happens to Histlewick Downs now?"

"I expect it will fall to the King of Caprian to decide that. Likely he'll award the barony to another Lord."

"So we are to become the subjects of a man who comes to us with neither connection nor affection. One who views us as little more than a political prize, and an inferior one at that. One for whom our entire worth will be measured by the taxes he can squeeze from us. His Lordship was a man of many failings, but as a whole, he did well by his people. If this is to be our fate, I, for one, shall mourn his passing."

Roman was speechless. "You'd say that, even though the man was a demon?"

"That knowledge gave us recourse. His Lordship knew if things ever got bad enough, someone among us would find a way to leak his secret. And yet, in all these long years, no one ever has."

"How do you know all this?" Roman asked.

Gwen's smile was enigmatic. "Life changes little here. When something does happen, we take note—and we remember."

"When did it happen?"

"His Lordship was new to his title when a mysterious woman and her young son came to him seeking sanctuary. It was for her he prepared the room in the tunnels—a place of comfort and safety intended to shelter her until her pursuers despaired of ever finding her."

"Are you saying she turned on him? After all he'd done for her, why would she do that?"

"For a while, the arrangement worked as planned. To eliminate any chance of discovery, His Lordship served her meals personally. As he was her only contact with the outside world, she craved his company—but never his love. That, of course, was the sticking point. As time went on, his obsession grew, as did his sense of entitlement for all he provided. When at last he could take it no more, he tried to force himself on her. He thought himself both clever and safe, having first taken the child hostage. He never stood a chance."

"So, how did you get Histlewick to tell you all this? It's not the sort of thing I'd expect he'd care to chat about."

"He didn't," Gwen said. "Before leaving, the woman spoke at length with one of my predecessors, who had apparently suggested the failed arrangement in the first place. Though grateful for His Lordship's aid, the woman couldn't allow his transgression to go unpunished. She left him as you saw him. According to the account, any feelings of arousal would trigger his transformation, and only the taste of blood would restore him. A fitting punishment, if you think about it. Lust now brought out the beast in him—literally as well as figuratively. I wonder if she had any idea how long his sentence would last?"

"A quaint story," Father Graves said. "If it's true, it suggests he must have taken Elyria for the purpose of blackmailing His Ordinence. The other obvious motive wouldn't have been an option."

I suddenly recalled Histlewick's mysterious late-night visit during the time I'd been the prisoner in that same room, and how eager he'd been to learn what Joanna was capable of.

"Not so fast," I said. "As far as we know, he never mentioned anything to anyone about holding Elyria as a hostage. We also know from what Joanna said that she'd made some sort of deal with him. Now I think I know what she was offering."

Roman's eyes widened in realization. "Of course! She promised to remove the curse."

The irony wasn't lost on me. Technically, Joanna, too, had managed to keep her part of their bargain.

CHAPTER FORTY

AND THE YOUTH SHALL SET YOU FREE

After Father Graves finally took custody of the jar, I ducked outside and found Buck loitering near the courtyard gate.

His whole face lit up. "Mr. Flinch," he cried. "I thought sure you was a goner. You live a charmed life, you do."

The bear hug shouldn't have taken me by surprise, but it did. Barely enough air remained in my lungs to whisper, but I managed. "You have no idea."

"Was it Mr. Sly's plan what did it? Gotcha free, I mean?"

"It sure helped. Buck, you're a true friend."

"Shucks. 'Tweren't nothin' you wouldn't a done for me."

"I've got another little job for us. It might be a little dangerous, though. Are you game?"

"What kinda deputy would I be if I was to say no?"

I stifled the stab of guilt and pressed on. "Good man. It's just down to the inn and back. Let's go."

I asked Buck to wait downstairs while I went up. Ramos

answered my knock. His hopeful expression faded the instant he recognized me. "Oh, it's you. What do you want?"

"Can I come in?"

He hesitated a moment, and then stepped aside.

"It's over," I said. "They've got Joanna. I wanted to warn you so you could get out of here before they came looking for you."

"You're lying," Ramos said. "They don't have that kind of power. No one has that kind of power."

"No?" I tossed the charm bracelet on the table.

Ramos gaped at it and gulped. "How?"

"You don't have time for stories. Think of Ilse and the boys."

A weight seemed to lift from him then. "You're right," he said. He grabbed a few things and stuffed them into a bag.

I picked up the bracelet and held it out. "Here," I said. "Make sure this finds a good home."

His eyes welled up as he turned it over in his hand. "You know, I think I'm going to regret what I did to you for a very long time. I can't tell you how sorry I am."

"I understand," I said. "Now get out of here."

A moment later I was alone.

On one of the chairs, I noticed a familiar crate. I lifted the lid to find Joanna's dress, just as Father Graves had left it. Ramos hadn't taken the matching burgundy hat or the cameo either. I gently placed them both in the crate and tucked it beneath my arm. Then I went to the top of the stairs and called for Buck.

By the time I threw open the manor doors, Joanna was arrayed as she had been the day I'd first seen her in the inn, right down to the feather on her hat. She deserved that much. Buck carried her lifeless form cradled in his massive arms.

I nudged my black-and-red-feathered hat to give it a jaunty tilt. "Victory is ours," I cried. "My promise is fulfilled—the demon is no more."

Roman crossed the room in an instant. "What do you think you're doing?"

Armand hobbled forward on his crutches. "That's her," he cried. "That's Joanna Hockery. Saints alive, he did it. The boy actually defeated the demon."

Sly slapped me on the back. "Good job, there, Flinch."

"My name's Thoren," I said. "Thoren Theratigan."

"Well then," he said with a grin, "let's make sure everybody knows it." He seized my hand and held it aloft. "Three cheers for Thoren Theratigan, demon hunter extraordinaire. Hip, hip, hooray!"

Armand took up the cheer immediately, and much to my chagrin, the entire room joined in. Though I can't say he looked entirely pleased, even Roman clapped a little. I braced myself for the inevitable dressing-down, but at that moment Darron sat up on his cot, blinking in confusion at the noise. After that, I suspect I was the last thing on Roman's mind.

Sometime later I pulled Gwen aside and explained about my parents, and how they might be Histlewick's other prisoners. I waited for her to volunteer to help me look. When an offer didn't materialize, I finally worked up the courage to ask, but I already knew the answer. Her eyes gave her away.

"My maps of the Lord's passages are sketchy at best. If you had a specific destination, I might be able to figure out a safe route, but without that, it would be a fool's errand. Those tunnels are more treacherous than you know."

"You got Elyria out."

"Only because I had a strong suspicion where to find her and a reasonably reliable map to get us there. Even then, it was risky. If we'd taken a wrong turn…"

"Was Histlewick really that paranoid?"

Gwen shook her head. "These dangers long predate His Lordship."

"Maybe Roman would let me take an Inquisitor or two."

"I wouldn't recommend it, unless you want their deaths on your conscience. Did Buck ever tell you about his grandfather's cousins?"

"The ones who got lost?"

Gwen shuddered. "They didn't get lost. That's just what they told the family. It was kinder that way."

"They're my parents. I've got to try. Are you going to help me or not?"

"With a new Lord taking over, these people are going to need me now more than ever. If there were any reasonable chance of making it back alive—but there isn't."

"Is there anyone else who could help me?"

"I'm sorry. His Lordship was the last."

The celebration no longer held any joy for me. I slunk away to my room. There, I lay on my pallet staring up through the darkness, tears trickling into my ears. I'd failed them. Someone else's need had always been more pressing, someone else's life more endangered, someone else's threat too imminent. Now it was too late.

If only Histlewick were still here.

My thoughts turned to Joanna. If she could come back after what had happened to her, why not Histlewick? Maybe Roman's question shouldn't have been viewed metaphorically after all. And yet, if Histlewick's soul had somehow been linked to one of the hundreds of things scattered about that room, how would I ever find the right one?

I buried my head in my hands—not from despair, but from embarrassment. The monocle, of course. How could I have missed something so obvious?

When I slipped it out of my pocket, my heart nearly stopped. The thing was blazing with color. I started breathing again when I remembered I still had the gecko in my other pocket, but something still didn't add up. From my recollection of the gecko's schematics, I could account for two colors, but not six.

I forced myself to breathe as I worked through the possibilities. It couldn't be the watch. The monocle had always responded to that by displaying all seven colors. It was the same for Joanna, and her charm bracelet too, for that matter. This had to be something else. Something in the room, perhaps?

I cracked the door. When I was quite certain nothing sinister lurked beyond it, I took off down the hallway. Even after I'd gone a considerable distance, all six colors remained. Retracing my steps, I laid the gecko on my pillow and headed down the hallway once more. This time the colors dissipated. It was definitely the gecko.

Since I hadn't checked it with the monocle before, I had no way of knowing if it had always been this way, or if these mysterious extra spells were recent additions. As I tried to recall every place the gecko had been since I'd first seen it, a tiny, desperate seed of hope took root in the back of my mind.

Dropping the gecko back into my pocket, I set off for the Marstow wing. With everyone still gathered in the lobby, the manor was eerily quiet, and I made it there without seeing a soul. I almost jumped out of my skin when I opened the door and nearly collided with Hollings. The man had the ability to rattle me like no one else.

"Hollings," I said. "What are you doing here?"

"I work here, Mr. Flinch."

"Sorry, stupid question. It's just that it's so dead in here you startled me."

"My apologies. Is there something you require?"

"Um, I have a question for Father Graves. Is he in?"

"I believe he's still in the lobby."

"Oh, it's too crowded down there. I wanted to speak to him in private. Maybe I'll just wait for him here."

"As you wish."

He stepped aside to let me pass, and then slipped out through the door before it had a chance to close. I waited barely long enough to hear the click of the latch before I darted off down the hallway. I continued right on past Father Graves' apartments, opening doors until I found the room with the rainbow motif. I was in luck. Amidst the chaos of the evacuation, Histlewick's duplicate had been overlooked.

I drew out the gecko as I approached, eager to test my theory, but uncertain how to go about it. I hesitated, forcing myself to think through the logic one more time, but the effort yielded no new insights.

Enough second-guessing. I reached out and fitted the gecko onto his ear.

Nothing. No flashes, no colors, no whirlwinds, nothing.

Even though I'd known it was a long shot, I still wasn't prepared for failure. I buried my face in Histlewick's rainbow coverlet and sobbed.

A gentle touch on my shoulder nearly loosened my bowels. I looked over to see Histlewick staring back at me, a wistful look in his eye.

"It's been a very long time since anyone's wept for me."

"You're alive?"

"So it seems. How did you manage it?"

"It wasn't me, it was the gecko. Father Graves said it attuned to the bearer. I wondered whether that might generate enough affinity so that when Joanna dispelled your Evoked body, your soul wasn't lost. Then I had to hope that even after all these years, your soul would have more affinity for your actual body than it did for the gecko."

"Actual body?"

"You probably didn't know about that. I found it while I was imprisoned in the catacombs. It had been sitting down there transformed into a table all these years, but whoever had done that had provided the means to turn it back. I happened across it by accident."

"But that would mean—"

"I'm sorry. I didn't have any way to restore the Evoked one."

Histlewick sat bolt upright. "I'm free," he cried. "Truly, utterly free."

At that moment, Roman kicked in the door and leveled a crossbow at Histlewick's chest. "Don't count on it, demon."

Hollings peered in over his shoulder. "See, I told you. I knew the boy was up to no good."

CHAPTER FORTY-ONE

ALL A MISUNDERSTANDING

I cried out and leapt onto the bed, desperate to block Roman's shot. "What are you doing?"

"Get out of the way, Mr. Flinch."

"You're making a terrible mistake."

"Tell it to the families of those who lost their lives to the last demon. Now step aside."

"He's not a demon. Not anymore."

"I'm not going to ask again."

Father Graves' voice echoed down the hallway. "I came as soon as I could." He skidded to a stop next to Hollings and his eyes bulged at what he saw. "If you were planning to kill the boy, wouldn't it have been better to do it before he became a hero?"

"Albert, he brought back Histlewick. A little Profanity here and there is one thing, but this—this is Demonology. Even I can't absolve that."

"He's not a demon," I said. "He's cured."

Roman took aim right at me. "Mr. Flinch, you were warned."

Albert reached over and pushed the weapon aside. "What do you mean, cured?"

"Don't you see? This body you see here wasn't a duplicate—it was the original. Histlewick's soul is now back right where it belongs. It's exactly like what Joanna did. When she created her demon, she had to vacate her original body to do it. That's what I brought back to you from the inn—her original body, emptied. The difference is she did it to herself, while Histlewick was an unwilling participant. Look at it this way. When Joanna Sacrificed all those Inquisitors, you didn't blame the Inquisitors for it, did you?"

Father Graves gave Roman a sidelong look. "As I recall, neither did he threaten the Ordinal for trying to heal them."

Roman aimed the crossbow again. "Don't you dare try to paint Histlewick as the innocent victim. What about his kidnapping of Elyria? What about his deal with Joanna Hockery?"

Father Graves pushed the crossbow aside again. "I daresay we've all done a thing or two we later had reason to regret—haven't we?"

Roman flushed crimson. "I suppose next you're going to tell me I should just ignore the entire incident."

"Not at all," Father Graves said. "As Inquisitor General, you have vast powers of discretion. Those powers are wasted unless you exercise them in broadest possible context. So, by all means, take this incident into account—but don't do it in isolation. Before deciding, examine all the implications. Determine whether this decision is the one most likely to achieve the greatest possible good. If it isn't, toss it out and choose the one that is."

"You're referring to that little speech from that Hutchins woman, aren't you?"

"Forget the fate of the barony," I said. "Histlewick's the only one who can rescue my parents."

Father Graves' eyes twinkled. "Speaking of the lad's parents, I seem to recall a certain promise to grant them clemency in the event he could find out what makes Histlewick tick. You can't argue he hasn't come through—indeed, he's proven it beyond all doubt."

The humor was lost on Roman. "I suppose that's one of those things you expect me to take into account?"

"A posthumous award of clemency might be a considered a tad disingenuous if you were responsible for preventing their rescue, no?"

Histlewick finally broke his silence. "I don't know where all this talk of rescue is coming from. The lad's parents are my guests, not my prisoners."

There was something a little too self-serving about his admission, and it rankled. "If that's true, then why didn't you tell me?"

Histlewick shrugged innocently. "They preferred to keep their stay a secret. After all they'd been through, can you really blame them? In my defense, I had planned to tell you during the hunt, but you sent Elyria in your stead. Charming girl, by the way."

"You don't seriously expect us to buy that," Roman said. "We have it from the girl you imprisoned her."

"I admit to locking the door, if that's what you mean. The catacombs beneath this manor are extensive and quite dangerous. What kind of host would I be if I allowed my guests to lose themselves in that maze?"

Roman didn't look convinced. "Albert, is there any way you can prove whether he's a demon?"

"I'm so glad you asked. The science of forensic demonoscopy has a long and checkered history. Most experts are now agreed that methods pioneered during the pre-Dreamweaver era were mostly tragic cases of opportunistic charlatanism."

"Albert, please. Can we skip ahead to the relevant stuff?"

"I'm just coming to that. Post-Dreamweaver, some techniques, although perhaps a bit extreme by today's standards, are nonetheless considered generally effective—chief among them, diagnostic decapitation."

"I can't just cut off his head—what if I'm wrong?"

"Theoretically, I suppose one could instead remove a fingertip and take note of whether the fingerprint changes."

"No offense," I said, "but you're not even asking the relevant questions. You shouldn't have any doubts as to whether the body is genuine. You had plenty of time to examine that. So, if the body's his, the only way a demon could still be involved is if the body is occupied by somebody else."

Roman raised the crossbow again. "Good Lord," he cried. "He couldn't actually be Hockery, could he?"

"If he were Joanna," I said, "I hardly think we'd be having this conversation, but if you're still not convinced, then at least that's something you can test. Joanna couldn't possibly have Histlewick's knowledge of the catacombs, right? So, make him lead us to my parents. If he can't do it, you'll have your proof."

Roman didn't lower the crossbow, but for a change he seemed more contemplative than combative. "Albert?"

"As usual, the lad's logic is sound, although I expect we could come up with any number of other Histlewick-specific questions."

"I'd just as soon use the boy's suggestion. If the parents end up being prisoners rather than guests, I'd like to hear their story before deciding how to proceed. Hollings, get me some shackles. It's time for Lord Histlewick's walk."

Histlewick was true to his word. He navigated the catacombs with a practiced ease that banished any lingering doubts as to his identity, though I don't think Roman was truly convinced until he saw me smothered in my mother's arms. I shuddered to think how close they had come to not making it. I was so relieved I almost fainted. I felt like the luckiest person alive.

The little room where we found them was hardly lavish, but neither had they been deprived. They confirmed that Histlewick had found them in the swamp and welcomed them to stay until the Inquisition left Histlewick Downs. There were many tears, much laughter, and tales aching to be told.

Father Graves stood to one side, beaming as Roman himself removed Histlewick's shackles.

It was an awkward situation, but I didn't see any way to avoid it. I took my parents over for introductions. "Mother, Father, allow me to introduce Father Albert Graves and Father Roman Goodkin. Roman was very recently appointed to the position of Inquisitor General."

"Inquisitor General?" my father said. "Why, you're just the man I want to see." He moved over to Roman's side and leaned in closer. "You know, I'm not normally one to complain, but I think there's been some sort of mistake. Inquisitors raided my shop recently. They must have been under the impression that I was a heretic or something. Do you think you might be able to clear that up?"

Roman shot me a sidelong look before addressing my father's question. "Mr. Theratigan," he said. "I'm mortified. I'll be sure to take care of that right away. Rest assured you'll have no more trouble with Inquisitors as long as I have anything to say about it."

My father turned then to my mother. "You see, Myra? I told you it was all a mistake."

CHAPTER FORTY-TWO

TЬE BROAÐEST POSSIBLE CONTEXT

The caravan ride to the Holy City alternated between stifling and soggy, depending on the vagaries of the terrain and the weather, but to me, it was magical. I remember most fondly the deep conversations with Father Graves, who was every bit as interested in philosophy, theology, and history as he was in his Profanities. Then there were the riding lessons. Darron, who had fully recovered, insisted on teaching me as much as he could in the short time we had. Kendall presided over raucous evenings filled with the reek of rakia and the plaintive lament of the gadulka. From him, I also finally learned to load and shoot a crossbow.

The few times I was called upon to attend Roman, he seemed subdued, almost resigned. I don't think it was anything personal—he had a lot on his mind. Though the Ordinal still clung to life, he had not regained consciousness. Elyria and Sly spent every waking moment tending him, praying there was something else that could be done for him once we arrived.

The Primal Palace took my breath away. Domes and arches, buttresses and bell towers went on as far as the eye could see. Before it lay a landscaped garden easily larger than the entire village of Histlewick Downs. All that splendor disappeared in a puff of nerves the instant I discovered I would be attending Roman when he delivered his report to the Primal. Fortunately I'd brought Jaccard's outfit with me.

The Primal's throne room reminded me of a theater. Huge banners bearing the flags of affiliated city-states lined the walls, Caprian's among them. The throne sat atop a small dais surrounded by a huge expanse of white silk. Two entire walls of stained glass lit the room, splashing the white silk with bold patterns in shimmering primary colors. A strip of red silk stretched between the throne and the front doors. Above those doors loomed several levels of balconies—which, after my experience in Histlewick's lobby, only served to amplify my jitters.

Roman and I waited on one of those balconies as the chamber slowly filled to capacity. I could tell the Ordinals by their silver relics, which on occasions like these, were worn outside their vestments. I counted eight.

As the time drew near, Father Graves approached us.

"I haven't forgotten," Roman said, "the entire truth, no embellishments."

Father Graves reached out for Roman's shoulder. "I know it hurts, but sometimes purging the wound is the only way for it to heal. You need to be whole again, whatever the cost. Come on, I'll walk you downstairs."

Roman took the red runner at a ceremonial pace. I'd been instructed to stay two steps behind and slightly to his right. It sounds easy, but the combination of the crowd, the incense and the glass-tinted sunlight bewildered me. It took intense effort to stay focused.

Ahead of us, the Primal stood tall before his throne, glittering in jeweled vestments. His craggy face played host to deep-set eyes and a bloodless thin-lipped smile. His steely gaze skewered Roman with an expression that conveyed an unsettling degree of self-confidence. Roman dropped to his knees at the edge of the dais, and I followed suit. Only after bestowing his benediction, did the Primal finally take the throne.

"We welcome the return of our Inquisitor General with keen anticipation. You may begin."

Roman rose to his feet.

"Thank you, Your Primacy. Following the untimely death of my predecessor, my early efforts to restore order were reasonably successful. However, all progress ground to a standstill when I discovered my son Armand had been taken hostage by Marshall Hockery's widow, Joanna."

The Primal leaned forward. "Also a heretic, I presume?"

Roman nodded. "Highly skilled and deadly. I lost five Inquisitors to her Sacrifices. Many more suffered serious injury. Still more deserted when they saw what she was capable of."

"What became of her?"

"I'm proud to say she was neutralized, primarily through the efforts of my young protégé, here, Mr. Theratigan."

"Neutralized?"

"There are some technicalities involved. Father Graves is preparing a full report. Suffice it to say, she no longer poses a threat."

"I see. And what's the status of the prisoners?"

"Injuries and desertions left us a bare skeleton crew. Despite that, we attempted to maintain the prison as best we could. However, when the enemy destroyed our entire supply of sedative, we suddenly found ourselves in an untenable position. Once the drug wore off, the heretics would have had sufficient numbers to overwhelm the guards and potentially go on the offensive."

"And yet, here you are. How did you resolve the crisis?"

Roman licked his lips and swallowed hard, but his voice didn't falter. "I ordered the prisoners to be executed."

The Primal's eyes widened, and a collective gasp rippled through the assembly.

"Executed? Without benefit of a hearing?"

"I'm afraid so, Your Primacy."

"Were those orders carried out?"

Roman's face lost all its color, and his hands trembled. "They were. Only the children were spared."

The Primal rose from his chair. "Goodkin, when I appointed you to this position, I admit I had low expectations. Frankly, you only ended up with the job because, after what happened to your predecessor, I couldn't find anyone else foolhardy enough to take it. Now you come back to me, and this is the report I get. I stand before you, utterly astounded."

Roman bowed his head. "I am prepared to accept whatever consequences you deem appropriate."

The Primal raised both arms aloft and addressed the crowd. "Let the assembly take notice. These abhorrent attacks on our brethren demonstrate beyond all doubt that Phrendonic heresy has progressed beyond a mere doctrinal deviation."

The Primal stepped off the dais and paced animatedly before his audience. "Gentlemen, we are at war. Unlike many of you, Roman Goodkin understands this. When the need arises, he is unafraid to take decisive action. He appreciates that in war, casualties are sometimes a necessary evil. He comes to us now, battered, but not beaten—humbled, but victorious. A true hero for our troubled times."

The chamber erupted in frenzied applause and wild cheers.

Roman gaped at the crowd's reaction, dazed.

The Primal stepped back up on the dais. "Roman Goodkin, are you truly prepared to accept the consequences of your actions?"

He glanced around the chamber one more time with the wide eyes of a trapped animal. "I am," he said at last.

"A few moments ago, I received the sad news of the passing of one of my most trusted Ordinals. I have decided to appoint you to take his place. Of course, you'll also continue as Inquisitor General until a suitable replacement can be found."

Roman's response was numb. "Yes, Your Primacy."

"We are well pleased, Father Goodkin. You may go."

Roman bowed, and stalked away. This time, there was nothing ceremonious about his stride.

He passed Father Graves in the doorway without even slowing down.

Father Graves shot me a quizzical look and took off after him. We caught up with him in a small side chamber. The minute we were inside, he slammed the door behind us and rounded on his confessor.

"You did that deliberately."

"Roman, what's gotten into you?"

"You knew. You knew he'd react like that to the deaths of those prisoners."

"I suspected it as a possibility, yes."

"I hope you're happy. You've just made me that mad man's shining example for the virtues of murdering suspects without a hearing."

"If that's true, then I'm also to blame for making you Ordinal."

"How could you do this to me?"

"You're not the only one who's occasionally called upon to exercise discretion. Besides, I thought you wanted the position."

"I did, but not like this. I wanted it as recognition for my effort and my successes, not as evidence of my most dismal failure. My tenure will be forever tainted."

"Good," Father Graves said. "It's a penance, after all, not a reward. Now, at least you'll have the wherewithal to begin to atone for what you've done."

"You see where he's going with this, don't you? He's going to escalate this conflict, not resolve it, and I'm to be his hatchet man. I thought you were my friend."

"Roman, I am. I'll be right by your side the entire time. Maybe together we can at least mitigate some of the damage."

"Damnit, Albert, you're more meddlesome even than my wife."

"Why, thank you, Roman. I consider that high praise, indeed."

ꜰᴀɪᴛʜ, ʜᴏᴘᴇ, ᴀɴᴅ ᴄʜᴀʀɪᴛʏ

I didn't remain with Roman for long after that. In gratitude for my aid in eliminating Joanna Hockery, the Primal awarded me a lifelong stipend, with the stipulation that the Church could call on my expertise at need. The arrangement was a little open-ended for my taste, but I found it difficult to refuse. Not only was my parents' shop destroyed, but the ongoing Inquisition would likely make it impossible for my father to start over. Even if Inquisitors could no longer target him directly, he would still need customers. I set it up so that they could cash my vouchers. It wouldn't be anything like what my father used to make, but they wouldn't starve either.

After staying with my parents a week or so, it was time for me to move on. I packed up my fancy dress clothes, my hats, my walking stick, my monocle, and my other most prized possession—a pickle jar. I gave it a little swirl just to hear the satisfying sound of the cameo charm rattling about the bottom, and slid it into my pocket. I wondered for a moment what magic the little charm I'd put in Father Graves' jar could do. I'd probably never know—I doubted anyone was going to risk opening that jar for a very, very long time. As for my own jar? Someday, maybe once everyone Joanna had reason to hate was long gone, I'd stake down a checkered tablecloth, pour a couple glasses of wine, and have me a little peep inside.

I found Armand sitting alone on the front porch of the empty pub. The crutches had been replaced by a sturdy cane.

He greeted me with a big smile. "Now here's an unexpected surprise. I trust my father is treating you well?"

"He did," I said, "but I've since left his employ."

Armand nodded. "I understand. The kind of life he leads is not for everyone. What brings you here?"

"I thought you might want to know your father took care of that little issue with the Archbishop for Sly and Elyria. They're planning an October wedding. You'll be invited, assuming they can find you."

"And Lisbet?"

"They're talking adoption. I think Elyria sees herself as a little young to have a daughter that old, but I'm pretty sure Sly's going to win."

Armand grinned. "They're going to have their work cut out for them."

"I know. No doubt Lisbet will make quite an impression at court."

"So, what's next for you, Mr. Theratigan?"

"I was considering trying to find work at a local charity. I think I'm a good candidate for the job. I'm willing to assist with the day-to-day operations according to the measure of my abilities, and I promise to give back as I have received. I trust those terms are not unduly onerous?"

Armand paused a moment while that sank in. When it did, he wiped his eye on his sleeve. "Forgive me," he said, "but that sounds a little too good to be true."

I put my arm around him and escorted him inside. "I assure you, sir, it is not. Oh, and call me Flinch. We don't use real names around here."

acknowledgments

Marilyn Gosz for a lifetime of encouragement and razor-sharp advice without which none of this would ever have happened.

Jean Jenkins, whose editorial spit and polish rubbed away the rough edges to leave a gleaming professional sheen.

Adeela Syed, who was among the first to convince me I could actually do this.

Daniel Mendyke, for a multitude of in-depth conversations about how the world works, and how it should work.

The Southern California Writers' Conference, for a wealth of information and resources.

Dorothy and Everett Bornemann, for everything, always.

And, of course, **Nero**, my friend and constant companion. My bright-eyed boy forever.

Nero

The Pocket Watch used for the cover image was designed and crafted by **Lady Pirotessa** (at www.Facebook.com/pages/Blue-Rose-Creations/170481426318076). I still marvel at it.

GLOSSARY OF TERMS

Attunement: This property determines what constitutes a single object for purposes of vesting a spell—two or more objects attuned and in contact means a spell cast on one will spread to all of them. In general, items that remain in close contact for extended periods of time (about a year or so) become naturally attuned to each other. Thus, if a dagger blade is attached to a handle, and the two remain together for long enough, they become a single object for purposes of vesting spells (as long as they remain in contact as the spell vests) (see Vest). Certain Phrendonic spells from the Category of Enchantment can accelerate this process. In general, objects that are 95 percent attuned to each other behave as though they are 100 percent Attuned, while objects less than 95 percent Attuned behave as though they are not Attuned. Thus, once separated, Attuned items can lose their Attunement comparatively rapidly.

Category: Phrendonic spells can generally be grouped into one of seven categories based on how they function. Category dictates not only a spell's function, but places limits on spells that affect it. For example, a Dispel spell cannot generally affect more than one category. Thus, if two spells on the same object hail from different Categories, to dispel both, two different Dispels are required—one tailored to each of the Categories represented by the affected spells. The seven Phrendonic Categories are Alteration Divination, Enchantment, Encryption, Evocation, Kinesis, and Summoning. Likewise, Flinch's monocle consists of seven segments, each devoted to detecting the presence of spells from a different Category.

Charge: Some spells, referred to as Numeni (plural of Numenus), require an energy supply to maintain their effects. Charge spells collect and provide that energy—termed a '"charge." A Numenus can only accept a new charge when it is empty of charge or very nearly so. A Reservoir spell can hold a charge until a Numenus vested on the same item is ready to receive one. Numeni, Charge spells and Reservoirs all possess a trait called Tolerance. A charge can flow from a Charge spell or Reservoir with a higher Tolerance to a Reservoir or Numenus with a lower Tolerance. If multiple receptive Numeni are available, the charge flows to the one with the lowest Tolerance. Once a Numenus receives a charge, it retains it until the charge is exhausted. Thus, if an Incinerate spell and a Light spell are both vested on the same item, casting a Charge spell on the item will have different results depending on the Tolerances of the three spells. If the Light spell has the lowest Tolerance of the three, the Light spell will receive the charge and the object will light up. If the Incinerate has the lowest Tolerance, the object will instead blow up. If the Charge spell has the lowest tolerance, the charge will have nowhere to go, and will dissipate without effect. Only the Tolerances of empty or (nearly-empty Numeni capable of accepting a Charge) are considered for purposes of distributing charges.

Demon/Daemon: A soul displaced from its native body. The Church uses the term "Demon," Phrendonic practitioners prefer "Daemon."

Diffract: A type of Suppression spell that works on radiant effects (effects that extend beyond the target object in a radius, such as Darkness). Typically, a Diffraction spell is limited to affecting spells within a single category, e.g. Summoning. Since it only suppresses the effect without disturbing the spell's pattern, a Diffraction will not prevent a spell of the Diffracted Category from vesting within its radius. For that, one would use a Hedge, which is the corresponding radiant Dispel. See Dispel.

Dispel: A spell of the category of Alteration that disrupts the pattern of another spell vested on the same object causing it to dissipate. It is distinguished from a Suppression, which disrupts the effect of another spell, but leaves the pattern intact. If a Dispel is subsequently removed, the affected spell is still gone (provided it wasn't Patterned). By contrast, if a Suppression is removed, previously suppressed spells can often reassert themselves. A given Dispel is generally limited to Dispelling only spells within a single category. To be successful, the Dispel must be inherently stronger than the spell to be dispelled.

Evoke: To use a spell from the Phrendonic Category of Evocation. Evocation encompasses a Category of magic in which surrounding gasses are recruited into the pattern of a spell as it vests. Thus, solid objects may be created from air, although the spell itself must generally be cast upon an object to seed the effect. If the Evocation is dispelled or expires, the gas returns to its previous gaseous state. See also Category.

Inquisition: An investigative division of the Church devoted to quashing heresy. Although the Church boasted a number of career Inquisitors who were responsible for conducting hearings, most lower-ranking Inquisitors were recruited from the general populace in times of need and were provided only minimal training. This practice resulted in a system plagued by widespread abuses. The official in charge of the Inquisition, the Inquisitor General, was not technically part of the regular Church hierarchy, instead reporting directly to the Primal and serving at his pleasure. The extent of the Inquisitor General's authority therefore depended in large measure on his standing with the Primal at any given time.

Numenus: See Charge.

Ordinal: During Flinch's time, the Primal served as the chief executive of the Church. Just beneath him in rank were nine Ordinals appointed by the Primal, customarily for life. Upon a Primal's death, the Ordinals voted to determine his successor. Beneath the Ordinals were Archbishops, Bishops and Priests, in that order.

Passive Charge: Passive Charges are a special form of Charge Spell that collect energy over time, and when full (usually after about an hour) dump the accumulated Charge into an available Reservoir or Numenus vested on the same item. Once emptied, they resume gathering energy, and the process repeats as long as the spell remains in effect. See also Charge.

Patterning: A Patterned spell is one that has undergone the process of Patterning to make the spell's pattern integral to that of the object on which it is vested. In essence, a Patterned spell becomes permanent, as long as the object it's vested on remains intact. Thus, a Color spell Patterned on a Promise Stick to turn it red would no longer have a duration—instead, the stick would remain red indefinitely. However, if the stick is broken in half, the spell dissipates like normal, except that if the stick is reassembled (provided the two halves remain attuned), the Patterned spell manifests once again and the red color returns. Patterned Numeni still require Charges to take effect. Like Attunement spells, Patterning spells reside in the Category of Enchantment.

Phrendonic Heresy: Practicing Phrendonic magic, as outlined in the work Practical Phrendonics, was officially declared heresy by the Edict of Caprian in the year 887. Some related practices, such as demonology, had been deemed heretical long before that. Prior to 887, a number of canon scholars viewed Phrendonic practices as already subject to those previous edicts.

To them, the Edict of Caprian was little more than a clarification of existing canon.

Profanity: This term is used by the Church to denote an object upon which a Phrendonic spell is vested. Since Phrendonic spells generally don't last long unless they've been Patterned, it is usually presumed that a Profanity bears spells that have been Patterned.

Promise Stick: In its simplest form, a Promise Stick is a stick notched so that it may be easily snapped in two, usually to quickly break a spell without the bother of having to dispel it. In general, once a spell is vested on an object, at least 80 percent of the object must remain intact, or the spell is broken. Thus, if a Color spell is cast upon such a stick to turn it red, when the stick is broken, the spell is broken as well, and both pieces return to their normal color. However, if the stick is broken unevenly such that one piece retains at least 80 percent of its mass, the spell remains in effect on the larger piece, and dissipates from the smaller.

Reservoir: See Charge.

Sacrifice (Incinerate): Incinerate is a Summoning spell that instantaneously converts a Charge into light and heat in a radius around the targeted object. During the Caprian Inquisition, a number of Phrendonic heretic prisoners used this spell to immolate themselves rather than endure torture that might induce them to betray their compatriots. Inquisitors who got too close were often injured or killed as well. The Church's term for the practice, Infernal Sacrifice, gained traction at that time. Such a Sacrifice was an avenue of last-resort for a heretic, usually attempted after having been bound and masked or blinded. By casting the Sacrifice on themselves, they obviated the general requirement for the caster to see a spell's target to vest it. Since it's a Numenus, the Incinerate additionally requires a Charge to take effect.

Slept: Term of art used by Phrendonic practitioners to indicate that someone under the influence of a Sleep spell.

Spell Radius: Radiant spells generally affect a 30-foot radius surrounding the targeted object. Skilled Phrendonic practitioners can modify radiant spells to have a smaller radius, but not a larger one. Spell Radius is to be distinguished from Casting distance, which is generally line-of-sight up to a maximum of 150 feet.

Spells vested on persons vs. Spells vested on objects: Spells vested on people or animals behave differently in some particulars than they do when vested on inanimate objects. For example, the maximum duration of a spell on a person is approximately an hour, whereas on an object, they can last up to a day. The difference is thought to result from an interaction between the spell and the person's soul.

Vest/vesting: The nearly instantaneous process whereby the pattern of a spell spreads across the target object. Once initiated by casting, a spell spreads to encompass all solid material that is both attuned to and touching the point at which the vesting initiated. Thus, if one were to cast a Color spell on the blade of a knife to turn it red, the spell would initiate at a point targeted by the caster and spread until it encompassed everything that was attuned to the blade. If the handle had been in association with the blade long enough, they would be Attuned, the spell would vest on the handle, and the handle would turn red as well. If the blade and handle were only recently assembled and therefore not Attuned, the Color spell would vest on the blade only, and the handle would not be affected.

About the Author

Doug Bornemann works, plays, and sometimes even writes, in sunny Southern California. By day, he's a mild-mannered geneticist, stoically altering the genomes of unsuspecting fruit flies to create and analyze models of Huntington's disease. By night, he engages in subtly directing the lives of myriad unsuspecting characters, all of whom are fiercely convinced of their own free will (except, of course, for quirky Uncle Rayen). His law degree comes in handy mostly for defending those characters against the pointed and persuasive arguments of the other characters. It has absolutely no value whatsoever in winning arguments with either his lovely and talented wife, or their neurotic cat, Nero.